PENGUIN BOOKS

THE JANE AUSTEN BOOK CLUB

Karen Joy Fowler is the author of *Sister Noon*, a PEN/Faulkner Prize finalist, *Sarah Canary*, *The Sweetheart Season* and the story collection *Black Glass*. She lives in Davis, California.

The book club was Jocelyn's idea, and she handpicked the members.

Jocelyn's best friend was Sylvia, whose husband of thirty-two years had just asked for a divorce. We felt she needed something to distract her.

At sixty-seven, Bernadette was the oldest. She'd recently announced that she was, officially, letting herself go. 'I just don't look in the mirror any more,' she'd told us. 'I wish I'd thought of it years ago.'

The next person Jocelyn asked was Grigg, whom we none of us knew. We'd known Jocelyn long enough to wonder whom Grigg was intended for.

Allegra was thirty, and really only invited because she was Sylvia's daughter.

Prudie was the youngest of us, at twenty-eight. She taught French at the high school and was the only one of us currently married, unless you counted Sylvia, who soon wouldn't be.

Our first meeting was at Jocelyn's house . . .

The Jane Austen
Book Club

KAREN JOY FOWLER

PENGUIN BOOKS

PENGUIN BOOKS

Published by the Penguin Group
Penguin Books Ltd, 80 Strand, London WC2R ORL, England
Penguin Group (USA) Inc., 375 Hudson Street, New York, New York 10014, USA
Penguin Group (Canada), 90 Eglinton Avenue East, Suite 700, Toronto, Ontario, Canada M4P 2Y3
(a division of Pearson Penguin Canada Inc.)
Penguin Ireland, 25 St Stephen's Green, Dublin 2, Ireland (a division of Penguin Books Ltd)
Penguin Group (Australia), 250 Camberwell Road, Camberwell, Victoria 3124, Australia
(a division of Pearson Australia Group Pty Ltd)
Penguin Books India Pvt Ltd, 11 Community Centre, Panchsheel Park, New Delhi – 110 017, India
Penguin Group (NZ), cnr Airborne and Rosedale Roads, Albany, Auckland 1310, New Zealand
(a division of Pearson New Zealand Ltd)
Penguin Books (South Africa) (Pty) Ltd, 24 Sturdee Avenue,
Rosebank, Johannesburg 2196, South Africa

Penguin Books Ltd, Registered Offices: 80 Strand, London WC2R ORL, England

www.penguin.com

First published in the United States of America by G. P. Putnam's Sons 2004
First published in Great Britain by Viking 2004
Published in Penguin Books 2005
This edition published for *SHE* magazine 2006

1

Copyright © Karen Joy Fowler, 2004
All rights reserved

The moral right of the author has been asserted

This is a work of fiction. Names, characters, places, and incidents either are the product of
the author's imagination or are used fictitiously, and any resemblance to actual persons,
living or dead, business establishments, events, or locales is entirely coincidental.

Set in 9/10½ pt PostScript Monotype Garamond
Typeset by Rowland Phototypesetting Ltd, Bury St Edmunds, Suffolk
Printed in England by Clays Ltd, St Ives plc

ISBN-13: 978-0-141-02934-4
ISBN-10: 0-141-02934-X

For Sean Patrick James Tyrrell.
Missing and forever missed.

Seldom, very seldom does complete truth belong to any human disclosure; seldom can it happen that something is not a little disguised, or a little mistaken.

— JANE AUSTEN, *Emma*

The Jane Austen Book Club

Prologue

Each of us has a private Austen.

Jocelyn's Austen wrote wonderful novels about love and courtship, but never married. The book club was Jocelyn's idea, and she handpicked the members. She had more ideas in one morning than the rest of us had in a week, and more energy, too. It was essential to reintroduce Austen into your life regularly, Jocelyn said, let her look around. We suspected a hidden agenda, but who would put Jane Austen to an evil purpose?

Bernadette's Austen was a comic genius. Her characters, her dialogue remained genuinely funny, not like Shakespeare's jokes, which amused you only because they were Shakespeare's and you owed him that.

Bernadette was our oldest member, just rounding the bend of sixty-seven. She'd recently announced that she was, officially, letting herself go. 'I just don't look in the mirror anymore,' she'd told us. 'I wish I'd thought of it years ago . . .

'Like a vampire,' she added, and when she put it that way, we wondered how it was that vampires always managed to look so dapper. It seemed that more of them should look like Bernadette.

Prudie had once seen Bernadette in the supermarket in her bedroom slippers, her hair sticking up from her forehead as if she hadn't even combed it. She was buying frozen edamame and capers and other items that couldn't have been immediately needed.

Bernadette's favorite book was *Pride and Prejudice*; she'd told Jocelyn that it was probably everyone's favorite. She recommended starting with it. But Sylvia's husband of thirty-two years had just asked for a divorce, and Jocelyn would not subject her, the news so recent and tender, to the dishy Mr Darcy. 'We'll start with *Emma*,' Jocelyn had answered. 'Because no one has ever read it and wished to be married.'

Jocelyn met Sylvia when they were both eleven years old; they were in their early fifties now. Sylvia's Austen was a daughter, a sister, an aunt. Sylvia's Austen wrote her books in a busy sitting room, read them aloud to her family, yet remained an acute and nonpartisan observer of people.

Sylvia's Austen could love and be loved, but it didn't cloud her vision, blunt her judgment.

It was possible that Sylvia was the whole reason for the book club, that Jocelyn wished only to keep her occupied during a difficult time. That would be like Jocelyn. Sylvia was her oldest and closest friend.

Wasn't it Kipling who said, 'Nothing like Jane when you're in a tight spot'? Or something very like that?

'I think we should be all women,' Bernadette suggested next. 'The dynamic changes with men. They pontificate rather than communicate. They talk more than their share.'

Jocelyn opened her mouth.

'No one can get a word in,' Bernadette warned her. 'Women are too tentative to interrupt, no matter how long someone has gone on.'

Jocelyn cleared her throat.

'Besides, men don't do book clubs,' Bernadette said. 'They see reading as a solitary pleasure. When they read at all.'

Jocelyn closed her mouth.

Yet the very next person she asked was Grigg, whom we none of us knew. Grigg was a neat, dark-haired man in his early forties. The first thing you noticed about him was his eyelashes, which were very long and thick. We imagined a lifetime of aunts regretting the waste of those lashes in the face of a boy.

We'd known Jocelyn long enough to wonder whom Grigg was intended for. Grigg was too young for some of us, too old for the rest. His inclusion in the club was mystifying.

Those of us who'd known Jocelyn longer had survived multiple setups. While they were still in high school, she'd introduced Sylvia to the boy who would become her husband, and she'd been maid of honor at the wedding three years after they graduated. This early success had given her a taste for blood; she'd never recovered. Sylvia and Daniel. Daniel and Sylvia. Thirty-plus years of satisfaction, though it was, of course, harder to take pleasure in that just now.

Jocelyn had never been married herself, so she had ample time for all sorts of hobbies.

She'd spent fully six months producing suitable young men for Sylvia's daughter, Allegra, when Allegra turned nineteen. Now Allegra was thirty, and the fifth person asked to join our book club. Allegra's Austen wrote about the impact of financial need on the intimate lives of women. If she'd worked in a bookstore, Allegra would have shelved Austen in the horror section.

Allegra got short, expensive haircuts and wore cheap, sexy shoes, but neither of those facts would have made any of us think twice if she hadn't also, on occasions too numerous to count, referred to herself as a lesbian. Jocelyn's inability to see what had never been hidden eventually became offensive, and Sylvia took her aside and asked why she was having so much trouble *getting it*. Jocelyn was mortified.

She switched to suitable young women. Jocelyn ran a kennel and bred Rhodesian Ridgebacks. The dog world was, as it happily turned out, awash in suitable young women.

Prudie was the youngest of us at twenty-eight. Her favorite novel was *Persuasion*, the last completed and the most somber. Prudie's was the Austen whose books changed every time you read them, so that one year they were all romances and the next you suddenly noticed Austen's cool, ironic prose. Prudie's was the Austen who died, possibly of Hodgkin's disease, when she was only forty-one years old.

Prudie would have liked it if we'd occasionally acknowledged the fact that she'd won her invitation as a genuine Austen devotee, unlike Allegra, who was really there only because of her mother. Not that Allegra wouldn't have some valuable insights; Prudie was eager to hear them. Always good to know what the lesbians were thinking about love and marriage.

Prudie had a dramatic face, deep-set eyes, white, white skin, and shadowed cheeks. A tiny mouth and lips that almost disappeared when she smiled, like the Cheshire cat, only opposite. She taught French at the high school and was the only one of us currently married, unless you counted Sylvia, who soon wouldn't be. Or maybe Grigg – we didn't know about Grigg – but why would Jocelyn have invited him if he was married?

None of us knew who Grigg's Austen was.

The six of us – Jocelyn, Bernadette, Sylvia, Allegra, Prudie, and Grigg – made up the full roster of the Central Valley/River City all-Jane-Austen-all-the-time book club. Our first meeting was at Jocelyn's house.

MARCH

CHAPTER ONE

in which we gather
at Jocelyn's
to discuss *Emma*

We sat in a circle on Jocelyn's screened porch at dusk, drinking cold sun tea, surrounded by the smell of her twelve acres of fresh-mowed California grass. There was a very pretty view. The sunset had been a spectacular dash of purple, and now the Berryessa mountains were shadowed in the west. Due south in the springtime, but not the summer, was a stream.

'Just listen to the frogs,' Jocelyn said. We listened. Apparently, somewhere beneath the clamor of her kennel of barking dogs was a chorus of frogs.

She introduced us all to Grigg. He had brought the Gramercy edition of the complete novels, which suggested that Austen was merely a recent whim. We really could not approve of someone who showed up with an obviously new book, of someone who had the complete novels on his lap when only *Emma* was under discussion. Whenever he first spoke, whatever he said, one of us would have to put him in his place.

This person would not be Bernadette. Though she'd been the one to request girls only, she had the best heart in the world; we weren't surprised that she was making Grigg welcome. 'It's so lovely to see a man taking an interest in Miss Austen,' she told him. 'Delightful to get the male perspective. We're so pleased that you're here.' Bernadette never said anything once if it could be said three times. Sometimes this was annoying, but mostly it was restful. When she'd arrived, she seemed to have a large bat hanging over her ear. It was just a leaf, and Jocelyn removed it as they hugged.

Jocelyn had two portable heaters going, and the porch hummed cozily. There were Indian rugs and Spanish-tile floors of a red that might hide dog hair, depending on the breed. There were porcelain lamps in the shape of ginger jars, round and Oriental, and with none of the usual dust on the bulbs, because it was Jocelyn's house. The lamps were on timers. When it was sufficiently dark out, at the perfect moment, they would snap on all at once like a choir. This hadn't happened yet, but we were looking forward to it. Maybe someone would be saying something brilliant.

The only wall held a row of photographs – Jocelyn's dynasty of Ridgebacks, surrounded by their ribbons and pedigrees. Ridgebacks are a matriarchal breed; it's one of their many attractive features. Put Jocelyn in the alpha position and you have the makings of an advanced civilization.

Queenie of the Serengeti looked down on us, doe eyes and troubled, intelligent brow. It's hard to capture a dog's personality in a photograph; dogs suffer more from the flattening than people do, or cats even. Birds photograph well because their spirits are so guarded, and anyway, often the real subject is the tree. But this was a flattering likeness, and Jocelyn had taken it herself.

Beneath Queenie's picture, her daughter, Sunrise on the Sahara, lay, in the flesh, at our feet. She had only just settled, having spent the first half-hour moving from one of us to the next, puffing hot stagnant-pond smells into our faces, leaving hairs on our pants. She was Jocelyn's favorite, the only dog allowed inside, although she was not valuable, since she suffered from hyperthy-roidism and had had to be spayed. It was a shame she wouldn't have puppies, Jocelyn said, for she had the sweetest disposition.

Jocelyn had recently spent more than two thousand dollars on vet bills for Sahara. We were glad to hear this; dog breeding, we'd heard, could make a person cruel and calculating. Jocelyn hoped to continue competing her, though the kennel would derive no benefit; it was just that Sahara missed it so. If her gait could be smoothed out – for Ridgebacks it was all about the gait – she could still show, even if she never won. (But Sahara knew when she'd lost; she became subdued and reflective. Sometimes someone was sleeping with the judge and there was nothing to be done about it.) Sahara's competitive category was Sexually Altered Bitch.

The barking outside ascended into hysteria. Sahara rose and walked stiffly to the screen door, her ridge bristling like a tooth-brush.

'Why isn't Knightley more appealing?' Jocelyn began. 'He has so many good qualities. Why don't I warm to him?'

We could hardly hear her; she had to repeat herself. The conditions were such, really, that we should have been discussing Jack London.

Most of what we knew about Jocelyn came from Sylvia. Little Jocelyn Morgan and little Sylvia Sanchez had met at a Girl Scout camp when they were eleven years old, and they were fifty-something now. They'd both been in the Chippewa cabin, working on their wood-lore badges. They had to make campfires from teepees of kindling, and then cook over them, and then eat what they'd cooked; the requirement wasn't satisfied unless the Scout cleaned her plate. They had to identify leaves and birds and poisonous mushrooms. As if any one of them would ever eat a mushroom, poisonous or not.

For their final requirement they'd been taken in teams of four to a clearing ten minutes off and left to find their own way back. It wasn't hard, they'd been given a compass and a hint. The dining hall was southwest of them.

Camp lasted four weeks, and every Sunday Jocelyn's parents drove up from the city – three and a half hours – to bring her the Sunday funnies. 'Everyone liked her anyway,' Sylvia said. This was hard to believe, even for us, and we all liked Jocelyn a ton. 'She was attractively ill informed.'

Jocelyn's parents adored her so, they couldn't bear to see her unhappy. She'd never been told a story with a sad ending. She knew nothing about DDT or Nazis. She'd been kept out of school during the Cuban missile crisis because her parents didn't want her learning we had enemies.

'It fell to us Chippewas to tell her about communists,' said Sylvia. 'And child molesters. The Holocaust. Serial killers. Menstruation. Escaped lunatics with hooks for hands. The Bomb. What had happened to the real Chippewas.

'Of course, we didn't have any of it right. What a mash of misinformation we fed her. Still, it was realer than what she got at home. And she was very game, you had to admire her.

'It all came crashing down on the day we had to find our way back to camp. She had this paranoid fantasy that while we were hiking and checking our compass, they were packing up and moving out. That we would come upon the cabin and the dining hall and the latrines, but all the people would be gone. Even more, that there would be dust and spiderwebs and crumbling floorboards. It would be as if the camp had been abandoned for a hundred years. We might have told her too many *Twilight Zone* plots.

'But here's the weird part. On the last day, her parents came to pick her up, and on the drive back, they told her that they'd gotten divorced over the summer. In fact, she'd been sent off just for this purpose. All those Sunday drives together bringing the funnies, and they couldn't actually stand each other. Her dad was living in a hotel in San Francisco and had been the whole month she was gone. "I eat all my meals in the hotel restaurant," he told her. "I just come down for breakfast and order whatever catches my fancy." Jocelyn said he made it sound as though that were the only reason he'd moved out, because restaurant eating would be so swell. She felt she'd been traded for shirred eggs.'

One day several years later he called her to say he had a touch of the

flu. Nothing for her to worry her darling head about. They had tickets
to a baseball game, but he didn't think he could make it, he'd have to
take a rain check. Go, Giants! It turned out the flu was a heart attack.
He didn't get to the hospital until he was already dead.

'No wonder she grew up a bit of a control freak,' Sylvia said. With
love. Jocelyn and Sylvia had been best friends for more than forty years.

There's no heat with Mr Knightley,' Allegra said. She had a very express-
ive face, like Lillian Gish in a silent movie. She frowned when she was
making a point, had done this since she was a tiny girl. 'Frank Churchill
and Jane Fairfax meet in secret and quarrel with each other and make it
up and lie to everyone they know. You believe they're in love because
they behave so badly. You can imagine sex. You never feel that with Mr
Knightley.' Allegra had a lullaby voice, low, yet penetrating. She was
often impatient with us, but her tones were so soothing we usually
realized it only afterward.

'That's true,' Bernadette agreed. Behind the lenses of her tiny glasses
her eyes were round as pebbles. 'Emma is always saying how reserved
Jane is, even Mr Knightley says so, and he's so perceptive about everyone.
But she's the only one in the whole book' – the lights came on, which
made Bernadette jump, but she didn't miss a word for it – 'who ever
seems desperately in love. Austen says that Emma and Mr Knightley
make an unexceptional marriage.' She paused reflectively. 'Clearly she
approves. I expect the word "unexceptional" meant something different
in Austen's day. Like, nothing to be ashamed of. Nothing to set tongues
wagging. Neither reaching too high nor stooping too low.'

Light poured like milk over the porch. Several large winged insects
hurled themselves against the screens, frantic to find it, follow it to the
source. This resulted in a series of thumps, some of them loud enough
to make Sahara growl.

'No animal passion,' said Allegra.

Sahara turned. Animal passion. She had seen things in the kennels.
Things that would make your hair stand on end.

'No passion at all.' Prudie repeated the word, but pronouncing it as if
it were French. Pah-see-*ohn*. Because she taught French, this wasn't as
thoroughly obnoxious as it might have been.

Not that we liked it. The month before, Prudie's beautician had
removed most of her eyebrows; it gave her a look of steady surprise. We
couldn't wait for this to go away. '*Sans passion, amour n'est rien,*' Prudie
said.

'*Après moi, le deluge,*' Bernadette answered, just so Prudie's words wouldn't fall into a silence that might be mistaken for chilly. Bernadette was really too kind sometimes.

Nothing smelly outside. Sahara came away from the screen door. She leaned into Jocelyn, sighing. Then she circled three times, sank, and rested her chin on the gamy toe of Jocelyn's shoe. She was relaxed but alert. Nothing would get to Jocelyn that didn't go through Sahara first.

'If I may.' Grigg cleared his throat, held up his hand. 'One thing I notice about *Emma* is that there's a sense of menace.' He counted off on his fingers. He wore no ring. 'The violent Gypsies. The unexplained pilferings. Jane Fairfax's boat accident. All Mr Woodhouse's worries. There's a sense of threat hovering on the edges. Casting its shadow.'

Prudie spoke quickly and decisively. 'But Austen's whole point is that none of those things is real. There is no real threat.'

'I'm afraid you've missed the whole point,' said Allegra.

Grigg said nothing further. His eyelashes dropped to his cheeks, making his expression hard to read. It fell to Jocelyn as hostess to change the subject.

'I read once that the *Emma* plot, the humbling of a pretty, self-satisfied girl, is the most popular plot of all time. I think it was Robertson Davies who said so. That this was the one story everyone was bound to enjoy.'

When Jocelyn was fifteen, she met two boys while playing tennis at the country club. One of them was named Mike, the other Steven. They were, at first glance, average boys. Mike was taller and thinner, with a prominent Adam's apple and glasses that turned to headlights in the sun. Steven had better shoulders and a nice smile but a fat ass.

Mike's cousin Pauline was visiting from New York, and they introduced themselves to Jocelyn because they needed a fourth for doubles. Jocelyn had been working on her serve with the club pro. She wore her hair in a high ponytail that summer, with bangs like Sandra Dee in *Take Her, She's Mine*. She had breasts, pointy at first, but now rounding. Her mother had bought her a two-piece bathing suit with egg-cup shaping, in which Jocelyn was exquisitely self-conscious. But her best feature, she always believed, had been her serve. Her toss that day was perfect, taking her to full stretch, and she spun the ball into the service court. It seemed she couldn't miss. Her spirits, as a consequence, were high and wild.

Neither Mike nor Steven spoiled things by being particularly competitive. They split games sometimes, and sometimes they didn't; no one really kept score but Jocelyn, and she did so only privately. They traded partners. Pauline was such a little snot, accusing people of foot faults in a friendly game, that Jocelyn looked better and better by comparison. Mike said she was a good sport, and Steven said she wasn't a bit stuck-up, not like most girls.

They continued to meet and play after Pauline went back home, even though three was such an awkward number. Sometimes when they rallied, Mike or Steven would try to run from one side of the net to the other to play on both teams at once. It never worked and they never stopped trying. Eventually some adult would accuse them of not being serious and throw them off the court.

After tennis, they'd change into their swimsuits and meet at the pool. Everything about Jocelyn changed with her clothes. When she came out of the women's locker room, her movements were cramped and tight. She'd wrap a towel around her waist and remove it only to slip into the water.

Still, she liked when they stared; she felt the pleasure of it all over her skin. They came in after her, touching her under the water, where no one could see. One or the other would swim down to put his head between her legs and surface with her knees hooked around his shoulders, the water from her ponytail streaming into the cup over her breast. One day one of them, she never knew which, pulled the knot of her top loose. She caught it just as it began to drop. She could have stopped this with a word, but she didn't. She felt dangerous, brazen. She felt all lit up.

She had no desire for anything further. She didn't actually like Mike or Steven that much, and certainly not in that way. When she lay in her bed or the bath, touching herself more intimately and successfully than they did, the boy she pictured was Mike's older brother, Bryan. Bryan went to college and worked summers as a lifeguard at the pool. He looked the way a lifeguard looks. Mike and Steven called him the boss, he called them the squirts. He had never spoken to Jocelyn, possibly didn't even know her name. He had a girlfriend who rarely got wet, but lay on a beach chair reading Russian novels and drinking Coca-Cola. You could tell how many she'd drunk from the maraschino cherries lined up along her napkin.

In late July there was a dance, and it was girl-ask-boy. Jocelyn asked Mike and Steven both. She thought they knew this, assumed they would talk about it. They were best friends. She thought it would hurt someone's feelings if she asked one and not the other, and she didn't want to hurt anyone. She had a strapless sundress to wear; she and her mother went out and bought a strapless bra.

Mike showed up at her house first, in a white shirt and a sports jacket. He was nervous; they were both nervous; they needed Steven to arrive.

But when he did, Mike was shocked. Hurt. Furious. 'You two have a great time,' he said. 'I got other things to do.'

Jocelyn's mother drove Jocelyn and Steven to the club and wouldn't be picking them up again until eleven o'clock. Three whole hours had to pass somehow. Glass torches lit the pathway to the clubhouse, and the landscape flickered. There were rose wreaths and pots of ivy animals. The air cool and soft, the moon sliding down the sky. Jocelyn didn't want to be with Steven. It felt like a date now, and she didn't want to date him. She was rude and miserable, wouldn't dance, hardly talked, wouldn't take off her cardigan. She was afraid he might get the wrong idea, so she was trying to clarify things. Eventually he asked some other girl to dance.

Jocelyn went out by the pool and sat in one of the lounge chairs. She knew that she'd been unforgivably mean to Steven, wished she'd never met him. She wasn't wearing stockings and her legs were cold. She could smell her own Wind Song perfume mixing with the chlorine.

Music floated over the pool. 'Duke of Earl.' 'I Want to Hold Your Hand.' 'There is a house in New Orleans.' Bryan sat down on the end of her chair, making her blood skip. Probably she was in love with him.

'Aren't you the thing?' he said. The only light around them came from under the water and was blue. He was turned away, so she didn't see his face, but his voice was full of contempt. 'There's a word for girls like you.'

Jocelyn hadn't known this, hadn't even known there were girls like her. Whatever the word was, he didn't say it.

'You had those boys in such a fever. Did you like that? I bet you liked it. Did you know they used to be best friends? They hate each other now.'

She was so ashamed. She'd known all summer there was something wrong with the way she was behaving, but she hadn't known what it was. She *had* liked it. Now she understood that the liking it was the wrong part.

Bryan gripped one of her ankles hard enough so that the next morning she had a bruise where his thumb had been. He slid the other hand up her leg. 'You asked for this,' he said. 'You know you did.' His fingers grabbed at her panties, pushed them aside. She felt the slick surface of his nails. She didn't tell him not to. She was too ashamed to move. His finger found its way inside her. He shifted his weight until he lay over her. He was wearing the same bay aftershave her father had worn.

'Bryan?' His girlfriend's voice, over by the clubhouse. 'True Love Ways' playing on the turntable – Jocelyn would never like Buddy Holly again, even though he was dead, poor guy – the girlfriend calling. 'Bryan? Bryan!' Bryan slid his finger out, let go of her. He stood up, shaking his jacket into place and smoothing his hair. He put his finger into his mouth while she watched, took it out. 'We'll catch up later,' he told her.

Jocelyn walked down the watery path through the torches and out to the road. The country club was in the country, up a long hill. It took twenty minutes to drive there. The roads twisted and had no sidewalks and were surrounded by trees. Jocelyn started home.

She was wearing sandals with one-inch heels. She'd painted her toenails, and in the moonlight, her toes looked as if they'd been dipped in blood. Already there was a raw spot on the back of one heel. She was very frightened, because ever since camp she'd lived in a world with communists and rapists and serial killers. Whenever she heard a car coming, she stepped away from the road and crouched until it passed. The headlights were like searchlights. She pretended she was someone innocent, someone who hadn't asked for anything. She pretended she was a deer. She pretended she was a Chippewa. She pretended she was on the Trail of Tears, an event Sylvia had recounted in vivid if erroneous detail.

She thought she'd be home before her mother left to pick them up. All she had to do was go downhill. But in the beam of a passing car, suddenly she didn't recognize anything. At the bottom of the hill was a crossroads she never came to, and now she was going up, which she shouldn't be doing, even for a short time. There were no street signs, no houses. She kept going forward only because she was too ashamed to go back. Hours passed. Finally she found a small gas station, which was closed, and a pay phone, which was working. As she dialed she was sure her mother wouldn't answer. Her mother might be out, frantically looking for her. She might have packed all her clothes into the car while Jocelyn was at the dance, and moved away.

It was midnight. Her mother made a horrible to-do about it, but Jocelyn convinced her that she'd only wanted some fresh air, some exercise, the stars.

But I think what we're supposed to see,' said Prudie, 'is not the lack of passion so much as the control of it. That's one of Jane's favorite themes.' She smiled and her lips waned.

We exchanged secret looks. *Jane*. That was easy. That was more intimate, surely, than Miss Austen would wish. None of the rest of us called her Jane, even though we were older and had been reading her years longer than Prudie.

Only Bernadette was too good to notice. 'That's very true,' she said. She had her fingers laced and was fiddling with which thumb should be on top. '*Sense and Sensibility* is all about that, and it's Austen's first book, but then she returns to it in *Persuasion*, and that's the last. An enduring theme. Good point, Prudie. Knightley is violently in love – I believe those are the words used, violently in love – but he's so much the gentleman that even this can't make him behave badly. He's always a gentleman first. Jocelyn, your tea is excellent. So flavorful. I could swear I was drinking the sunshine itself.'

'He's a scold,' Allegra said. 'I don't find that so gentlemanly.'

'Just to Emma.' Grigg sat with one foot resting on the other knee. His leg was bent in two like a chicken wing. Only a man would sit that way. 'Just to the woman he loves.'

'And of course that makes it all right!' Prudie cried out. 'A man can do anything to the woman he loves.'

This time it was Sylvia who changed the subject, but she was acting as Jocelyn's agent; we saw Jocelyn look at her just before she spoke. 'Forget Knightley,' she said. 'Emma's the hard one to defend. She's adorable, but she's also an unrepentant snob.'

'But she's the only one of Austen's heroines who gets the book named after her,' Jocelyn said, 'so I think she must be the favorite.'

One of the dogs in the kennel was barking steadily. There was a long enough pause between outbursts to trick us into thinking each was the last. The barks were frayed – deceptively, cunningly weary. What fools we were, poised there above our books for a silence that would never come.

'I do believe the fog is rising.' Allegra's tone expressed satisfaction, her lovely mobile face joy. The moon shone down unimpeded, but its time was coming. Out over the fields the air was beginning to seep. Between barks we heard the sound of a distant train. 'Didn't I say so, Mother? Didn't I say we should meet in town instead of out here? We'll be lucky to get home now. Nothing more dangerous than these country roads in the fog.'

Grigg was instantly on his feet. 'I should probably go, then. My car's not too reliable. I'm not used to driving in the fog.'

Bernadette, too, was standing.

'Please, no,' said Jocelyn. 'Not yet. We're in a hollow here. On the road there'll be no fog at all. The moon is so bright. I have refreshments, please stay for them, at least. I'll get them right now. We haven't even talked about Harriet.'

*

In her junior year Sylvia transferred to Jocelyn's high school. They hadn't seen each other since camp, had written two letters each, the first very long, the second much less so, and then both stopped writing. But this was neither one's fault more than the other's, and they were excited to find each other again, sitting in Mr Parker's English class only two rows apart, equally bewildered by what was the deal with Ibsen. It was an enormous relief to Sylvia to discover that she already knew someone at her new school.

Now it was Jocelyn who was the expert, knowing where you were allowed to smoke, and who was cool to hang out with, and who, even if you secretly liked them, would make your reputation suffer. She had a boyfriend with a car and quickly arranged a boyfriend for Sylvia so they could all go to the movies together, or the shopping center, or the beach on weekends when the weather was nice enough. When they were out as a foursome, mostly Sylvia and Jocelyn talked to each other. Daniel and Tony drove, and when they went to the movies, Daniel and Tony paid.

Tony was Sylvia's boyfriend. He was a swimmer, and during the competitive season, he shaved every hair off his body so he was smooth as plastic. Sylvia got him at this time, somewhat marked down. After they'd been dating several weeks, he let his hair grow back. It was lovely hair, soft and brown. He was a good-looking guy.

Jocelyn was dating a boy named Daniel. Daniel had an after-school job at a bike shop called Free Wheeling, and adult responsibilities. His youngest brother was retarded, a Mongoloid child with big ears, sticky affections, and a careless gravity so powerful the rest of the family had fallen into orbit about him.

Jocelyn had quit the country club right after the dance. Even so, she made the tennis team her junior year, in the fourth spot. The first and second girls were ranked sixth and eleventh in the state; it was a powerful team. No one in the school cared about girls' sports, though. More people came to see the boys' team play, when they weren't nearly so good, and no one, even among the girls, thought this wasn't the way it should be.

One day during an away match Jocelyn noticed Tony sitting in the stands. It had begun to cloud; the match stopped and started and stopped for good. 'I came because of the weather,' Tony told her. 'Daniel asked me to drive you home if it rained.'

This was a lie. Ten minutes after they left the courts it was pouring so hard that Tony couldn't see. He pulled over to wait for it to ease up. Jocelyn was still sweaty from the match, and he kept the heat going for fear she'd chill. The car steamed like a teakettle, the windows coated so no one could look in. Tony began to write with his finger in the water on the glass. *I love you*, he wrote. Again and again. All over the driver's-side window and above the steering wheel. He hadn't said a word. The rain clattered on the roof, bounced on the hood. Tony's face was white, his eyes unnaturally large. Silence inside the car and the din without.

'Sylvia couldn't come with you?' Jocelyn asked. She was still hoping the words on the windows weren't for her.

'I don't care about Sylvia,' Tony said. 'I don't think you care about Daniel.'

'I do.' Jocelyn spoke quickly. 'And Sylvia is my best friend.'

'I think you like me,' Tony said.

Jocelyn was dumbstruck. She couldn't think of a single thing she'd done that might give that impression. 'I don't.'

The weather hadn't let up, and the windows were still sealed with steam. Tony began to drive again anyway, inching forward, peering through the *I love you*s written above the dash. They were already filling in. He accelerated.

'Don't drive if you can't see,' Jocelyn told him. She herself could see nothing of the road, only the rain sliding by in sheets. There was a crash of thunder right above.

'I can't sit here with you and not kiss you,' Tony said. 'If you won't let me kiss you, then I have to drive.' He accelerated again. The car tipped as he left the shoulder, righted as he straightened. 'That was a close one,' he observed. 'There was a tree right there.' He accelerated.

Jocelyn was squeezed into the door on her side, holding on with both hands. Once again she was barely dressed – short, short tennis skirt, sleeveless shirt cut away from the shoulders. Why, in these situations, was she always so disadvantageously clothed? Tony began to sing. 'In the chilly frozen minutes oven certain tea, I long to be . . .' He was completely unhinged, so nervous he couldn't even carry a tune. The speed of the car, the crash of the thunder – nothing frightened Jocelyn as much as his singing.

She snapped the radio on to the pearly voice of the d.j. '. . . out to a special, special lady in the South Bay.' Tony singing, the heater puffing, rain and more rain. Thunder.

'Dee dee, dee da la da, dee da dee dee.' Tony accelerated again. 'Dee – da dum.'

'Stop,' Jocelyn said. 'Pull over this instant.' She used the same tone she used with Daniel's brother when it was really important that she be obeyed.

Tony wouldn't look at her. 'You know my price.'

He had obviously laid his plans carefully. He tasted of breath mints.

Jocelyn made everyone a bowl of oatmeal. A nice basin of gruel, she said. We enjoyed the joke as soon as we understood that it *was* a joke and that slices of Kentucky bourbon cake, both lemon and crème de menthe squares, and almond crescent cookies were waiting for us in the kitchen as well. We told Jocelyn it was the best gruel we'd ever had, neither too thick nor too thin, too hot nor too cold. We all said we would be the better for eating it, though only Grigg did.

We had forgiven him by now for whatever it was that had set us off; in truth we couldn't remember what it had been. 'You've said very little,' we told him encouragingly. 'Speak up! Speak out!'

But he was frowning and fetching his jacket. 'I'm afraid the fog is getting worse. I really think I should go.' He took two almond crescents for the road.

Bernadette gave us all a stern look. Even her unkempt hair was suddenly sternly unkempt. 'I hope he'll be back next time. I hope we didn't run him off. We could have been a bit nicer, I think. It must have been awkward to be the only man.'

Prudie took a tiny, affected bite of oatmeal. 'I'm sure *I* enjoyed his interesting opinions. But then, I've always been a person who likes a bit of provocation. Anyone who knows me will tell you that!'

Jocelyn knew that she had to tell Daniel and Sylvia what happened, but she was afraid. At the time she'd seemed to have only two choices – she could kiss Tony repeatedly, or she could die in a tragic rainy-day car crash, like the girl in 'Last Kiss.' But she couldn't think how to tell the story in a way that made this clear enough. She didn't even believe it herself, and she'd been there.

Two days later she still hadn't said anything. She was dressing for school when the doorbell rang. Her mother called to her, and her voice had a pinched sound. Someone, her mother couldn't imagine who, had left a puppy on the doorstep, in an orange crate, with a big bow threaded through a card that said 'I belong to Jocelyn.' The handwriting was unmistakable when you'd seen so many samples of it in the condensation on a car's windows.

'Who would take it on themselves to give someone a puppy?' her mother demanded. 'I thought Daniel was a sensible boy. I must say I'm quite surprised, and *not* in a good way.' Jocelyn had never been allowed to have a dog. A dog, in her mother's opinion, was just a story with a sad ending coming.

The puppy was of mixed parentage, white and curly-haired, and so excited to see them that he stood on his hind legs and balanced, his front paws paddling in the air. When Jocelyn picked him up he went straight for her face, sticking his tiny tongue up her nostril. There was no talk of giving him away. In two seconds Jocelyn had fallen head over heels.

Sylvia and Tony, Jocelyn and Daniel met that day, as usual, on the high school's south lawn for lunch. 'Who would give you a puppy?' Tony kept asking, long after the others would have let it drop.

'It's got to be your mother,' Daniel said. 'Whatever she says. Who else would presume? A dog is a big responsibility.'

Tony gave Jocelyn a conspiratorial smile, let his knee fall carelessly against her leg. She remembered the feel and taste of kissing him. When he wasn't smiling at her mischievously, he was staring pleadingly. How could the others not notice? She had to say something. The more time passed, the worse things became.

Sylvia opened her lunch bag to find that her mother had packed two pieces of bread with nothing between them. It was hard to think of new things to pack in a lunch day after day after day. Her mother had cracked under the pressure. Jocelyn had a Hostess cupcake and a hard-boiled egg. She tried to give them to Sylvia, but she wouldn't take them.

That evening, on his way home from work, Daniel came to meet the dog. 'Hey, little guy,' he said, holding out his fingers for a good chew, but he seemed less enchanted than distracted. 'Here's the thing,' he said to Jocelyn, and then said nothing else for a long time. They were at opposite ends of the couch so the puppy could race over the flowered surface between them. This distance also prevented Daniel from kissing her, which Jocelyn had decided she couldn't allow until she'd told him everything.

'I hope that dog's not on the furniture,' Jocelyn's mother called from upstairs. She respected Jocelyn's privacy too much to come in, but she often listened.

'The thing is,' Daniel said.

He seemed to be trying to tell her something. Jocelyn was not ready for an exchange of secrets. She told him how Mr Parker had tried to lecture on the class issues in Ibsen's *An Enemy of the People* but they'd managed to make him talk about the Smothers Brothers instead. She made a long story of it, and the punch line was 'Stupid chickens!' When she could think of nothing more to add on that subject she moved on to math class. She only had to keep talking without pause for twenty minutes or so. Daniel would never put his mother, who had enough to deal with, through the worry and trouble of his being late to dinner.

Bedtime had come to the kennels at last. There was still an occasional bark, but it led to nothing, no one took it up. The dogs were dreaming in their houses. We women were deep inside the fog now, floating in the warm, bright porch as if encased in a bubble. Sahara crawled closer to one of the heaters and lay with her head between her paws. We could see the stitching of her spine, rising and falling with her breath. In the cottony peace outside we heard the stream rinsing and spitting. Jocelyn gave us coffee in cups painted with tiny violets.

'I feel,' she said, passing among us with the cream, but not stopping at Sylvia since she knew how Sylvia liked her coffee, and had already fixed it that way, 'I feel Austen working hard to persuade us that Frank Churchill's behavior is less repulsive than it is. Too many good people in the book would be hurt if he were felt to be as bad as her usual handsome, charming villain. The Westons would be hurt. Jane Fairfax.'

'He's neither a good man like Knightley nor a bad one like Elton,' Bernadette said. When she nodded, her glasses slipped ever so slightly down her nose. We couldn't see this; we knew only because she pushed them back. 'He's complicated. I like that about him. He should come to see Mrs Weston immediately and he doesn't, but he's attentive and thoughtful when he does. He shouldn't encourage Emma into speculations about Jane that will embarrass her later, but he doesn't hold them against her. He shouldn't flirt so with Emma, but he knows somehow that she is safe from him. He needs the subterfuge, and he can see that Emma won't misunderstand it.'

'That's just what he can't know!' Jocelyn's anguished tone made Sahara get up and come to her, tail wagging tentatively. 'That's just exactly what people are always misunderstanding,' she added, with an apologetic lessening of intensity.

She offered the sugar to Allegra, who shook her head, frowning and gesturing with her spoon. 'Harriet thinks that Knightley likes her. Emma thinks that Elton doesn't like her. The book is full of people getting that wrong.'

'Elton *doesn't* like Emma,' Prudie said. 'His real interest is money and position.'

'Even so.' Jocelyn returned to her place on the couch. 'Even so.'

We thought how the dog world must be a great relief to a woman like Jocelyn, a woman with everyone's best interests at heart, a strong matchmaking impulse, and an instinct for tidiness. In the kennel, you just picked the sire and dam who seemed most likely to advance the breed through their progeny. You didn't have to ask them. You timed their encounter carefully, and leashed them together until the business was done.

On the weekend after the aborted tennis match, the weather was so lovely Jocelyn's mother suggested a picnic. They could go to the park with the puppy, now named Pride and called Pridey, and then he could piss and shit anywhere he liked and no one who had never wanted a dog in the first place would have to clean it up. Ask Sylvia, she suggested, since Sylvia had hardly been over to play with Pridey yet.

In the end they all went, Pridey, Sylvia, Tony, Daniel, Jocelyn, and Jocelyn's mother. They sat on the grass on a scratchy plaid car blanket and ate chicken legs fried while wrapped in strips of bacon, and finished the meal by dipping fresh berries in sour cream and brown sugar. The food was good but the company awkward. Every word out of Jocelyn's mouth was a guilty word. Tony played it bright and brittle. Sylvia and Daniel hardly spoke. And why in the world had her mother come along?

Pridey was so happy he blurred at the edges. He ran up the seesaw and did not weigh enough to tip it until the very end. The downward plunge frightened him, and he jumped straight into Jocelyn's arms, but two seconds later, completely recovered, he wiggled his way loose, grabbed a leaf in his teeth, and raced off, dropping it only when he found a dead robin in the grass. Pridey lived in the moment, and a moment with a dead robin in it was a very good moment. Jocelyn had to pick up the bird with a paper napkin and put it in the trash, where it lay on a half-eaten ham sandwich and a moldering apple. She never touched it, but its weight in her hand was so – well, dead – so stiff but rubbery, and the black eyes were filmed over like a window slick with steam. She went to the restroom and washed. On the wall someone had written 'Ride the train' in blue ballpoint and drawn a locomotive with the name Erica on it, and then a phone number. Of course, this might be about a train, though Jocelyn knew what Sylvia would say.

When she got back, Pridey was so happy to see her again he pissed himself. Even this didn't cheer Jocelyn up. Her mother had lit a cigarette and was breathing smoke out of her nose as if she intended to stay to the bitter end. Sometimes she drove Jocelyn crazy. She wore these slippers at home and some evenings just the sound of them shuffling in the hall was more than Jocelyn could stand.

'I was thinking,' Jocelyn said. 'Isn't it funny that I feel so dirty now, because I picked up a dead bird, but a dead bird is exactly what we all ate for lunch.'

Her mother tapped the ash loose. 'Honestly, dear! Those were drumsticks.'

'And delicious,' Tony said. 'I like that way of cooking them.'

He was an idiot, Jocelyn decided. They were all idiots. 'Don't you have somewhere to be?' she asked her mother. 'Errands to run? A life?'

She watched her mother's face fall. She had never thought about that phrase before, but it was exactly right. Everything slid downward.

Her mother put out her cigarette. 'I do, actually.' She turned in the general direction of Daniel and Sylvia. 'Thanks for letting me tag along, kids. Daniel, you'll bring Jocelyn home for me?' She packed up the picnic things and left.

'That was kind of mean, Jocelyn,' Daniel said. 'After she cooked all that food and all.'

'Bits of dead bird. Dead bird legs. It just bugged me that she wouldn't admit it. You know know how she is, Sylvia.' Jocelyn turned, but Sylvia wasn't even meeting her eyes. 'She always has to put such a gloss on everything. She still thinks I'm four years old.'

Pridey had forgiven her for the robin. He chewed through Jocelyn's shoelace as a gesture of forgiving and forgetting; he was so fast Jocelyn hadn't noticed it was happening. She had to limp to Daniel's car in order to keep the shoe on.

We are not the saints that dogs are, but mothers are expected to come a close second. 'That was fun,' was the only thing Jocelyn's mother ever said to her about the afternoon. 'You have such nice friends.'

Daniel drove her home, Pridey standing on her lap with his little paws barely reaching the window, his breath making a small, sticky cloud on the back of Jocelyn's hand. She was sorry now for having been rude to her mother. She loved her mother. She loved her mother's chicken fried with bacon strips. The guilt she was feeling over Tony was coming to a boil, and the easiest thing in the world would have been to start to cry. The hardest thing would have been to stop.

'The thing is,' Daniel said, 'that I really like Sylvia. I'm sorry, Jocelyn.' The words came from a distance, like something that had been said several days before and was just now sinking in. 'She feels terrible about it.' Daniel came to a standstill at an empty intersection. He drove so carefully and responsibly. 'She can hardly face you. We both feel terrible about it. We don't know what to do.'

The next day at school, Daniel was Sylvia's boyfriend and Tony was Jocelyn's. It was much talked of in the halls. Jocelyn had made no objection, because if she went along, it would be the first time in the history of the world that such a rearrangement suited all parties equally, and also because she wasn't in love with Daniel. Now that she thought about it, Daniel really was perfectly suited to Sylvia. Sylvia needed someone more serious than Tony. Someone who would calm her down on those occasions when she saw that the world was too awful to live in. Someone who wouldn't spend an afternoon kissing her best friend.

Besides, Tony had given her Pridey. And kissing Tony hadn't been too foul. It probably would be worse, though, without the rain and the steam and the guilt. Jocelyn had figured out enough about the way things worked to know *that*.

What makes me unhappiest about *Emma*,' said Allegra, 'are the class issues about her friend Harriet. In the end, Emma, the new, improved Emma, the chastened Emma, understands that Harriet wasn't good enough to marry the odious Elton after all. When there was some hope that her natural father was a gentleman, she would have been, but once it's established that he was in trade, then Harriet is lucky to get a farmer.'

It was now late enough that the heaters never cycled off. They hummed and puffed, and those of us seated next to them were too hot, the rest too cold. No coffee remained but the nasty bits at the bottoms of the cups, and the crème de menthe squares were gone – clear signs that the evening was coming to an end. Some of us had headaches.

'The class stuff in *Emma* is complicated.' Bernadette was settled back in her chair, her belly mounding under her dress, her feet tucked up like a girl's. She had taken yoga for years and could put her feet into some astonishing places. 'First, there's the fact of Harriet's illegitimacy, about which Austen seems quite liberal.'

She was by no means finished, but Allegra interrupted. 'She says it's a stain if unbleached by nobility or wealth.' We had just begun to suspect that Allegra might not like Austen as much as the rest of us. So far it was only a suspicion; nothing she'd said had been unfair. We were keeping watch, but *honi soit qui mal y pense*.

'I think Jane is being ironic there,' Prudie suggested. She was next to a heater. Her pale, polished cheeks were delicately flushed. 'She has an ironic wit, I think some readers miss that. I'm often ironic myself, especially in e-mail. Sometimes my friends ask, Was that a joke?'

'Was that a joke?' Allegra asked.

Bernadette went steadily on. 'Then there's the case of Robert Martin. Surely we're intended to take Mr Knightley's side on the question of

Robert Martin. Only a farmer, but at the end Emma says it will be a great pleasure to get to know him.'

'We all have a sense of level,' said Jocelyn. 'It may not be based on class exactly anymore, but we still have a sense of what we're entitled to. People pick partners who are nearly their equal in looks. The pretty marry the pretty, the ugly the ugly.' She paused. 'To the detriment of the breed.'

'Was that a joke?' Prudie asked.

Sylvia had spoken very little all night and Jocelyn was worried about it. 'What should we read next?' Jocelyn asked her. 'You pick.'

'I'm in the mood for *Sense and Sensibility*.'

'I love that one,' Bernadette said. 'It's maybe my favorite, except for *Pride and Prejudice*. Though I love *Emma*. I always forget how much until I reread it. My very favorite bit is about the strawberries. Mrs Elton in her hat, with her basket.' She thumbed through the pages. The relevant corner had been folded back, but so had several other corners; it was little help. 'Here we have it,' she said. '"Mrs Elton, in all her apparatus of happiness, her large bonnet and her basket, was very ready . . . Strawberries, and only strawberries, could now be thought or spoken of . . . 'delicious fruit – only too rich to be eaten much of – inferior to cherries . . .'"'

Bernadette read us the whole thing. It was a wonderful passage, though quite long when done aloud.

Jocelyn's relationship with Tony lasted into their senior year, and its end was unfortunately timed so as to make her miss the Winter Ball. She'd already bought a dress, a tiered, lacy, off-the-shoulder silver thing that she loved so much she would have made things go another couple of weeks if she'd been able. But by then every word he said was an irritation to her, and he did insist on continuing to talk.

Three years later Sylvia and Daniel married, and it was a formal affair, not quite their style. Jocelyn always suspected it had been planned that way so she would finally have a place to wear her dress. She brought a date, one in a series of boyfriends and lasting no longer than the others, but immortalized in the wedding pictures – raising his glass, standing with his arm around Jocelyn, seated at a table with Jocelyn's mother, the two of them deep in serious conversation.

Sylvia and Jocelyn were in college now, and they joined a consciousness-raising group that met on campus, second floor of the International House. At their third meeting, Jocelyn spoke about the summer of Mike and Steven. She hadn't meant to take a great deal of time with it, but she'd never told anyone, not even Sylvia, much about the night of the dance. She found herself crying all through the telling. She'd forgotten, until she was in the midst of it, how Bryan had looked at her to be sure she was watching, and then stuck his finger into his mouth and pulled it out.

The other women were outraged on her behalf. She'd been raped, some of them argued. It was a shame no charges had been pressed.

A shame. After the initial relief, now that the story existed in the open air and could be looked at, what Jocelyn noticed most was how unresisting she'd been. She saw, as if from above, her own inert body in the strapless dress and thin cardigan, reclining on the lounge chair. The suggestion that Bryan should have been made to face some consequences came at her like an accusation. She should have done something. Why hadn't she put up a fight? The whole time Bryan was fingering her, she was still hoping to win his good opinion!

No one else blamed her. Culturally programmed passivity, they said. The fairy-tale-princess imperative. But Jocelyn grew more and more humiliated. There were two women in the group who really *had* been raped, one of them by her own husband and repeatedly. Jocelyn felt she'd made a big deal over nothing. With her silence, she'd given Bryan a power he didn't deserve. She wasn't about to let some frat-boy asshole have a thing to say about who she was.

Who was she?

'What's wrong with me?' she asked Sylvia later. It wasn't a question for the group. 'The simplest thing. Falling in love. Falling. Why can't I do that?'

'You love dogs.'

Jocelyn waved that angrily away. 'It doesn't count. That's too easy. Hitler did that.'

She didn't go back to a fourth evening. Raising her consciousness had turned out to be one more thing that left her feeling ashamed, and she was done with feeling ashamed.

Daniel became a lobbyist in Sacramento, for an Indian tribe, a wild-river group, and the Japanese government. He was urged, from time to time, to run for office, but this was easily resisted. Politics, he said, was a foot-to-mouth occupation. Sylvia worked at the state library, in the California History Room. Jocelyn managed accounts at a small vineyard; her own dog kennel was still some years in her future and would never provide for her complete support. Pridey lived to be sixteen, and his last day on earth, it was Sylvia and Daniel who took off work to drive him to the vet with Jocelyn. They sat with her on the speck of grass outside the office, where Jocelyn held him while he died. Then they all sat in the car together. No one was able to stop crying long enough to see the road home.

How are you doing?' Jocelyn asked Sylvia. They had one minute alone together in the kitchen and a hundred things to say that could not be said in front of Allegra. Allegra was Daniel's darling, his only daughter, and though she'd immediately taken her mother's side and stuck there, it was unnatural and made us all sad.

The kitchen was, of course, beautifully done, with counters of blue and white tile, brass fixtures, and an antique stove. Sahara sat by the sink, turned to show her fine African profile. After everyone had gone and there was no one to see, Sahara would be given the plates to lick, but this was a secret and Sahara could keep a secret.

Jocelyn was rinsing the glasses. The water in town was so hard that they got scratched if they were put in the dishwasher, and therefore had to be done by hand.

'Dead woman walking,' Sylvia said. 'You know how Daniel used to drive me crazy? It turns out I was very happily married. For thirty-two years. I miss him like my heart has been torn from my chest. What are the odds?'

Jocelyn put down a glass and took Sylvia's cold hands in her own slippery, soapy ones. 'I've been very happily unmarried all those same years. Everything is going to be all right.' It was occurring to her for the first time that she was losing Daniel, too. She'd handed him over, but she'd never given him up. Now, while she was breeding her dogs and dusting her lightbulbs and reading her books, he had packed his bags and moved away. 'I love you very much,' she told Sylvia.

'How could I have let myself forget that most marriages end in divorce?' Sylvia asked. 'You don't learn that in Austen. She always has a wedding or two at the end.'

Allegra, Prudie, and Bernadette appeared as she spoke, carrying their coffee cups, napkins, plates. There was something, perhaps created by Sylvia's words, of the bridal procession about it. The way the golden light reflected in the windows. The silence of the fog outside. The women coming, one after another, into the kitchen, with their dirty dishes held before them, until we were all gathered together.

'*Le monde est le livre des femmes*,' Prudie offered.

Whatever that meant. We could still see her lips, so she might have been perfectly serious, unless it was more of her ironic wit. Either way, we could think of no polite response.

'My dearest, most beloved Sylvia,' Jocelyn said. A tiny, lady-like drop of drool plinked from Sahara's mouth to the stone floor. Our forks and spoons slid under the foam of soap in the sink. Allegra put her arms around her mother and her head on her mother's shoulder. 'We haven't come to the end yet.'

Jocelyn explains the dog show:

The judge generally begins by asking all handlers to gait their dogs around the edge of the ring and then stack them in a line along one side. As the dogs move, the judge stands in the center, assessing grace, balance, soundness.

When the dogs are stacked – a pose designed to display the dog to best advantage – the judge conducts a hands-on examination of the bite, depth of chest, spring of ribs, shoulder angulation, coat, and body condition. On males, the judge manually confirms two testicles.

After this, the handlers gait their dogs again, each in turn now, first moving away so the judge can evaluate from behind, then coming back so the judge can see from the front. The judge watches for movement faults: Does the dog move true, or do his feet cross over? Is his stride free or tight, easy or restricted? In the final stages, the judge may ask competing handlers to gait two at a time so a direct comparison can be made, before selecting a winner.

The dog show emphasizes bloodline, appearance, and comportment, but money and breeding are never far from anyone's mind.

APRIL

CHAPTER TWO

in which we read
Sense and Sensibility
with Allegra

A partial list of things not found in the books of Jane Austen:

    locked-room murders
    punishing kisses
    girls dressed up as boys (and rarely the reverse)
    spies
    serial killers
    cloaks of invisibility
    Jungian archetypes, most regrettably, doppelgängers
    cats

But let's not focus on the negative.

'I don't think there's anything better in all of Austen than those pages where Fanny Dashwood persuades her husband, step by step by step, not to give his stepmother and sisters any money,' Bernadette said. She repeated the same point in a variety of unilluminating ways while Allegra listened to the soft percussion of rain on the roof, the windows, and the deck. Bernadette was dressed today in something resembling desert robes, only periwinkle blue. Her hair had been cut, which left it less scope for improvisation, and she looked very nice, which was all the more remarkable for being a bit of magic done without mirrors.

It was cold out, and wet, the way it gets in April just when you've convinced yourself that spring is here. Winter's last laugh. The book club was circled about the woodstove in Sylvia's huge living room, with the stove door open and the flames wrapped tight about the logs. Overhead, a hundred bird's-eyes in the high bird's-eye-maple ceiling looked down on the little gathering.

Allegra's elbow often ached when it rained, and she rubbed it without noticing she was doing so until she saw her mother look at her, which made her stop and think of something diverting to say. 'I like a progression,' she agreed. 'Repetition is tedious' – this aimed at Bernadette, but Allegra wouldn't have said it if Bernadette had been likely to get it –

'because there's no direction to it. I especially like a progression that turns things completely over. Takes you pole to pole.'

Allegra was a creature of extremes – either stuffed or starving, freezing or boiling, exhausted or electric with energy. She'd moved back home the month before, when her father had moved out. Jocelyn looked at Allegra approvingly. She was a very good daughter. Sylvia would have been very lonely there without her.

No one could be lonely with Allegra in the house. Such a vivacious presence, her company must be a great comfort. Except that – really Jocelyn didn't wish to even be thinking this – Allegra, well, she felt things very deeply. It was one of her delightful qualities; she wept with those who wept.

Sylvia's boys could be very comforting, too, especially Diego. Andy couldn't manage a sustained sympathy, though he was good for an hour or two. It was too bad Diego couldn't come. Of course, he couldn't; he had a job and his family. But Diego would have cheered Sylvia up. While Allegra sometimes felt things so deeply you ended up consoling her even when the tragedy was entirely your own.

Jocelyn imagined Sylvia compelled to put a good face on things for Allegra's sake. To have to appear happy when she was so miserable. Who would require it? She imagined Sylvia making Allegra soups and running her baths, Allegra collapsed on the couch, tucked up in shawls and plied with tea. Really, it seemed too much, that Sylvia should be caring for Allegra at such a time. A surreptitious look at the CD cases scattered about the player told Jocelyn that someone had been indulging in a good wallow, and this someone was not Sylvia, not unless she'd developed a sudden taste for Fiona Apple. How could Allegra be so selfish?

But then, she'd always been a difficult child. Beautiful, beyond a doubt. She had Sylvia's dark eyes and Daniel's bright hair, her face the best possible combination of the two, her figure like Sylvia's, but sexier. Yet none of her parents' steadiness or placidity. When happy, she was uncontrollable, when sad, inconsolable, until she changed – fast as a finger snap – long after you'd given up. Sylvia had a repertoire of tricks that had worked on the boys when they were little. 'If you were a dog I'd cheer you up by rubbing you behind your ears,' she'd say, rubbing as described. 'If you were a cat, I'd scratch under your chin,' scratching. 'If you were a horse, I'd pet your nose. If you were a bird, I'd stroke your stomach' – doing so – 'but since' – quickly lifting his shirt – 'you're a boy' – she would blow wet, loud blasts of air onto his belly until he was gasping with laughter. This same scene would send Allegra into a fury.

One day when she was four years old, while leafing through Sylvia's beauty magazines, Allegra had taken offense at how much white space she found. 'I don't like white,' she'd said. 'It's so plain.' She burst into tears. 'It's so plain and there's so much of it.' She sat for more than an hour, sobbing, working her way through the pages, coloring in the whites of people's eyes, their teeth, the spaces between paragraphs, the frames around ads. She was sobbing because she could see that she would never be done; her whole life would be used up in the hopeless, endless task of amending this single lapse in taste. She would grow old, and there would still be white sheets, white walls, her own white hair.

White snow. 'The whole beginning sequence has something of the fairy tale about it,' Grigg said. 'With a lovely twist. Once upon a time, after the death of her beloved husband, a gentle stepmother was forced to live in a house ruled by her wicked stepdaughter.'

Allegra was sort of our hostess this month, but it was Sylvia's house and Sylvia's food, so it was sort of Sylvia. In this role, whatever role this was, Sylvia was determined to treat Grigg well today. He'd been the last to arrive, which had made her wonder whether he was coming, and therefore all the more pleased when he showed. Bernadette would never forgive them if he left early again. He had just made a very interesting point.

'Such an interesting point,' said Sylvia. 'In fact, in a society where money passes to the eldest son, this can't have been an unusual case? But how often does it appear in books? The problems of older women don't interest most writers. Trust Miss Austen!'

'But the book isn't really so much about Mrs Dashwood as about the young, beautiful daughters,' Prudie pointed out. She had come straight from a meeting of the teachers' union and was, therefore, uncommonly lipsticked and politicized. Her eyebrows had grown back in a bit, or else she'd painted over the deficiency; that was a relief, but the voice she was using was a public-speaking voice and that was an aggravation. It was, Sylvia supposed, an occupational hazard, more to be pitied, and so on. Her articulation would surely become more normal as the evening progressed. 'Once it actually gets going. Colonel Brandon's not much younger than Mrs Dashwood, but he falls in love with her youngest daughter, never her. An older man can still fall in love. An older woman better not.'

Prudie had spoken without thinking, but the thinking came rapidly behind. What a faux pas she'd just made, though, in justice, she felt that she wasn't the sort who often stumbled that way. Of course, this only made it more obvious when she did. Rumor had it that Daniel was seeing someone, had, in fact, left Sylvia not because the marriage had gone bad, but because he'd been hit by the thunderbolt. Prudie looked for something to add that would make it clear she hadn't been speaking of Sylvia, though, honestly, not that Sylvia wasn't attractive enough for her age, but what could her prospects be at fifty-whatever?

'Not,' Prudie said, but Bernadette had spoken at the same time and Bernadette was the one who carried through. Bernadette was the one who carried on. The rain ticked off the time while she spoke. The fire turned from blue to orange, pole to pole. The log in the stove fell.

Bernadette was capable of speaking and enjoying the stillness of the scene at the same time. Nothing disturbed her peace less than the sound of her own voice. Sylvia's house was so much quieter than Jocelyn's. Sylvia lived downtown, near campus but back from the street, directly behind the Phi Beta Pi sorority, unless it was the Pi Beta Phi. This was a hidden, tranquil location, except during rush, when the girls gathered on the lawn for a week, singing, 'I want to be a Phi Beta Pi [or the other], boom, boom,' like sirens to sailors. Of course, the club wouldn't have met here if it had been rush week. If Daniel had moved out during rush week, Bernadette would have completely understood. Jocelyn had told her that Daniel was seeing someone young enough to be his sister.

Jocelyn knew how a child felt when her father decamped. But surely it was different when the child was grown-up and had a place of her own. Allegra had every right to miss her father, just not the way Sylvia did. Sylvia was daily deserted; Allegra had merely had her Christmases spoiled. From now on there would be no place to come where she felt entirely at home. Her holidays would be split down the middle, like a grapefruit.

December was still months away, but Jocelyn knew enough about Allegra to guess that she'd already thought of it. Christmas had always been such a big deal to her. As a child she'd spent the days leading up to it sick with apprehension, so afraid that she wouldn't like her gifts, that the wishes closest to her heart would go unattended. She would cry herself to sleep at night, anticipating her disappointment. By Christmas morning she'd have the whole family exhausted and peevish.

In fact, her requests were never difficult or expensive, and there was no reason not to indulge them. From the moment the actual getting began, Allegra was wild with delight. She loved surprises and ripped her presents open, with cries of joy for whatever was inside. 'For me?' she'd ask, as if it were too much to believe. 'More for me?'

Every year she'd be given a sum of money with which to buy presents as well, and she spent it thoughtfully, but it never went far enough. So she added things that she'd made, drawings for her brothers and books of stapled pictures for her parents and Jocelyn. Ashtrays and ornaments. Stones and pine cones painted with glitter. Bookends and calendars. As she grew older these handmade gifts outstripped the store-bought ones. She was not – she was quite insistent on this point – an artist. But she was clever. Her father taught her to use power tools, and she opted for shop in high school rather than the cooking class. By then she was designing furniture and jewelry. The glass-top coffee table on which Jocelyn had just set her purse was something Allegra had made back then, and it was as nice as anything you saw anywhere.

Now she sold her things in stores, online, and at craft fairs. Her current project was to collect damaged jewelry at flea markets, dinged beads and bad cameos, and crush them, pressing the resulting bits into fish-scale mosaics. Sylvia was wearing a new bracelet made of mismatched earrings caught together in a delicate chain. It was a great deal prettier than it sounded, and showed that Allegra's heart, as always, was in the right place. The year before this she'd joined a caroling group in San Francisco and spent her Christmas Eve singing second soprano in a round of hospitals and nursing homes. Sylvia had a picture of her on the mantel, wearing a purple robe and carrying a lit candle. A silver frame of Allegra's own making. A madonna with fire-bright cheeks, eyes like mirrors.

Austen's minor characters are really wonderful,' said Grigg. 'Good as Dickens's.' Sylvia was very glad to have Grigg speaking right up this way. She wouldn't have taken issue for the world, and anyway, what was there to possibly take issue with? There were authors whose names she didn't like to use in the same sentence with Austen's, but Dickens had written some very good books in his day. Especially *David Copperfield*.

'And speaking of Dickens,' Grigg said – were they never to be done speaking of Dickens! – 'I was trying to think of contemporary writers who devote that same care to the secondary characters, and it occurred to me that it's a common sitcom device. You can just imagine how today Austen would be writing 'The Elinor Show,' with Elinor as the solid moral center and the others stumbling into and out of her New York apartment with their wacky lives.'

Sylvia could imagine no such thing. It was all very well to point out fairy-tale themes in Austen; Sylvia had done this herself. *Pride and Prejudice* as 'Beauty and the Beast.' *Persuasion* as 'Cinderella,' et cetera, et cetera. It was even all right to suggest that Dickens also did well what Austen did superbly. But 'The Elinor Show'! *She did not think so*. What a waste those eyelashes were on a man who watched sitcoms.

Even Bernadette was silent with disapproval. The rain drummed on the roof, the fire sputtered. The women looked at their hands or at the fire, but *not* at one another. It was Allegra who finally spoke. 'Good as the secondary characters are, I do think Austen gets better at them in her later books. The women – Mrs Jennings, Mrs Palmer, and that other one – are kind of a mishmash. Hard to keep straight. And I loved Mr Palmer's acid tongue, but then he reforms and disappears very disappointingly.'

In fact, Allegra had instantly recognized herself in the sour Mr Palmer. She, too, often thought of sharp things to say, and she said them more often than she wished. Mr Palmer didn't suffer fools and neither did Allegra, but it wasn't something she was proud of. It didn't spring, as Austen suggested, from the desire to appear superior, unless lack of patience was a superior quality. 'Plus' – Allegra allowed herself one more moment's irritation over the silencing of Mr Palmer – 'I do think *Sense and Sensibility* stretches our credulity at the end. I mean, the sudden marriage of Robert Ferrars and Lucy Steele! The later books are more smoothly plotted.'

'It requires some hand-waving,' Grigg agreed. (That stern moment of silence utterly lost on him! What would it take?) 'You see, of course, the effect Austen's going for, that moment of misdirection, but you wish she hadn't had to go to such lengths for it.'

The Austen-bashing was getting out of hand. Sylvia looked to Jocelyn, whose face was stoic, her voice calm but firm. 'I think Austen explains it very well. My credulity remains unstretched.'

'I don't have any trouble with it,' Sylvia said.

'Perfectly in character,' said Prudie.

Allegra frowned in her pretty way, chewing on a fingernail. You could see that she worked with her hands. Her nails were short, and the skin around them rough and dry. You could see that she took things to heart. Hangnails had been teased loose and then stripped, leaving painful peeled bits by her thumbs. Prudie would have liked to take her somewhere for a manicure. When your fingers were long and tapered like that, you might as well make the most of them.

'I suppose,' Allegra conceded, 'if the writer's not allowed to pull an occasional rabbit out of a hat, there would be no fun in writing a book at all.'

Well, Prudie thought, Allegra would be the one to know where writers found their fun. Prudie herself had no problems with girl-on-girl. She opened her mouth to tease Allegra about her book-writing girlfriend, which would certainly make this point, as well as alert Grigg to the lay of the land.

But Grigg was agreeing again. Really, he had become very agreeable where Allegra was concerned! He was seated next to her on the couch, and Prudie tried to remember how this had come about. Had it been the only seat left, or had he schemed for it?

Usually Allegra managed to work her sexuality into any conversation. This was a point of contention with her mother, who thought it rude to press sexual details onto slight acquaintances. 'Your paperboy doesn't need to know,' she'd say. 'Your mechanic doesn't care.' Allegra would never believe that homophobia wasn't at the bottom of this. 'I won't be closeted,' she declared. 'It's not in my nature.' But now, just when the information might be usefully shared, she was suddenly, irritatingly silent on the subject.

'How's Corinne?' Prudie asked impishly. 'Speaking of writers.'

'Corinne and I have gone our separate ways,' Allegra answered, which Prudie then remembered she'd been told. Allegra's face had turned to stone. But that business with Corinne had been months ago, surely. Prudie trusted that it wasn't too sensitive a subject to be raised *now*. No one had told her they were never to mention Corinne's name, because she was certainly capable of holding her tongue when necessary.

Grigg was flipping through his enormous complete-works-of. Why did men always have to have the biggest books? It wasn't clear he'd even heard.

While Allegra liked to describe herself as a garden-variety lesbian, she knew that the truth was more complicated. Sexuality is rarely as simple as it is natural. Allegra was not entirely indifferent to men, just to men's bodies. She was often attracted to the men in books; they seemed, as a rule, more passionate than the women in books, though actual women seemed more passionate than actual men. As a rule.

Allegra was aroused most by passion itself. Poems of the confessional sort. Vistas, all kinds, even swampy. Swelling music. Danger. She needed to feel to feel alive.

Adrenaline was her drug of choice. This was *not* something she talked much about, and especially not to people who knew her mother. Sylvia believed in being careful, though she also believed that being careful was often not enough. She saw the world as an obstacle course. You picked your way across it while the terrain slipped about and things fell or exploded or both. Disasters arrived in the form of accidents, murders, earthquakes, disease, and divorce. She'd tried to raise sensible, cautious children. During the high school years, when Allegra knew that Sylvia had been congratulating herself on her daughter's good appetite, good grades, sweet friends, sober habits, Allegra had been cutting herself.

Allegra and Corinne met in a small plane on Allegra's twenty-eighth birthday. She'd spent the night with her parents, and her dad had made her waffles in the morning. Then she'd left, telling them she was meeting friends back in the city. Instead she'd gone to a tiny airport in Vacaville for an appointment she'd made months earlier. This was her very first solo jump. She hesitated at the last minute, with the sky roaring past her – she wasn't insane – and wondered whether she was going to go through with it. She was more afraid than she'd been on her first tandem jump. She'd been warned of this, but it still surprised her. If she could have backed down without anyone's knowing, she would have. Instead, merely to save face, she threw herself out. She pulled the cord too soon. The instant she did, she wished she were free-falling again. That was the best part, and she saw she would have to do this again, and better next time. The chute opened, jerking her upward, taking her breath, the straps compressing her breasts. She grabbed the cords, pulled herself into a better position. How odd, to be minding the uncomfortable straps at the very moments in which she was plunging to earth from a plane. 'That's one small step for a man, and it's a bit hot in this spacesuit.'

The fall became quiet, contemplative. She was surprised at how long it seemed to last, how she experienced each second of it with such clarity. She came down hard, landing on her butt and then tipping so that she crushed the point of her elbow, and her butt hurt immediately, but she didn't feel her elbow at first. She lay, looking up, with the chute spilled behind her. Clouds floated, birds flew. Her blood was still plummeting deliciously. Corinne and the tandem master drifted over her. Allegra could see the bottoms of Corinne's boots, which meant Corinne was in the wrong position. Like Mary Poppins.

Allegra tried to stand, and as she tipped herself upright, a white-hot wire shot through her arm. Her ears were full of sea sounds; her eyes were full of light. There was a smell like tar. She took a step, pitched forward into the void.

She came to with Corinne speaking. 'Are you all right? Can you answer me?' The words passed over like the shadows of birds, and then the darkness spread silently out from those shadows. The next time she awoke, she was in Corinne's arms.

It was an irresistible way to meet. By the time they got to the hospital they were partners in crime. Sylvia mustn't be told about the jump, but

Allegra was still too faint, too fading in and out, to trust herself on the phone with her mother. 'Don't tell her anything,' Allegra said. She remembered how she'd broken her foot years before, in kindergarten, falling off the monkey bars. She'd spent a night in the hospital and Sylvia had stayed the whole time, sitting by the bed in one of those awful plastic chairs, never closing her eyes. Allegra would have said she was closer to Daniel than to Sylvia – even within the family there was something guarded about Sylvia – but now, with her arm hurting horribly, she wanted her mother. 'Make her come.'

She lay on the gurney, her mind drifting over the white swirling contours of the ceiling like snow. Corinne punched her cell phone and then picked up Allegra's unhurt hand while she talked, stroking it with her thumb. 'Mrs Hunter?' Corinne said. 'You don't know me, but I'm a friend of Allegra's. Allegra is fine. We think her arm is broken, but I'm here at the Vacaville Kaiser with her and she's going to be fine.' Corinne described, in great detail, an unfortunate chain of events. A friendly dog, a boy with a ball, a pebbly patch of road, Allegra on a bicycle. Sylvia bought it all. These things happened, even when dogs were friendly, even when bike helmets were worn. Allegra had always been so careful to wear her bike helmet. But sometimes it just didn't matter how careful a person was. She and Daniel would be there as soon as they could. They'd hope to thank Corinne for her kindness in person.

Allegra was impressed. Anyone who could lie as effortlessly as Corinne was someone to keep on the right side of. You would want her lies told for and not to you.

But Corinne turned out not to be the thrill-seeker Allegra assumed. Later, when Allegra mentioned some ideas that might add a touch of adrenaline to their lovemaking, Corinne was unreceptive. She'd been skydiving only as an antidote to writer's block. She'd hoped to shake something loose. She saw the void as the blank page; she was throwing herself onto it. The skydiving had been a metaphor.

But it hadn't helped, and she would be a fool to repeat the experiment. 'You broke your arm!' she would say, as if Allegra didn't know this. Corinne kept herself on the ground, at safe speeds, inside her apartment, drinking cups of fretful tea. She was a dental hygienist, but not a passionate one – she'd chosen it because it seemed like a job that would allow her time to write. Really, she lived the most boring life, though Allegra was totally in love with her before she saw this. The only part of Corinne that Allegra had seen clearly in those hours at the hospital when she was flying on painkillers and falling falling falling in love was the lying.

*

Sylvia had uncorked a nice Petit Syrah, something that went well with cheese and crackers, the rain and the fire. Jocelyn had drunk just enough to feel companionable, not quite enough to feel witty. She was holding up her glass so the firelight came through it. It was a heavy, faceted crystal, a wedding gift once, now unfortunately clouded by thirty-two years of hard water in the dishwasher. If only Sylvia had taken proper care.

'*Sense and Sensibility* features one of Austen's favorite characters – the handsome debaucher,' Jocelyn said. 'She's very suspicious of good-looking men, I think. Her heroes tend to be actively nondescript.' Twirling her glass so the ruby-colored wine rose in thin sheets and fell again. Daniel was a nondescript man, though Jocelyn wouldn't say it and Sylvia would never concede it. Of course, in Austenworld, that was all to his credit.

'Except for Darcy,' Prudie said.

'We haven't gotten to Darcy yet.' There was a warning in Jocelyn's voice. Prudie took it no further.

'Her heroes have better hearts than her villains. They're deserving. Edward is good people,' said Bernadette.

'Well, of course,' in Allegra's smoothest, most melodious tones. Probably only her mother and Jocelyn would know how impatient such an obvious point made her. Allegra took a gulp of wine so big Jocelyn could hear it going down.

'In real life,' said Grigg, 'women want the heel, not the soul.' He spoke with great bitterness, eyelashes pumping. Jocelyn knew a lot of men who believed this. Women don't want nice men, they cry out over beers, to any woman nice enough to listen. They condemn themselves loudly, lamenting their uncontrollable, damnable niceness. In fact, when you got to know these men better, lots of them weren't as nice as they believed themselves to be. There was no percentage in pointing this out.

'But Austen's not entirely unsympathetic to Willoughby in the end,' Bernadette said. 'I love that bit where he confesses to Elinor. You can feel Austen softening just the way Elinor does, in spite of herself. She won't allow that he's a good person, because he's not, but she lets you feel for him, just for a moment. She has to balance it on a knife edge – too much and you'll be wishing him with Marianne after all.'

'Structurally that confession bookends the long story Brandon tells her.' Another writerly observation from Allegra. Corinne might be gone, Jocelyn thought, but her ghost certainly remained, reading Allegra's books, making Allegra's points. Perhaps Jocelyn had been too hard on Allegra earlier. She'd neglected to factor in Corinne when calculating the loss of Daniel. Poor darling.

'Poor Elinor! Willoughby on one side, Brandon on the other. She is quite *entre deux feux*.' Prudie had a bit of lipstick on her teeth, or else it was wine. Jocelyn wanted to lean across and wipe it off with a napkin, the way she did when Sahara needed tidying. But she restrained herself; Prudie didn't belong to her. The fire sculpted Prudie's face, left the hollows of her cheeks hollow, brightened her deep-set eyes. She wasn't pretty like Allegra, but she was attractive in an interesting way. She drew your eye. She would probably age well, like Anjelica Huston. If only she would stop speaking French. Or go to France, where it would be less noticeable.

'And Lucy, too,' Bernadette said. 'Something about Elinor. Everyone wants to tell her their secrets. She encourages intimacy without meaning to.'

'Why doesn't Brandon fall in love with her, I wonder?' Jocelyn asked. Jocelyn would never second-guess Austen, not in a million years, but that was the match she would have tried to make. 'They're perfect for each other.'

'No, he needs Marianne's animation,' said Allegra. 'Because he has none of his own.'

Corinne craved confession. Where Allegra wished to be teasingly intimidated before lovemaking, Corinne wished to be soothed with secrets afterward. 'I want to know everything about you,' she said, which was just what a lover should say, and roused no suspicions. 'Especially the things you've never told anyone.'

'Once I say them, they'll change,' Allegra protested. 'They won't be secrets anymore.'

'No,' said Corinne. 'They'll be *our* secrets. Trust me.'

So Allegra told her:

1. There was a special class at my grammar school. A class for retarded children. Sometimes we saw them, but mostly they were kept away. They had a different recess, a different lunch-time. Maybe they only came for half the day.

One of these children was a boy named Billy. He carried a basketball wherever he went, and he sometimes talked to it. Nonsense, gibberish. I used to think that he was only aping human conversation, that he didn't understand it involved actual words and people who talked back. He wore a hat, squashed down on his head, which made his ears stick out like Dopey in *Snow White*. His nose ran a lot. It made me unhappy to think about him, or about any of them. Mostly I didn't.

One day I saw him at the edge of the playground, where he wasn't supposed to be. I thought he'd get in trouble if anyone else saw him. The teacher for the special class always seemed to be shouting at someone. So I went up to him, congratulating myself the whole time on how caring I was, how I could talk to Billy just as if he were a real boy. But when I got close I saw he had his penis in his hand. He showed it to me, laid it flat along his palm for me to look at. It twitched there, like it was being poked with pins. I went back to my friends.

A few weeks later, there was a day when my father picked me up after class. He was distracted by something; I felt ignored. So I told him how there was this boy at school who'd made me look at his penis. An older boy. Daddy was more upset than I'd bargained for; right away I wished I'd kept my mouth shut. He demanded the boy's name, stopped to look the family up in the phone book at the drugstore, drove over to their house, banged on the front door. A woman came. She had braids like a child, but gray hair; it struck me as odd. She wore those winged glasses. Daddy started to talk and she started to cry. But angrily at first. 'None of you give a damn about us,' she said. I wasn't used to people swearing, so I was shocked. And then she wasn't angry anymore; it was more like despair. 'What do you expect me to do?'

'I expect you to talk to your boy –' Daddy was saying, when Billy appeared behind her, holding his stupid ball and muttering. Daddy stopped mid-sentence.

Daddy had a younger brother who was retarded. He died when he was fifteen, hit by a car. I've always been afraid that I wouldn't love a child unless it was beautiful. I've always been afraid to have children because of that. But Daddy says his mother loved her retarded child best. She always said that a mother's love goes where it's needed.

After his brother died, Daddy tried to get his mother to go out more. He and Mom tried to take Grandma to movies and concerts and plays. But she usually said no. He would drop by to see how she was doing, and she'd be sitting at the kitchen table, staring out the window. 'I can't think of a blessed thing I want to do anymore,' she'd say.

So Billy was standing behind his mother, talking to his basketball with more and more agitation in his voice. Daddy was apologizing, but Billy's mom was having none of it. 'What do you know?' she asked. 'With your pretty little girl going off to college one day. Marrying. Having more pretty children for you.'

We got back in the car and drove home. Daddy said, 'I wouldn't have added to that woman's troubles for anything in the world.' He said, 'You must have known there was an important part of the story you were leaving out.' He said, 'Why didn't you tell me? I would have handled things very differently.' 'Go to your room,' he said. I hadn't known I could make him that angry. I was afraid he'd stopped loving me. He wouldn't take my hand. He wouldn't look at me.

I couldn't defend myself, even to myself. I tried. I thought about how I'd had no idea he would get so upset, no idea she would get so upset. I didn't know there would be tears. I wouldn't have said a word if I'd known. But why had I said a word? I'd just been idly angling for attention. I hadn't told Daddy that Billy was retarded, because I knew I'd get more attention doing it the other way. I hadn't even minded when Billy showed me his penis. It seemed kind of friendly.

2. One time we went to a museum where there were paintings by van Gogh. I liked how thick they were. Daddy said that artists paint the way they actually see, or maybe he said something else, but I heard it that way. I thought about van Gogh looking out from his eyes at a world thick like that. I'd never wondered if I saw the world the way everyone else did or if I saw something better or wrong or different. How would you know? How would van Gogh say, Does everything look sort of thick to you? He wouldn't even think to say it.

The next day I lay out on the grass in our backyard and I looked straight into the sun, the way my mother had told me never to do because it would damage my eyes. I thought that I would grow up to be a famous artist and everything and everyone I saw, everything and everyone I painted, would be blinding to look at.

3. My parents believed children should have lots of free time. They believed in dreaming. I had piano lessons briefly, but they didn't take, and I didn't do after-school sports or anything until I was in high school. I read a lot and I made things. I looked for four-leaf clovers. I watched ant colonies. Ants have very little unscheduled time. Places to go, people to see. I adopted a particular nest, out by a stepping-stone in Mom's mission garden. I was very good to my ants at first. I brought them bits of cookies with sprinkles; I landscaped with shells and thought how *I'd* like to find a shell so big I could climb inside, go exploring.

I made tiny newspapers of ant events, stamp-sized papers at first, then a bit bigger, too big for ants, it distressed me, but I couldn't fit the stories otherwise and I wanted real stories, not just lines of something that looked like writing. Anyway, imagine how small an ant paper would really be. Even a stamp would have been like a basketball court.

I imagined political upheavals, plots and coups d'état, and I reported on them. I think I may have been reading a biography of Mary Queen of Scots at the time. Did you read those orange biographies as a child? The ones all about the childhoods of famous people, and the last chapter would be the accomplishments that made them famous? God, I loved those books. I remember Ben Franklin and Clara Barton and Will Rogers and Jim Thorpe and Amelia Earhart and Madame Curie, and one about the first white child born in the Roanoke colony – Virginia Dare? – but I guess that must have all been made up.

Anyway, there was this short news day for the ants. I'd run out of political plots, or I was bored with them. So I got a glass of water and I created a flood. The ants scrambled for safety, swimming for their lives. I was kind of ashamed, but it made good copy. I told myself I was bringing excitement into their usual humdrum. The next day, I dropped a rock on them. It was a meteorite from outer space. They gathered around it and ran up and over it; obviously they didn't know what to do. It prompted three letters to the editor. Eventually I torched them. I was always way too interested in matches. Things got a little out of hand and the fire spread from the anthill into the garden. Only a little, not as bad as that sounds. Diego came and stamped it out, and I remember crying and trying to get him to stop, because he was stepping on my ants.

But what a horrible, heartless queen I turned out to be. I will never seek the presidency.

4. There was this boy I fucked when I was twenty-two, just because he wanted it so much. He was a student from Galway, and we met in Rome and traveled together for three weeks. On our last night together, the night before I had to go home, we were in Prague. We went to dinner and then out to the bars, and I drank until I was wetly sentimental, and demanded an exchange of tokens. He gave me a photograph of him holding a cat. I forced my silver ring onto his finger. It caught at the knuckle, but I pushed it down.

He said how touched he was. He swore he'd never take it off, and then he tried to take it off and he couldn't. His finger began to swell and turn odd colors. We went to the restroom of the pub and tried to soap it loose, but it was too late, the finger far too swollen. We asked for butter and got it, but that didn't work either. His face was now turning an odd color as well, sort of a fishy white. You know how pale the Irish are; they never go outdoors there. We went back to the hostel and I tried to take his mind off it by fucking him, but this was only a temporary diversion. His finger was round as a sausage and he couldn't bend it anymore.

So we went looking for a taxi to take us to a hospital. By now it was about three in the morning; the streets were dark, cold, and silent. We walked several blocks, and he was actually starting to whine, like a dog. When we did finally find a ride, the driver spoke no English. I made siren sounds and pointed, again and again, to the finger. I pantomimed a stethoscope. When you picture this, you have to picture me very drunk. I don't know what the driver thought initially, but he did get it at last, and then the hospital turned out to be less than a block away. He coasted forward and let us out. He was saying something as he drove off. We couldn't understand it, but we could guess.

The hospital was closed, but there was an intercom and we spoke on it to someone else who didn't speak English. He begged us to be intelligible and then gave up and buzzed us in. All the hallways were dark, and we walked down several until we saw some lights in a waiting room. I used to have dreams like that, dark hallways, echoing footsteps. Labyrinths that twisted and circled, with the directions printed on the walls in some alien alphabet. I mean I had the dreams before this happened, and I still have them sometimes: I'm lost in a foreign city; people talk, but I can't understand them.

So we followed the light and found a doctor, and he spoke English, which was a bit of luck, really. We explained about the ring and he stared at us. 'You're in internal medicine,' he said. 'I'm a heart surgeon.' I was prepared to go back to the hostel rather than put up with such embarrassment, but then it wasn't my finger. (Though it was my ring.) But Conor – that was his name – was not leaving.

'It hurts more than I can say,' he said. Which is sort of a koan, if you think about it. Anyway, I was thinking about it.

'You're drunk, yes?' the doctor asked. He took Conor away and removed the ring, screwing it off by force. Apparently this was astonishingly painful, but I slept through it in the waiting room.

Afterward I asked Conor where the ring was. He'd left it in the doctor's office. I pictured it lying in one of those blue kidney-shaped dishes. Conor said it had been badly dented in the removal, but I'd made it myself, so I was the tiniest bit hurt that he'd forgotten it. I would have gone back for it if the doctor hadn't been so cross. 'I wanted you to have it as a keepsake,' I told Conor.

'I guess I'll remember you, all right,' he said.

*

The phone rang in the kitchen and Allegra went to answer it. Daniel was on the other end. 'How's your mom doing, sweetpea?' he asked.

'*Bueno*. She's lovely. We're having a party. Ask her yourself,' Allegra said. She put the phone down and went back into the living room. 'It's Dad,' she told Sylvia. 'It's a guilt call.'

Sylvia went to the phone, carrying her wine. 'Hello, Daniel.' She turned off the kitchen light and sat in the dark, her glass in one hand and the phone in the other. The rain was loud; one of the gutters on the roof emptied right outside the kitchen.

'She'll hardly speak to me,' he said.

Sylvia hoped she wasn't being asked to intercede. That would be too much. But she knew how Daniel loved Allegra; she couldn't help feeling sorry for him, order herself as she would to stop. The refrigerator gave one of its funny rattles; the familiarity, the hominess of the sound nearly undid her. She pressed her glass against her face. A moment passed before she could trust herself to speak. 'Give her time.'

'I have someone coming on Saturday to look at the upstairs shower. You needn't be there, I'll come and deal with it. I'm just giving you fair warning. You and Allegra. In case you don't want to see me.'

'It's not your house anymore.'

'Yes, it is. I'm leaving the marriage, I'm not leaving you. As long as you're in the house, I'll take care of the house.'

'Fuck off,' said Sylvia.

There was a burst of laughter from the living room. 'I'll let you get back to your guests,' Daniel said. 'I'll be there between ten and twelve Saturday. Go to the farmer's market, buy those pistachios you like so much. You won't even know I've been by, except that the shower will be fixed.'

Corinne joined a writing group that met once a week. She hoped it would function as a kind of deadline, forcing her to work. She did seem to be spending more time at the computer, and occasionally, Allegra heard the keys. Corinne's mood had improved, and she talked a lot at dinner now about point of view and pacing and deep structure. All very abstract.

The writing group met at a Quaker meeting hall, and initially there'd been some question, the Quakers being so kind as to allow the use of their space without remuneration, whether the group shouldn't honor Quaker principles in the work they brought there. Was it right to accept this gift and then share work with violent or unwholesome themes? The group decided, after much discussion, that a work might need to be violent in order to espouse nonviolence effectively. They were writers.

They, of all people, must resist censorship in whatever guise. The Quakers would expect no less of them.

The other writers in the group became important to Corinne, so much so that Allegra minded that she was evidently never to meet them. She heard about them, but only in abridged versions. The critique circle was built on trust; there was an expectation of confidentiality, Corinne said.

Corinne was not good at keeping secrets. Allegra heard that one woman had brought in a poem on abortion, written in red ink to represent blood. One man was doing a sort of French bedroom farce, only without any actual humor to it, and the text messily annotated with arrows and cross-outs, so it was no pleasure to read; yet week after week he reliably turned in another plodding chapter of cocks and cuckoldings. Another woman was writing a fantasy novel, and it had a good plot, ticked right along, except everyone in it had amber eyes, or emerald or amethyst or sapphire. Nothing the other members said could persuade her to substitute brown or blue or not mention the goddamn eyes at all.

One evening Corinne said casually over dinner that she was going out that night to a poetry reading. Lynne, from her writing group, was reading an erotic set at Good Vibrations, the sex-toy store. 'I'll go with you,' Allegra said. Surely Corinne didn't expect her to stay home while racy poetry was being read aloud in a landscape of whips and dildos.

'I don't want you making fun of anyone.' Corinne was obviously very uncomfortable. 'You can really be severe when you think someone has no taste. We're all just novices in the group. If I hear you make fun of Lynne, I'll know that I'm probably ridiculous, too. I can't write if I think I'm being ridiculous.'

'I would never think you're ridiculous,' Allegra protested. 'I couldn't. And I love poetry. You know that.'

'You love your sort of poetry,' Corinne said. 'Poems about trees. That's not what Lynne will be reading.' Corinne never actually said that Allegra could go, but Allegra did, since she was now anxious to prove that she could behave, in addition to getting some glimpse of Corinne's other life. Corinne's real life, as she sometimes thought. The life she wasn't to be any part of.

Good Vibrations had set up fifty chairs, of which seven were taken. Inflatable crotches hung on the walls behind the podium in various stages of openness, like butterflies. There were cabinets in which corsets and strap-ons had been scattered together. Lynne was charmingly nervous. She read, but she also talked about the issues, personal and artistic, that her poetry raised for her. She'd just finished a piece in which a woman's breast spoke in several stanzas about its past admirers. The poem had a formal structure, and Lynne confessed that she wondered whether this was really the way to go. She begged her audience to regard it as a work in progress.

Even the breast spoke in a poetry-reading voice, with that lilt at the end of each line, like Pound or Eliot or whoever it was who had started the unfortunate custom. The audience clapped at the hot parts, and Allegra was careful to clap, too, although what she found hot was apparently different from what others found hot. Afterward she went with Corinne to congratulate Lynne. She said how much she'd enjoyed the evening, as blameless a statement as anyone could make, but Corinne shot her a sharp look. She could see that her presence was making Corinne unhappy. She had forced her way in, when she'd known Corinne didn't want her. Allegra excused herself to use the bathroom. She took her time, washing her face, combing her hair, and all on purpose so that Corinne could talk to Lynne without Allegra there to hear.

That weekend Sylvia and Jocelyn came down for a dog show at the Cow Palace and Allegra met them for lunch. Corinne had been invited, but the words were suddenly flowing, she'd said, she couldn't risk stopping. Jocelyn was in a very good mood. Thembe had taken Best of Breed, the judge noting his great reach and drive, as well as his beautiful topline. He would compete in Hounds in the afternoon. Plus, Jocelyn had in her pockets the cards of several promising studs. The future looked bright. The Cow Palace was thunderous and odorous. They took their lunches to the picnic tables so as not to eat in front of the dogs.

It was a great relief to Allegra to be able finally to tell someone about the poetry reading. She remembered particularly choice lines; Sylvia laughed so hard she spit her sandwich into her lap. Afterward Allegra was contrite. 'I wish Corinne would let me in a bit,' she said. 'She's afraid to be laughed at. As if I'd laugh at her.'

'I once broke up with a boy because he wrote me an awful poem,' Jocelyn said. ' "Your twin eyes." Don't most people have twin eyes? All but an unfortunate few? You think it shouldn't matter. You think how nice the sentiment is and how much work went into it. But the next time he goes to kiss you, all you can think is "Your twin eyes." '

'I'm sure Corinne's a wonderful writer,' Sylvia said. 'Isn't she?'

And Allegra said yes! She was! Wonderful! In fact, Corinne had yet to show Allegra a word. The books she liked to read were all really good books, though.

'The thing is,' said Allegra, and in Jocelyn's experience, good things rarely followed those words, 'if she had to choose between writing and me, I know she'd choose writing. Should I mind that? I shouldn't mind that. I'm just sort of an all-out person, myself.'

'The thing is,' Sylvia answered, 'she doesn't have to choose. So you never have to really know.'

When Allegra got home, much to her surprise, she met Lynne just leaving the apartment. They stopped for a moment on the step to exchange pleasantries. Allegra had walked several blocks uphill from the only parking place she'd been able to find – she might as well have left the car in Daly City – and was hot, cross, and out of breath. But she managed to say again how much she'd enjoyed Lynne's poetry. This wasn't a lie. She had thoroughly enjoyed it. 'I brought some cookies by to thank you both for coming,' Lynne said. 'I was so happy to find Corinne working. She's such a talent.'

Allegra felt the bite of jealousy because Lynne had seen Corinne's work. Even the woman who wrote abortion poems in red ink had seen Corinne's work. 'Wonderful stories,' Lynne said, hitting the first syllable of 'wonderful' like a gong. 'Her piece about the retarded boy? "Billy's Ball"? Like Tom Hanks in that castaway thing, only genuinely moving.'

'Corinne wrote a story about a retarded boy?' Allegra asked. And she hadn't even changed his name? Corinne wouldn't do such a thing. *Our secrets. Trust me.*

Lynne covered her mouth with her hand, smiling through her fingers. 'Oh! Everything that happens in critique is absolutely classified. I so shouldn't have said that. Of course, I thought she'd have shown *you*. You have to promise you won't tell. Please don't tell on me.' She persisted with such a distasteful, flirty girlishness that Allegra made the promise just to make it stop.

Allegra went inside, walked into the study, where Corinne was still working at the computer, and watched her hit Sleep, the words disappearing from the screen in the time it took Allegra to cross the room. 'No more writer's block?' she asked. One touch on any key would bring the words back.

'No,' said Corinne. 'The muse has returned to me.'

That night Corinne asked for a story even though they hadn't made love. Allegra propped herself up on the pillow and looked at her. She had her eyes closed, an ear poking through the hair on one side of her head. Her chin tilted upward, her neck a snowy slope. Her nipples visible through her tank top. Seductive innocence.

Allegra said:

*

5. There was this girl I knew in high school who got pregnant. I liked her when I first met her, and I felt sorry for her when she got pregnant – you should have heard the things boys said about her. But by then I didn't really like her much anymore. There's a whole middle to the story, but I'm too tired to tell it.

Allegra had gotten drunk. She didn't think she was the only one. She could see that Prudie had flushed cheeks and glassy eyes. The Petit Syrah had disappeared like magic, and Jocelyn had sent her to the kitchen for a bottle of Graffigna Malbec and to see how Sylvia was doing since she had never come back after Daniel's phone call. When Allegra stood up, she knew she was drunk.

Sylvia was sitting in the dark kitchen with the phone back in its cradle. 'Hey, darling,' she said, and her voice was fine.

There was no need for such a charade, especially in front of Allegra. 'How do you take it so calmly?' she asked. 'You hardly seem to care.' She knew she was out of line. She could hear her drunk, out-of-line voice coming out of her mouth.

'I care.'

'You don't have to hide it. No one out there will think any worse of you if you throw a glass or scream or go to bed or tell them all to get the fuck out.'

'You'll have to let me be who I am, dear,' Sylvia said. 'Do you know where we were when Daniel told me he wanted a divorce? He'd taken me out to dinner. To Biba's. I'd always wanted to go to Biba's, but we'd never been able to get in. So that's what just occurred to me. That he had to make a reservation way in advance and then pretend for weeks that everything was okay. Such a thoughtful way to dump your wife.'

'I'm sure he wasn't planning the evening like that! I'm sure he didn't know what he'd say or when he'd say it. Some people do things without planning them all through like you.'

'You're probably right. A person's no more sane falling out of love than falling into it, I guess. Thank God it's raining. We didn't get enough rain this year.'

Sylvia's face was dimly reflected in the kitchen window. Allegra thought how she was seeing both sides of her face at once. Her mother had been such a pretty woman, but after holding her own for quite some time, she'd aged all of a sudden a few years back. You could see how the aging would go on now; you could see where the hammer would hit next.

Allegra knelt unsteadily and put her head into her mother's lap. She felt her mother's hands combing through her hair. 'What do we know about it, you and I?' Allegra asked. 'We're not the sort who fall out of love, are we?'

Allegra got up when she was sure Corinne was sleeping, and went into the study. She emptied the wastebasket onto the floor. There wasn't much, and what there was had been torn into tiny, despairing bits, none looking as if they'd come from Corinne's printer. Allegra found the word 'Zyzzyva' embossed on one piece. She persisted, sorting by color, until she had three piles. She was wearing nothing but the knee-length T-shirt she slept in, so she dragged a blanket out of the linen closet and lay on the floor, swaddled, piecing bits of paper together.

'We must regretfully pass on the story you've sent us,' she read at last. ' "Billy's Ball" has much to recommend it, and although it didn't seem exactly right for us, we would be willing to see other work from you in the future. Good luck with your endeavors, the Editors.'

Fifteen minutes later: 'We are returning your story "Goodbye, Prague" to you as we are only interested in lesbian material. We highly suggest you familiarize yourself with our magazine. A subscription form is enclosed. Thank you, the Editors.'

Ten minutes later: A form rejection – 'does not suit our purposes at this time' – but someone had penned a single sentence across the bottom in ballpoint ink: 'Who among us has not tormented ants?'

Allegra swept the pieces up, mixed them back together, dumped them into the wastebasket. She felt as if she'd been stripped and then strip-mined. So Corinne's desire to keep her away from her writing friends had nothing to do with Allegra's sarcastic tongue. How unkind of Corinne to make her feel that she was the one at fault.

Of course, this small unkindness was nothing compared with the betrayal of trust. It had begun to rain, but Allegra didn't know that until she went outside. She hardly felt it even then, though she was wearing only her T-shirt. She walked three blocks to her car, drove two hours to her parents' house – longer than usual, because she'd forgotten to bring money for the bridge toll (forgotten even her driver's license) and she had to pull over to the side, get out undressed as she was, to talk about this. Eventually she was waved through, such was the persuasive power of crying uncontrollably when you were practically naked.

It was after three in the morning when she arrived home, soaking wet. Her father made her a cup of hot milk; her mother put her straight to bed. For three days, she got up only to go to the bathroom. Corinne phoned several times, but Allegra refused to speak to her.

How dare Corinne write up Allegra's secret stories and send them off to magazines to be published?

How dare Corinne write them so poorly that no one wished to take them?

It wasn't Jane Austen's fault that love went bad. You couldn't even say she didn't warn you. Her heroines made out well enough, but there were always other characters in the book who didn't finish happily – Brandon's Eliza in *Sense and Sensibility*; in *Pride and Prejudice*, Charlotte Lucas, Lydia Bennet; in *Mansfield Park*, Maria Bertram. These were the women to whom you should be paying attention, but you weren't.

Allegra was trying very hard not to express any of Corinne's opinions, but every time she spoke, Corinne's words came out. Corinne was in no mood to praise a writer like Austen, who wrote so much about love when the world was full of other things. 'Everything in Austen is on the surface,' Allegra said. 'She's not a writer who uses images. Image is the way to bring the unsaid into the text. With Austen, everything is said.'

Prudie shook her head vigorously; her hair flew about her cheeks. 'Half of what Jane says is said ironically. Irony is a way of saying two things at once.' Prudie was trying to express something she hadn't completely worked out yet. She opened her hands, like two halves of a book, clapped them closed. Allegra was mystified by the gesture, but she could see that whatever Prudie was trying to say, it was something she deeply believed. 'The thing you've said and that opposite thing you've said at the same time,' she cried out. She had the carefully constructed dignity of someone drunk. Prudie's dignity always felt slightly manufactured, so the difference was a subtle one. A tiny slur, a bit of spit.

'Yes, of course.' Of course, Bernadette had no more idea what Prudie was going on about than Allegra did. She was just choosing agreement because it seemed more polite than opposition, even when one had no idea what point was being made. 'And I think it's her humor that keeps us reading her two centuries later. At least, that's what I respond most to. I don't think I'm alone in this. Tell me if I'm alone in this.'

'People like a romance,' Grigg said. 'Women do, anyway. I mean, I do, too. I didn't mean that I didn't.'

Sylvia came back into the room. She stirred the fire so that it threw off sparks, spinning like pinwheels up the flue. She added another log, crushing the life out of what little flame had remained. 'Brandon and Marianne,' she said. 'At the end, doesn't it feel just as if Marianne's been sold? Her mother and Elinor, both pushing so hard. It reads as if she fell in love with Brandon, but only *after* she married him. He's been such a good man that her mother and Elinor are determined he'll get his reward.'

'But that's my point,' Prudie said. 'Jane *intends* you to feel that uncomfortableness. The book ends with that marriage and the thing Austen isn't saying about it.'

Sylvia sat down next to Allegra, which forced Grigg to move aside. 'It just makes me sad. Marianne can be self-centered and all, but who really wants her sobered up, settled down? Nobody. Nobody could ever want to see her be anything but exactly what she is.'

'Do you want her with Willoughby, then?' Allegra asked.

'Don't you?' said Sylvia. She leaned forward to address Prudie. 'I think you should let Jocelyn drive you home tonight. Don't worry about your car. Daniel will bring it round in the morning.' There was a silence. Sylvia put her hand over her mouth.

'I'll do that,' said Allegra. 'I'll bring you your car.'

When Allegra finally rose from her bed, only three days after she'd fled her apartment in nothing but her T-shirt, she drove to the Vacaville skydiving school. At first she was told that no one would take her. She had no appointment; she knew the rules. And if she was back because of the broken arm, they weren't responsible for that; there were certain forms she might remember having signed. She needed to go home and think it through, they said. She needed to make an appointment and come back after she'd thought more about it.

Allegra argued. She laughed a lot, so that no one would get the wrong idea about her mood and intentions. She flirted. She let the men flirt back. She told them that this was a skydiving emergency, and finally, Marco, who'd been one of her instructors and was apparently still unclear on her sexuality – not that she hadn't told him often enough, but her behavior today had obviously raised the question again – agreed to be her tandem master. Tandem was not what she wanted; she was definitely in the mood for solo, but solo wasn't happening.

Allegra put on the ridiculous orange suit and they went up. Marco clipped himself to the back of her shoulders and hips. 'Are you ready?' he asked, and before she could answer, he'd pushed her out. There was a smiley-face sticker inside the plane, just where you put your hand before you jumped. The words 'Go Big' were written in marker beneath.

They slid through the air. The wind was rough, Marco close. But she got what she wanted. Blue sky above, brown hills below. Behind her, the university stretching out its vast agricultural fields of unnatural tomatoes, burrowing owls, dairy cows. Somewhere to the east, her parents were having lunch. Her parents, who loved her. Marco pulled the cord, and she heard the parachute spinning out, felt it catching. Her parents who loved her and her brothers and her nieces and each other, and they always would.

Dear Miss Austen:
  We must regretfully inform you that your work does not suit our current needs.

In 1797, Jane Austen's father sent *First Impressions* to a publisher in London named Thomas Cadell. 'As I am well aware of what consequence it is that a work of this sort should make its first Appearance under a respectable name I apply to you,' he wrote. He asked what it would cost to publish 'at the Author's risk,' and what advance might be offered if the manuscript were liked. He was prepared to pay himself, if necessary.

The package came back immediately, with 'Declined by Return of Post' written across the top.

The book was published sixteen years later. Its title had been changed to *Pride and Prejudice*.

In 1803, a London publisher named Richard Crosby bought a novel (later titled *Northanger Abbey*) from Jane Austen for ten pounds. He advertised it in a brochure, but never published it. Six years passed. Austen then wrote to Crosby, offering to replace the manuscript, if it had been lost and if Crosby intended to publish it quickly. Otherwise, she said, she would go to another publisher.

Crosby wrote back, denying that he was under any obligation to publish the book. He would return it to her, he said, only if she returned his ten pounds. *Northanger Abbey* was not published until five months after Austen's death.

Jane Austen's books, too, are absent from this library. Just that one omission alone would make a fairly good library out of a library that hadn't a book in it.

MARK TWAIN

I am at a loss to understand why people hold Miss Austen's novels at so high a rate, which seem to me vulgar in tone, sterile in artistic invention, imprisoned in their wretched conventions of English society, without genius, wit, or knowledge of the world. Never was life so pinched and narrow ... All that interests in any character [is]: has he (or she) the money to marry with? ... Suicide is more respectable.

RALPH WALDO EMERSON

MAY

CHAPTER THREE

in which we read
Mansfield Park
with Prudie

Her perfect security in such a tête-à-tête . . . *was unspeakably welcome to
a mind which had seldom known a pause in its alarms or embarrassments.*
(MANSFIELD PARK)

Prudie and Jocelyn had met two years before, at a Sunday matinee of
Mansfield Park. Jocelyn was sitting in the row behind Prudie when the
woman to Prudie's left began a whispered monologue to a friend about
high jinks at some local riding stable. Someone was sleeping with one of
the farriers – a real cowboy type, boots and blue jeans and a charm that
seemed unstudied, but anyone who could gentle horses knew perfectly
well how to get a woman into bed. The horses, of course, were the ones
to suffer. Rajah was not eating at all. 'Like he thinks he's *hers*,' the woman
said, 'just because I let her ride him from time to time.'

Prudie was pretty sure this was about the horse. She hadn't spoken
up. She sat and seethed over her Red Vines and thought about moving,
but only if it could be done without an implied accusation; she was, ask
anyone, courteous to a fault. She was just beginning to take an unwelcome
and distracting interest in Rajah's appetite when Jocelyn leaned forward.
'Go gossip in the lobby,' Jocelyn said. You could tell that she was not a
woman to be trifled with. Send her to deal with your cowboy types. Send
her to feed your oh-so-sensitive horses.

'Excuse me,' the woman responded resentfully. 'Like your movie is so
much more important than my real life.' But she fell silent, and Prudie
didn't really care that she was offended, an offended silence being just as
silent as a flattered one. This silence lasted the whole movie, which was
all that mattered. The gossipers left at the credits, but the true Janeite
was truly gracious, and stayed for the final chord, the white screen. Prudie
knew without looking that Jocelyn would still be there when she turned
to thank her.

They talked more as they threaded through the seats. Jocelyn turned
out to like fiddling about with the original story no better than Prudie
did. The great thing about books was the solidity of the written word.

You might change and your reading might change as a result, but the book remained whatever it had always been. A good book was surprising the first time through, less so the second.

The movies, as everyone knew, had no respect for this. All the characters had been altered -- Fanny's horrid aunt Mrs Norris was diminished simply by lack of screen time; her uncle Mr Bertram, a hero in the book, was now accused of slave-dealing and sexual predations; and all the rest were portrayed in broad strokes or reinvented. Most provocative was the amalgamation of Fanny with Austen herself, which scraped oddly at times, as the two were nothing alike – Fanny so shrinking and Austen so playful. What resulted was a character who thought and spoke like Jane, but acted and reacted like Fanny. It made no sense.

Not that you couldn't understand the screenwriter's motivation. No one loved Austen more than Prudie, ask anyone. But even Prudie found the character of Fanny Price hard going. Fanny was the prig in your first-grade class who never, ever misbehaved and who told the teacher when anyone else did. How to keep the movie audience from loathing her? While Austen, by some accounts, had been quite a flirt, full of life and charm. More like *Mansfield*'s villainous Mary Crawford.

So Austen had given Mary all her own wit and sparkle, and none of it to Fanny. Prudie had always wondered why, then, not only Fanny but also Austen seemed to dislike Mary so much.

Saying all this took time. Prudie and Jocelyn stopped at the Café Roma to have a cup of coffee together and examine their responses more minutely. Dean, Prudie's husband, left them there and went home to reappraise the movie in solitude while catching the second half of the 49er – Viking game.

On her first reading, *Mansfield Park* had been Prudie's least favorite of the six novels. Her opinion had improved over the years. So much so that when Sylvia picked it for May, Prudie volunteered to host the discussion, even though no one is busier than a high school teacher in May.

She expected a lively exchange and had so much to say herself, she'd been filling index cards for several days in order to remember it all. Prudie was a great believer in organization, a natural Girl Scout. She had lists of things to be cleaned, things to be cooked, things to be said. She was serious about her hosting. With power – responsibility.

But the day began, ominously, with something unexpected. She appeared to have picked up a virus in her e-mail. There was a note from her mother: 'Missing my darling. Thinking of coming for a visit.' But then there were two more notes that had her mother's return address plus attachments, when her mother hadn't mastered attachments yet. The e-mails themselves read, 'Here is a powful tool. I hope you will like,' and 'Here is something you maybe enjoy.' The identical 'powful tool' message came again in another e-mail. This one seemed to be from Susan in the attendance office.

Prudie had planned to send out a reminder that, because of the heat, the book club would meet at eight instead of seven-thirty that night, but she didn't wish to risk spreading the infection. She shut down without even answering her mother's note.

The predicted temperature for the day was a hundred six. This, too, was bad news. Prudie had planned to serve a compote, but no one was going to touch anything hot. She'd better stop by the store after work and get some fruit for a sherbet. Maybe root beer floats. Easy, but fun!

Dean lurched out of bed just in time to kiss her good-bye. He was wearing nothing but a T-shirt, which was a good look for him, and how many men could you say that about? Dean had been staying up at night to watch soccer. He was in training for the World Cup, for those games that would soon be shown live from whatever time zone Japan and Korea occupied. 'I'll be late today,' he told her. He worked in an insurance office.

'I've got book club.'

'Which book?'

'*Mansfield Park*.'

'I guess I'll skip that one,' Dean said. 'Maybe rent the movie.'

'You've already been to the movie,' Prudie answered. She was a tiny bit distressed. They'd been to it together. How could he not remember? Only then did she see that he was teasing her. It was a measure of how distracted she was, because she was usually quick to catch a joke. Anyone could tell you that.

> '*How long ago it is, aunt, since we used to repeat the chronological order of the kings of England, with the dates of their accession, and most of the principal events of their reigns!*' '*. . . and of the Roman emperors as low as Severus; besides a great deal of the Heathen Mythology, and all the Metals, Semi-Metals, Planets, and distinguished philosophers.*'
> (MANSFIELD PARK)

Prudie gave her third-period students a chapter of *Le Petit Prince* to translate – '*La seconde planète était habitée par un vaniteux*' – and took a seat in the back of the classroom to finalize her notes for book club. (The secret to teaching was to place yourself where you could see them but they couldn't see you. And nothing was more deadly than the reverse. Chalkboards were for chumps.)

It was already way too hot. The air was still, with an odor faintly locker-room. Prudie's neck was streaked with sweat. Her dress was fastened onto her back, but her fingers slid on the pen. The so-called temporary buildings (they would last no longer than Shakespeare's plays) in which she taught had no airconditioning. It was hard to keep the students' attention in May. It was always hard to keep the students' attention. The temperature made it impossible. Prudie looked about the room and saw several of them wilted over their desks, limp as old lettuce leaves.

She saw little sign of work in progress. Instead the students slept or whispered among themselves or stared out the windows. In the parking lot, hot air billowed queasily over the hoods of cars. Lisa Streit had her hair in her face and her work in her lap. There was something especially brittle about her today, the aura of the recent dumpee. She'd been dating a senior and, Prudie had no doubt, pressured daily to give it up to him. Prudie hoped she'd been dumped because she hadn't done so rather than dumped because she had. Lisa was a sweet girl who wanted to be liked by everyone. With luck she would survive until college, when being likable became a plausible path to that. Trey Norton said something low and nasty, and everyone who could hear him laughed. If Prudie rose to go see, she believed, she'd find Elijah Wallace and Katy Singh playing hangman. Elijah was probably gay, but neither he nor Katy knew it yet. It was too much to hope the secret word would be French.

In fact, why bother? Why bother to send teenagers to school at all? Their minds were so clogged with hormones they couldn't possibly learn a complex system like calculus or chemistry, much less the wild tangle of a foreign language. Why put everyone to the aggravation of making them try? Prudie thought that she could just do the rest of it – watch them for signs of suicide or weapons or pregnancy or drug addiction or sexual abuse – but asking her to teach them French at the same time was really too much.

There were days when just the sight of fresh, bright acne or badly applied mascara or the raw, infected skin around a brand-new piercing touched Prudie deeply. Most of the students were far more beautiful than they would ever realize. (There were also days when adolescents seemed like an infestation in her otherwise comfortable life. Often these were the same days.)

Trey Norton, on the other hand, was beautiful and knew it – wounded eyes, slouched clothes, heavy, swinging walk. *Beauté du diable.* 'New dress?'

he'd asked Prudie while taking his seat today. He'd looked her over, and his open assessment was both unsettling and infuriating. Prudie certainly knew how to dress professionally. If she was exposing more skin than usual, that was because it was going to be a hundred-fucking-six degrees. Was she supposed to wear a suit? 'Hot,' he'd said.

He was angling for a better grade than he deserved, and Prudie was just barely too old to be taken in. She wished she were old enough to be impervious. In her late twenties, suddenly, unnervingly, she found herself wishing to sleep with nearly every man she saw.

The explanation could be only chemical, because Prudie was not that sort of woman. Here at school every breath she took was a soup of adolescent pheromones. Three years of concentrated daily exposure – how could this not have an effect?

She'd tried to defuse such thoughts by turning them medicinally, as needed, to Austen. Laces and bonnets. Country lanes and country dances. Shaded estates with pleasant prospects. But the strategy had backfired. Now, often as not, when she thought of whist, sex came also to mind. From time to time she imagined bringing all this up in the teachers' lounge. 'Do you ever find yourself . . .' she would begin. (As if!)

She'd actually been sexually steadier her first time through high school, a fact that could only dismay her now. There was nothing about those years to remember with satisfaction. She had grown early and by sixth grade was far too tall. 'They'll catch up,' her mother had told her (without being asked, that's how obvious the problem was). And she was perfectly right. When Prudie graduated, most of the boys had topped her by a couple of inches at least.

What her mother didn't know, or didn't say, was how little this would matter by the time it happened. In the feudal fiefdom of school, rank was determined early. You could change your hair and clothes. You could, having learned your lesson, not write a paper on *Julius Caesar* entirely in iambic pentameter, or you could not tell anyone if you did. You could switch to contact lenses, compensate for your braininess by not doing your homework. Every boy in the school could grow twelve inches. The sun could go fucking nova. And you'd still be the same grotesque you'd always been.

Meanwhile, at restaurants, the beach, the movies, men who should have been looking at her mother began to look at Prudie instead. They brushed past her in the grocery store, deliberately grazing her breasts. They sat too close on the bus, let their legs fall against her at the movies. Old men in their thirties whistled when she walked by. Prudie was mortified, and this appeared to be the point; the more mortified she became, the more pleased the men seemed to be. The first time a boy asked to kiss her (in college) she'd thought he was making fun of her.

So Prudie was not pretty and she was not popular. There was no reason she couldn't have been nice. Instead, to bolster her social position at school, she'd sometimes joined in when the true outcasts were given their daily dose of torment. She'd seen this as a diversionary tactic at the time, shameful but necessary. Now it was unbearable to remember. Could she have really been so cruel? Someone else perhaps had tripped Megan Stahl on the asphalt and kicked her books away. Megan Stahl, Prudie could now see, had probably been slightly retarded as well as grindingly poor.

As a teacher Prudie watched out for such children, did her best for them. (But what could a teacher do? No doubt she made things worse as often as she made them better.) This atonement must have been the real reason she'd chosen the career, although at the time it had seemed to be about loving France and having no inclination for actual scholarship. Probably every high school teacher arrived with scores to settle, scales to tip.

Precious little in *Mansfield Park* supported the possibility of fundamental reform. 'Character is set early.' Prudie wrote this on a notecard, followed it with examples: Henry Crawford, the rake, improves temporarily, but can't sustain it. Aunt Norris and cousin Maria are, throughout the book, as steadfast in their meanness and their sin as Fanny and cousin Edmund are in their propriety. Only cousin Tom, after a brush with death and at the very, very end of the book, manages to amend.

It was enough to give Prudie hope. Perhaps she was not as horrible as she feared. Perhaps she was not beyond forgiveness, even from Jane.

But at the very moment she thought this, her fingers, slipping up and down her pen, put her in mind of something decidedly, unforgivably un-Austenish. She looked up and found that Trey Norton had swung about, was watching her. This was no surprise. Trey was as sensitive to any lewd thought as a dowser to water. He smiled at her, and it was such a smile as no boy should give his high school teacher. (Or no high school teacher should attribute such things to the mere act of baring one's teeth. My bad, Jane. *Pardonnez-moi*.)

'Do you need something, Trey?' Prudie asked. She dropped the pen, wiped her hands on her skirt.

'You know what I need,' he answered. Paused a deliberate moment. Held his work up.

She rose to go see, but the bell rang. '*Allez-vous en!*' Prudie said playfully, and Trey was the first on his feet, the first out the door. The other students gathered their papers, their binders, their books. Went off to sleep in someone else's class.

'This chapel was fitted up as you see it, in James the Second's time.'
(MANSFIELD PARK)

Prudie had a free period, and she walked through the quad to the library, where there was air-conditioning as well as two computer stations with Internet access. She wiped the sweat from her face and neck with her hand, wiped her hand on her hem, and looked at her e-mail. Kapow to the offers to consolidate her debts, enlarge her penis, enchant her with X-rated barnyard action, provide craft tips, recipes, jokes, missing persons, cheap pharmaceuticals. Kapow to anything with a suspicious attachment; there were six more of these. Deleting all this took only a minute, but it was a minute she begrudged, because who'd asked for any of it? Who had the time? And tomorrow every bit of it would be back. She had *la mer à boire.*

Cameron Watson settled into the terminal next to her. Cameron was a slope-backed, beak-nosed kid who looked about eleven but was really seventeen. He'd been in Prudie's class two years before and was also a neighbor from three houses over. His mother and Prudie were members of the same investment group. Once this investment group had seen some heady returns. Once fiber-optics companies and large-cap tech stocks had hung like grapes from a vine. Now everything was a shambles of despair and recrimination. These days Prudie saw little of Cameron's mother.

Cameron had told Prudie that he had a friend in France. They e-mailed, so he wanted to learn the language, but he'd shown no aptitude, although his excellent homework made Prudie suspect the French friend did it for him. Clearly bright as a bee, Cameron had that peculiar mix of competence and cluelessness that marks the suburban computer geek. Prudie went to him with all her computer problems and did her best, in return, to genuinely like him.

'I'm afraid to send anything from home just now,' she told him, 'because I've been getting e-mails that seem to've come from people in my address book but didn't. There are attachments, but I haven't downloaded them. Or read them.'

'Doesn't matter. You've been infected.' He wasn't looking at her, leaning into his own screen. Mouse clicking. 'Self-replicating. Tricky. The work of a thirteen-year-old kid in Hong Kong. I could come clean it up for you faster than I could tell you how.'

'That would be so great,' Prudie said.

'If you had DSL I could do it from home. Don't you hate being so – geographical? You should get DSL.'

'You live *three* houses from me,' Prudie said. 'And I spent so much money last time out.' (Cameron had advised her on every purchase. He knew her setup better than she did.) 'Just two years ago. Dean won't see the need. Do you think I could get a substantial upgrade without buying a whole new computer?'

'Don't *go* there,' Cameron said, apparently not to Prudie but to the screen. Although it might have been to Prudie. Cameron liked Dean a ton and would hear no criticism about him.

Three more students walked in, ostensibly on a research assignment. They punched up the catalogue, wrote things in their notebooks, conferred with the librarian. One of these students was Trey Norton. There was a second boy, whom Prudie didn't know. One girl, Sallie Wong. Sallie had long polished hair and tiny glasses. Good ear for languages, lovely accent. She was wearing a blue tank top with straps that crossed in the back, and her shoulders gleamed with sweat and that lotion with glitter all the girls were using. No bra.

When they went into the stacks, they went in three different directions. Trey and Sallie met up immediately somewhere in poetry. Through the glass window of the computer station, Prudie had a clear view down four of the aisles. She watched Trey take Sallie's hair in his hands. He whispered something. They ducked into the next aisle just before the other boy, a heavy young man with an earnest, baffled expression, appeared. He was obviously looking for them. They were obviously ditching him. He tried the next aisle. They doubled back.

Cameron had been talking this whole time, talking with passion, although still scrolling down his own screen. Multitasking. 'You need bandwidth,' he was saying. 'Your upgrade now, it's not about processors and storage anymore. You need to *situate* yourself on the Web. That desktop paradigm – that's over. That's beached. Stop thinking that way. I can get you some killer freeware.'

Trey and Sallie had surfaced in the magazines. She was laughing. He slid his hand under one strap of her top, opened his fingers over her shoulder. They heard the other boy coming, Sallie laughing harder, and Trey pulled her down another aisle and out of Prudie's sight.

'Like a free long-distance line,' Cameron was saying. 'Streaming live real-time video, IRC. You'll be able to fold your computer like a handkerchief. You'll be living inside it. You'll be global.' Somehow they'd morphed into *The Matrix*. Prudie hadn't been paying attention and might not have known when it happened even if she had been. The air-conditioning was starting to chill her. Nothing a brisk walk to her classroom wouldn't cure.

Trey and Sallie reappeared in the magazines. He backed her into *National Geographic* and they kissed.

'Your computer's not a noun anymore,' Cameron said. 'Your computer's a f-fricking *verb*.'

The heavy young man came into the computer station. If he had turned around he'd have seen Sallie Wong's lips closing over Trey Norton's tongue. He didn't turn around. 'You're not supposed to be in here,' he told Cameron accusingly. 'We're all supposed to be working together.'

'I'll be there in a minute.' Cameron sounded neither apologetic nor concerned. 'Find the others.'

'I can't.' The boy took a seat. 'I'm not going to do anything by myself.'

Sallie was holding on to the back of Trey's neck, arching slightly. The air-conditioning was no longer a problem for Prudie. She forced herself to stop watching, swung back to Cameron.

'I'm not going to do the whole assignment by myself and then put all your names on it,' the boy said, 'if that's what you think.'

Cameron continued to type. He could spot a hoax in seconds, but he had no sense of humor. He thought the graphics for Doom were totally awesome – his fingers twitched spasmodically when he talked about them – but he'd fainted dead away when *Blood on the Highway* was shown in driver's ed. Although this was a fatal step for his high school rep, it consoled Prudie when she heard about it. This was not a boy who would open fire in the hallway anytime soon. This was a boy who still knew the difference between what was real and what wasn't.

For an instant, like an ambush, a picture came into Prudie's mind. In this picture she was backed into *National Geographic*, kissing Cameron Watson. She deleted the image instantly (good God!), kept an expressionless face, concentrated on whatever the hell Cameron was saying. Which was –

'What if they changed the paradigm and no one came?' Cameron did something strange with his hands, thumbs touching at the tips, fingers curled above.

'What's that?' Prudie asked him.

'A smiley face. Emoticon. So you'll know I'm joking.'

He wouldn't look at her, but if he had, she wouldn't have been able to look back. How lucky his generation was, making all these friends they'd never actually meet. In cyberspace, no one gets pantsed.

'*If any one faculty of our nature may be called more wonderful than the rest, I do think it is memory . . . The memory is sometimes so retentive, so serviceable, so obedient – at others, so bewildered and so weak – and at others again, so tyrannic, so beyond controul!*' (MANSFIELD PARK)

Prudie liked the beginning of *Mansfield Park* most especially. This was the part about Fanny Price's mother and aunts, the three beautiful sisters, and how they all married. It bore some resemblance to the story of the Three Little Pigs. One sister had married a wealthy man. One had married a respectable man with a modest income. One, Fanny's mother, had married a man of straw. Her poverty became so pronounced that Fanny Price was sent all alone to live with the wealthy aunt and uncle. Everything changed them into 'Cinderella' and the real story began. Someone else had talked about fairy tales last time. Was it Grigg? Prudie had read a million fairy tales as a child. And reread them. Her favorite was 'The Twelve Swans.'

One thing she'd noticed early – parents and adventures did not mix. She herself had no father, only a picture in the hallway of a young man in uniform. He'd died, she'd been told, on some secret mission in Cambodia when she was nine months old. Prudie had no reason to believe this and, in spite of its obvious appeals, didn't. Her mother was the problem; no matter what Prudie did, she showed no inclination to give Prudie away.

Prudie's mother was sweet, affectionate, tolerant, and cheerful. She was also strangely tired. All the time. She claimed to work in an office, and it was this work, she said, that so wore her out that even lying on the couch watching television was sometimes too taxing. She spent the weekends napping.

It made Prudie suspicious. It was true that her mother left the house after breakfast and didn't come back until dinnertime, it was true that Prudie had gone to visit her at her office building (though never unannounced) and there she would always be, but she was never actually working when Prudie did visit. Usually she was talking on the telephone. Her mother should try a day at day care! 'I'm too tired' cut no mustard there.

On Prudie's fourth birthday her mother was unable to rouse herself to the demands of a party at which many of the guests would presumably be four years old. For several days she told Prudie that the birthday was coming up – the day after tomorrow, or maybe the day after after – until she finally gave Prudie a present (not wrapped) of a *Sesame Street* record and apologized for its being late. Prudie's birthday, she now admitted, lay somewhere vaguely behind them.

Prudie threw the record and herself onto the floor. She had all the advantages of justice on her side, as well as four-year-old tenacity. Her mother had only twenty-three-year-old cunning. The whole thing should have been happily resolved in less than an hour.

So it was with considerable confidence that Prudie lay on the rug, drumming her toes, thudding her fists, and she could hardly hear what her mother was saying over her own wailing. But the bits she caught when she paused for breath were so outrageous as to silence her completely. Yes, Prudie's birthday was over, her mother was now contending. But, of course, there'd been a party. Prudie's mother described this party. Balloons, cupcakes with pink frosting and sprinkles, a piñata shaped like a strawberry. Prudie had worn her unicorn shirt and blown out all the candles. She was such a good hostess, such a wonderful, uncommon child, that she'd opened all the presents and then insisted the guests take them back, even though one had been the stuffed squirrel that sucked its thumb, which she'd seen in the toy section at Discoveries and been whining after ever since. None of the other parents could believe how unselfish she was. Prudie's mother had never been so proud.

Prudie looked up through a screen of wet and knotted hair. 'Who were the guests?' she asked.

'No one you know,' Prudie's mother said, not missing a beat.

And her mother refused to back down. On the contrary, over the next few days, she embellished. Scarcely a meal went by (a favorite dinner was bagels with butter, which left only a single knife to be washed afterward) without a vivid description of a treasure hunt, pirate hats as party favors, pizza just the way four-year-olds like it, with nothing on it but cheese and not a lot of that. She even produced an opened package of napkins from the back of the cupboard, with ladybugs on them. 'Left over,' her mother said.

The other children had not behaved as well as Prudie had. Someone had been pushed down the slide and needed a Band-Aid. Someone had been called a chicken noodle and cried over it. And her mother provided all of this detail with a conspiratorial twinkle. 'Don't you remember?' she would ask periodically, inviting Prudie to join her inside the rich, rewarding world of the imagination.

Prudie held out less than a week. She was drinking orange juice from a little plastic orange that her mother had said they would rinse out and she could keep after. The prospect had her charmed almost to the point of sedation. 'I remember a clown,' Prudie offered carefully. 'At my birthday.' She was, in fact, beginning to recall the party, or bits of it. She could close her eyes and see: wrapping paper stamped with stars; the cheese sliding in a sheet off her pizza slice; a fat girl with sparkly glasses she'd once seen at the park winning the ring toss. She'd already told Roberta at day care about the piñata. But the clown was a gambit, one last attempt to resist. Prudie hated nothing so much as clowns.

Once again her mother eluded the trap. She gave Prudie a hug, her chin pressing into the top of Prudie's head and then retracting, like a pen point. 'I would never bring a clown into this house,' she said.

The stratagem had been such a success it was reemployed on Halloween, and then whenever it suited her mother's purposes. 'I got milk at the store this morning,' she might say. 'You already drank it.' Or, 'We've seen that movie. You didn't like it.' Always with a smile, as if it were a game they were playing together. (When they did play games, Prudie's mother let her roll the dice and move her token for her. She always let Prudie win.)

Sometimes it seemed to Prudie that she'd had a childhood filled with wonderful parties, trips to Marine World, dinners at Chuck E. Cheese, where grownup-sized rodents played guitar and sang Elvis songs to her. Surely some of these things must have happened. But she was often not certain which. She began to keep a diary, became a maker of lists, but it proved surprisingly hard to write things down accurately.

It was especially hard to be honest about her own behavior, and she began to feel, long before she could put it into words, that there was something manufactured about her, not just in the diaries, but in the real world. (Whatever the hell that was.) The years receded behind her like a map with no landmarks, a handful of air, another of water. Of all the things she had to make up, the hardest was herself.

One evening when she was eight or nine, during a commercial break in the middle of *The Greatest American Hero* (Prudie's mother was a sucker for the sad, guilt-ridden lives of superheroes. In *The Greatest American Hero*, a high school teacher was given a magical red suit and superpowers, which he then used to battle spies and criminals; as if the classroom isn't the place superpowers are really needed), her mother recalled a Christmas when they'd gone to meet Santa at Macy's. 'We had breakfast there,' she said. 'You ate chocolate chip pancakes. Santa came and sat at the table with us and you asked him for Matchbox cars.'

Prudie paused with her dinner (spoonfuls of peanut butter taken with milk) softening in her mouth. Something unfamiliar bloomed inside her chest, expanding until it took up all the empty space around her heart. This something was a conviction. She had never, in her whole life, wanted Matchbox cars. She swallowed, and the peanut butter rolled down her throat in a life-threatening clump. 'That wasn't me,' she said.

'The menus were shaped like snowflakes.'

Prudie gave her mother what she imagined was a look of steel. 'I'm a poor orphan. No one takes me to see Santa.'

'Santa had just eaten a Christmas cookie. He had red and green sugar sprinkled all through his beard. *I'm* your mother,' Prudie's mother said. She blinked once, twice, three times. She took the low road. 'What would I do without my little crumble-cake?'

But an eight- or nine-year-old has no heart, except maybe where baby animals are concerned. Prudie was unmoved. 'My mother is dead.'

'What of?'

'Cholera.' Prudie had *The Secret Garden* very much in mind. If she'd been reading *Irish Red* it would have been rabies. (Not that anyone in *Irish Red* got rabies. They nearly died of starvation in a snowstorm on a mountain when they went out hunting martens. Rabies was not even mentioned. It was just that any dog book made one think of *Old Yeller*.)

Her mother was in no mood for small mercies. 'I see,' she said slowly. Her face was melted sadly around the eyes and lips. 'Cholera. That's a nasty death. Vomiting. Diarrhea. Really, really painful. Like you're turning inside out. Puking your guts up.'

Prudie had pictured something less rude. 'I loved her very much,' she offered, but it was too late, her mother was already rising.

'I didn't know you liked to pretend you were an orphan,' she said, and bull's-eye! How many times had Prudie imagined her mother dead? How many ways? Riptides, car crashes, kidnapping by bandits, misadventures at the zoo. She began to cry with the shame of being such a horrible daughter.

Her mother went to her room and closed the door, even though the show had come on again – William Katt, who, her mother always said, was hot, hot, hot, and anyone who preferred Tom Selleck wasn't using the eyes God gave them. If they *had* been playing a game, Prudie couldn't have told if she'd just won or just lost. But if it was a game, that was the sort of game it would be, the kind where you wouldn't know.

For her tenth birthday Prudie saved her allowance for four months in order to buy her own invitations, which she then addressed herself, and an ice cream cake, which she served on Ewok plates with matching napkins. She asked seven girls she knew from school, and on the day she gave out the invitations she had one lunchtime in which she was the center of attention. This turned out to be more alarming than enjoyable.

On the day of the party, because her mother had measured her for a dress she'd seen in the Sears catalogue, but then not gotten around to ordering it, she let Prudie wear her pearl-drop necklace from Hawaii.

The chain was too long for Prudie, so they strung the pendant on a black cord that could be tied at any length she liked.

Prudie was given three books, all too young for her, a kite, children's Trivial Pursuit, a bicycle bell, and a plastic goldfish in a plastic goldfish bowl, none of which she gave back. The presents and the party struck her as lame. The girls behaved very nicely. It was all a sad comedown from what she was used to.

It was a very proper wedding. The bride was elegantly dressed – the two bridesmaids were duly inferior . . . her mother stood with salts in her hand, expecting to be agitated – her aunt tried to cry – (MANSFIELD PARK)

Prudie had brought a magazine to read in the teachers' lounge at lunch. She was prepared to socialize if there was interesting conversation, but two of the teachers had developed bunions and were commiserating over it. Prudie was too young to be told that shopping for shoes could ever become a nightmare. Nurses' shoes were suggested. Orthotics. It was horrible. Prudie opened her magazine. She saw that Dean had already taken the quiz, a set of questions to determine which of the *Sex and the City* girls you were most like. She checked out his answers:

To make a good impression on a Saturday night, Dean would '(a) wear a flirty top and a pencil skirt.' If a hot guy stood next to him at a bar, Dean would '(d) tell him he has great biceps – and ask him to flex.'

Prudie and Dean had first met at a bar. She was in college, out with her friends Laurie and Kerstin, celebrating something or other. Finals or the week before finals or the week before that. 'We just need some girl time,' Kerstin had told him warningly, but the words had no impact. Dean leaned past her without so much as a look and asked Prudie to dance.

Everyone else was dancing fast. Dean put his arms around her, pulled her in. His mouth was right beside her ear; his chin brushed her neck. Al Green's 'Don't Look Back' was playing. 'I'm going to marry you,' he told her. Laurie thought it was weird. Kerstin thought it was scary. It wasn't their ear; it wasn't their neck.

Dean had that specific confidence that comes from nothing else but being popular in high school. He had been a high school jock, made the college soccer team as a freshman, was a scoring left wing with a fan section. He was the sort of guy who, a few years before, wouldn't have even seen Prudie standing in front of him. Now he picked her out in a crowded bar. She was flattered, though she assumed she was not the first woman he'd vowed to marry in this fashion. (She found out later that she was.)

Didn't matter. His heavy-lidded eyes, his cheekbones, athlete legs, orthodontic teeth – none of it mattered. Forget the fact that he would look *so good* walking in next to her at her high school reunions. Some people would be so surprised.

No, the only thing that turned out to matter was that the first time he laid eyes on her he thought she was pretty. Love at first sight was as ridiculous as it was irresistible. In fact, Prudie wasn't pretty. She just pretended to be.

She'd assumed from this beginning that Dean was a romantic sort of guy. Her mother saw him clearer. 'There's a young man with his feet on the ground,' she had said. Prudie's mother didn't much care for young men with their feet on the ground. (Though she turned out to really like Dean. They both watched *Buffy the Vampire Slayer* every Tuesday night and phoned each other afterward to discuss the week's developments. Dean was a sucker for the sad, guilt-ridden lives of superheroes. Now he had her mom rooting desperately for the no-superpowers-at-all U.S. soccer team and talking about offside traps as if she knew what they were and when to use them.)

Prudie heard the criticism implied in her mother's assessment and forced it in Dean's favor. What was wrong with a solid sort of guy? Did you want a marriage full of surprises, or did you want a guy you could depend on? Someone who, when you looked at him, you knew what he'd be like in fifty years?

She asked Laurie, because Laurie had a theory about everything. 'It seems to me,' Laurie had said, 'that you can marry someone you're lucky to get or you can marry someone who's lucky to get you. I used to think the first was best. Now I don't know. Wouldn't it be better to spend your life with someone who thinks he's lucky to be there?'

'Why can't you both be lucky?' Prudie asked.

'You can wait for that, if you like.' (But Laurie was the one who hadn't married yet.)

Of course Prudie had to plan the wedding herself. It was a modest affair in her mother's backyard. She heard later that the food had been good, strawberries and oranges and cherries with chocolate and white chocolate dipping sauces. She was too busy to eat any of it. Too dazed. When she looked at the pictures – her pleated dress, the flowers, Dean's politely drunken friends – she hardly remembered being there. It was a very nice wedding, people said afterward, and the minute they said it, Prudie realized she hadn't wanted a very nice wedding. She'd wanted something memorable. They should have eloped and never told anyone.

But it was the marriage that was important; Jane Austen rarely even bothered to write about the wedding. Prudie had married Dean, who, for no reason that Prudie could see, thought he was lucky to get her.

She was still learning how lucky she was. Dean was so much more than solid. He was generous, friendly, easygoing, hard-working, good-looking. He shared the housework and he never complained and you never had to ask. For their wedding anniversary, he'd bought two tickets to Paris. This very summer Prudie and Dean were going to France.

And that was the problem. Prudie loved France; she'd made a life out of loving France. She'd never been, but she could imagine it perfectly. Of course, she didn't want to actually go. What if the trip was a disappointment? What if, once there, she didn't like it at all? Then what? It seemed to her that her husband, the love of her life, should have understood her well enough to know this.

Kerstin's husband did impressions. He could do people, but he could do objects as well – lawn mowers, corkscrews, cake beaters. He could do the whole cast of *Star Wars*, especially an excellent Chewbacca. Dean was a thoughtful lover with no objections to oral sex, even when it was *his* mouth. Even so – if Prudie had an itch one night for Chewbacca, there wasn't a thing Dean could do about it. He was always himself.

Prudie had thought that was what she wanted. Someone dependable. Someone with no pretense. Most of the time she was deeply in love with Dean.

But just occasionally she felt more lucky in her marriage than contented with it. She could imagine something better. She knew who to blame for this, and it wasn't Dean. The girl on *Sex and the City* that Dean was most like was Miranda.

It would be the last – in all probability the last scene on that stage; but he was sure there could not be a finer. The house would close with the greatest éclat. (MANSFIELD PARK)

Prudie had a terrible headache. The air was so hot all the oxygen seemed to have been squeezed out of it. She took two aspirin and drank lukewarm water from the only fountain whose nozzle wasn't blocked with a wad of gum. Careless of her makeup, she splashed some water on her face. By the time she arrived at her fifth-period class, her headache was survivable, though she still felt it in her temples like a distant drum.

Karin Bhave was waiting for her with a note: Ms. Fry, the drama teacher, asked if Karin could be excused for the period. The school production of *Brigadoon* was having its first dress rehearsal this afternoon and its second this evening, and the blocking for some of the scenes was still not working.

Karin had played Maria in *The Sound of Music* her sophomore year, Marian the librarian her junior. The day the cast list for *Brigadoon* had gone up, Prudie had come upon her sobbing alone in the bathroom, tears streaking the blusher on her cheeks, turning it to war paint. Prudie had assumed, naturally enough, that the lead had gone to someone else. She'd said something well intentioned, that one didn't want to do the same thing over and over again, even when that something was something good. She'd said it in French, because everything sounded better in French. Prudie was a better person in French – wiser, sexier, more sophisticated. '*Toujours perdrix*,' she'd finished, exhilarated by the idiom. (When she'd thought back on it later, she realized there was little chance Karin had understood her. The straight path, the English version, would have served better. Her ego had gotten in the way of her purpose. *Tout le monde est sage après le coup.*)

As luck would have it, she'd misjudged the problem anyway. Karin had once again been given the female lead. Of course she had. No one else had her bell-like voice and her slender figure and her innocent face. Karin was crying because the male lead had gone to Danny Fargo and not, as she'd secretly hoped, to Jimmy Johns, who was, instead, playing the part of Charlie Dalrymple. So Karin was going to have to fall in love with Danny Fargo in front of the whole school. They would kiss with everyone watching, and in order to do so, they would have to practice kissing. This was what her future held – numerous kissings of Danny Fargo while Ms. Fry stood at her elbow, demanding more and more passion. 'Look into his eyes first. Slower. Naked longing.' Karin had kissed under Ms. Fry's direction plenty of times before.

Plus, there were no other imaginable circumstances under which a girl like Karin could hope to kiss a boy like Jimmy. Jimmy had surprised everyone by even trying out when the show would pose such an obvious conflict with the baseball season. Jimmy's coach had told the team they couldn't do any other sports. Not in his wildest dreams had it occurred to him to out-law the musical.

Jimmy was his only reliable closer. Accommodations were made, though the choice of a musical over baseball had left Coach Blumberg at first stunned and then dispirited. 'I don't have so many seasons left in me,' he'd told a group of women in the teachers' lounge.

The whole thing had cruelly raised Karin's hopes. If Jimmy had gotten the part of Tommy, they would have spent a lot of time together. He might have actually looked at her. He might have noticed that she could, in makeup and with her hair done, look just like a star in a Bollywood musical. Danny Fargo might have the same revelation, but who wanted him to?

'Are you coming to see us?' Karin asked Prudie, and Prudie said she wouldn't miss it. (Though how hot was the theater going to be? How would she herself respond to the spectacle of Jimmy Johns, with his closing-pitcher arms, singing 'Come to Me, Bend to Me'?)

She gave her sixth-period class the same section of *The Little Prince* to translate, but as they were third-years, English to French instead of the other way around. 'The second planet was inhabited by a conceited man.'

Prudie returned to her index cards. It had occurred to her over lunch that none of Jane's other heroines was anywhere near as devout as Fanny. The book club had yet to even mention religion.

Austen's other books were filled with clergymen's livings – promised, offered, desired – but these posed more financial concerns than spiritual ones. No heroine but Fanny spoke so approvingly of worship or seemed to admire the clergy so much. Six books. So many scenes of village life, so many dances and dinners carefully depicted. Not a single sermon. And Jane's father had been a clergyman himself. There was much here to discuss! Bernadette would surely have things to say about this. Prudie filled five new cards before the heat got to her.

Her headache was making a comeback. She pressed on her temples and looked at the clock. Sallie Wong had written a note, folded it like a crane, brushed it off the desk with her elbow. Teri Cheyney picked it up, unfolded it, read it. Oh my God, she mouthed. (And not *Mon dieu*.) Probably Trey's name was in that note somewhere. Prudie considered confiscating it, but that would involve standing. She was so hot she thought she might actually faint if she stood. What might the students not do if she were unconscious? What romps and frolics? Little black spots swam through her vision like tadpoles. She put her head on the desk, closed her eyes.

It was, thank God, almost time to go home. She would do some light cleaning before the book club came. Quick vacuum. Casual dusting. Perhaps it would be cool enough by eight to meet out on the deck. That might be lovely if the Delta breeze came in. The noise level in the classroom was rising subtly. She should sit up before it got out of hand, open her eyes, clear her throat loudly. She was determined to do so, and then the bell rang.

And then, instead of going straight home, Prudie found herself outside the multipurpose room. The kids who did drama were an interesting group. Mostly into pot, which distinguished them from the ones who did student government (alcohol) or played sports (steroids) or did yearbook (glue). So many distinct sets and subsets. There was something quite mandarin about the complexity of it. Prudie sometimes wished she'd studied anthropology. There would have been papers to write. Of course, that was the bad news as well as the good. Writing papers would have been an effort. She wasn't her mother's daughter for nothing.

She could hear music, muffled through the multipurpose room door. Behind that door was the Scottish highlands. Mists and hills and heather. It sounded lovely and cool. While going home, desirable in every other way, involved getting into a car that had been in the parking lot with the windows up since eight that morning. She would have to wrap her hand in her skirt to open the door. The seat would be too hot to sit on, the steering wheel too hot to hold. She would spend several minutes actually, technically, baking as she drove.

None of this would improve with delay, but the prospect was so unappealing that Prudie chose door B. She was rewarded with a wash of air-conditioning over her face. Some kid who'd never taken French was playing the bagpipe. Onstage the players rehearsed the chase of Harry Beaton. Ms Fry was having them run through the scene, first in slow motion, and then up to speed. From her seat, Prudie could see the stage, and also the actors waiting in the wings. Meanwhile, in the back, the bagpipe practiced for Harry's funeral. Without exactly liking the instrument, Prudie admired the performance. Where would a kid from California have learned to blow and squeeze that way?

The boys jumped down off the stage, kilts flying. Jimmy Johns put his arm around the blond sophomore girl who was playing his fiancée. In Brigadoon, their love had broken Harry's heart; at Valley High, the broken heart was Karin's. She sat a few rows back and alone, a careful distance from Danny.

Prudie found herself in sudden sympathy with Coach Blumberg. How wise was it, after all, to encourage these children to play at great love? To tell them that romance was worth dying for, that simple steadfastness was stronger than any other force in the world? What Coach Blumberg believed – that there was something important about nine boys outpitching, outhitting, and outrunning nine other boys – seemed, by contrast, a harmless fraud. Jane Austen wrote six great romances, and no one died for love in any of them. Prudie observed a moment's silence in honor of Austen and her impeccable restraint. Then she was just quiet with no purpose to being so.

Trey Norton slid into the seat beside her. 'Should you be here? Don't you have class?' she asked him.

'It was a hundred fourteen in the Quonset. Some geek had an actual thermometer on him, we were let out. I'm picking up Jimmy.' Trey was smiling at Prudie in a disconcerting way that wasn't his usual disconcerting way. 'I saw you in the library. You were watching me.'

Prudie felt herself flush. 'A public display of affection is public.'

'Okay, public. I wouldn't call it affection, though.'

It was long past time to change the subject. 'The boy playing the bagpipes is really good,' Prudie said.

If only she'd said it in French! Trey made a delighted noise. 'Nessa Trussler. A girl. Or something.'

Prudie looked at Nessa again. There was, she could see now, a certain plump ambiguity. Maybe Trey wouldn't tell anyone what she'd said. Maybe Nessa was perfectly comfortable with who she was. Maybe she was admired throughout the school for her musical ability. Maybe pigs could jig.

The best thing you could say for Nessa was that she had only three years here. Then she could go as far away as she liked. She could never come back if that was what she wanted. Prudie was the one staying. She had a sudden revelation that this was Brigadoon, where nothing would ever change. The only people who would age were the teachers. It was a terrifying thing to think.

She had a more practical idea. 'I'm not wearing my contacts,' she offered. Lamely and late.

'Yes you are.' Trey was looking deep into her eyes; she could smell his breath. It was slightly fishy, but not in a bad way. Like a kitten's. 'I can see them. Little rings around your irises. Like little dinner plates.'

Prudie's heartbeat was quick and shallow. Trey lifted his chin. 'And a good thing. PD of A to starboard.'

Prudie turned around. There, right there, in the wings, with the stage empty but a fair number of kids still scattered about the auditorium, Mr Chou, the music teacher (unmarried) slipped his hands over Ms Fry (married)'s breasts, squeezed them as if he were testing cantaloupes. And clearly not for the first time; those hands knew those breasts. What was it about this school! Prudie's headache upped its tempo. The bagpipe exhaled forlornly.

Prudie's second reaction was to calm down. Maybe this was not so bad. It would distract Trey from her unfortunate faux pas about Nessa. Nessa was an innocent here; Prudie didn't regret the exchange.

As for Ms Fry and Mr Chou, Prudie couldn't even pretend to be surprised. Ms Fry had large breasts. Take pheromones, add music, rehearsals day and night, people dying for love. What could you expect?

One of the things that troubled Prudie about *Mansfield Park* was the way things ended between Mary Crawford and Edmund. Edmund had wished to marry Miss Crawford. It looked to Prudie as if, whatever other excuses he might offer, he'd finally cast her aside because she wished to forgive her brother and his sister for an adulterous affair. Edmund accused Mary of taking sin lightly. But he himself preferred to lose his sister forever rather than forgive her.

Prudie had always wanted a brother. It would have been nice to have someone with whom to cross-check memories. Had they ever been to Muir Woods? Dillon Beach? Why were there no pictures? She'd imagined that she would love this brother very much. She'd imagined he would love her in return, would see her shortcomings – who would know you better than a brother did? – but with fondness and charity. In the end, Prudie disliked Edmund so much more than she disliked his scandalous, selfish, love-stricken sister.

Of course, attitudes changed over the centuries; you had to allow for this. But an unforgiving prick was an unforgiving prick. 'Oo-la-la,' Trey said.

Prudie's own feelings on adultery were taken from the French.

'The evergreen! – How beautiful, how welcome, how wonderful the evergreen!'
(MANSFIELD PARK)

The climate in the Valley was classified as Mediterranean, which meant that everything died in the summer. The native grasses went brown and stiff. The creeks disappeared. The oaks turned gray.

Prudie got into her car. She rolled down the windows, started the AC. The seat burned the backs of her bare legs.

Some bird had shat on the windshield; the shit had cooked all day and would have to be scoured off. Prudie couldn't face doing this in the full sun. Instead she drove home while peering around a large continent – Greece, maybe, or Greenland. Using the water and wipers would only make things worse. None of the driving was freeway, and she had mirrors, so it wasn't really as reckless as it sounded.

Without any particular affection for her eldest cousin, her tenderness of heart made her feel that she could not spare him; and the purity of her principles added yet a keener solicitude, when she considered how little useful, how little self-denying his life had (apparently) been. (MANSFIELD PARK)

The curtains were drawn and the air conditioner was on, so Prudie walked into a house that was dark and tolerably cool. She took two more aspirin. Now that it came to it, she didn't have the energy for further cleaning. Her lists were a comfort to her, an illusion of control in a turvy-topsy world, but she was no prisoner to them. Things came up, plans changed. Holly, the housekeeper, had been by last week. The place was clean enough by anyone's standards but Jocelyn's. Prudie would have to go out shopping again, there was no help for that, or serve a salad made from a romaine already browned at the edges.

She took a cold shower, hoping that would pep her up, and dressed in a sleeveless T-shirt and cotton pajama pants printed with various sorts of sushi. Someone rang the doorbell while she was toweling her hair.

Cameron Watson stood on her porch, sweat running down the peak of his sharp nose. 'Cameron,' Prudie said. 'What's this about?'

'I said I'd clean up your machine.'

'I didn't know you meant today.'

'You want to be able to e-mail,' he said, in surprise. How could anyone go twenty-four hours without e-mail?

There was a time when Prudie had worried that Cameron had a little crush on her. Now she knew better. Cameron had a little crush on her computer, which he had, of course, picked out himself. Cameron had another little crush on Dean's video games. Cameron didn't even see that she was wearing nothing but her pajamas. If this were a Jane Austen book, Prudie would be the girl courted for her estate.

She stood aside to let Cameron in. He had cords and peripherals slung across his body like a bandolier, disks in a plastic case. He went straight to the family room, began running his diagnostics, working his magic. She'd thought to take a nap, but she couldn't do that now, not with Cameron in the house. She dusted instead, indifferently, even resentfully. This was certainly a poor trade for sleeping.

Because she didn't feel the gratitude Cameron deserved – really this was very nice of him – she made a show of it. She brought him a glass of lemonade. 'I'm downloading you some deadware,' he said. 'Emulator programs.' He took the lemonade, set it aside to sweat in its glass all over the top of the desk. 'We should get you Limux, too. Nobody uses Windows anymore.' (And pigs can jig.)

She looked down on the white line of scalp that showed through at the part in his hair. He had large, dead flakes of dandruff. She felt an impulse to dust him. 'What do emulator programs do?'

'You can play old games on them.'

'I thought the point was new games,' Prudie said. 'I thought the games were just getting better and better.'

'So you can play the *classics*,' Cameron told her.

Perhaps that was a bit like rereading. Prudie returned to the living room. She was chasing a thought now about rereading, about memory, about childhood. It had something to do with how Mansfield Park seemed a cold, uneasy place to Fanny until she was banished back to her parents'. The Bertram estate became Fanny's home only when she was no longer in it. Until then, she'd never understood that the affection of her aunt and uncle would prove more real in the end than that of her mother and father. Who else but Jane would think to turn the fairy tale this way? Prudie meant to get the index cards from her purse, write some of this down. Instead, in spite of Cameron, she fell asleep on the couch.

She woke up with Dean stroking her arm. 'I had the strangest dream,' she said, and then couldn't remember what it had been. She sat up. 'I thought you said you'd be late.' She looked at his face. 'What's wrong?'

He picked up both her hands. 'You need to get right home, honey,' he said. 'Your mom's been in an accident.'

'I can't go home.' Prudie's mouth was dry, her head fuzzy. Dean didn't know her mother the way she did, or he'd know there was nothing to be concerned about. 'I have my book club coming.'

'I know. I know you've been looking forward to that. I'll call Jocelyn. You have a plane reservation in an hour and a half. I'm so sorry, darling. I'm so sorry. You really have to hurry.'

He put his arms around her, but it was too hot to be hugged. She pushed him off. 'I'm sure she's fine. I'll go tomorrow. Or this weekend.'

'She hasn't been conscious since the accident. The Baileys called my office. No one could get through to you. I've been trying the whole way home. Busy signal.'

'Cameron's on the computer.'

'I'll send him off.'

Dean packed Prudie's bag. He told her that by the time she got to San Diego he'd have a car waiting for her, to look for a driver with her name on a card in baggage claim. He said he'd call the school for a substitute, cancel his own appointments. Find someone more responsible than Cameron to feed the cat. He'd think of everything. She should think only about her mom. And herself.

He'd follow as soon as he could. He'd be at the hospital with her by tomorrow morning at the latest. Late tonight if he could manage it. 'I'm so sorry,' he kept saying, 'I'm so sorry,' until she finally got the message that he thought her mother was dying. As if!

A year earlier Dean could have accompanied her to the gate, held her hand while she waited. Now there was no point in even going in. He dropped her at the curb, went home to make the rest of the arrangements.

A man went through security in front of her. He had a gym bag and a cell phone and he walked on his heels the same way Trey Norton did. He was pulled aside, made to remove his shoes. Prudie's fingernail clippers were confiscated, and also her Swiss Army knife. She wished she'd remembered to give this to Dean; she liked that knife.

Her reservation was on Southwest. She'd gotten a boarding pass in the C group. She could still hope for an aisle seat, but only if she was right at the front, and maybe not even then.

While fishing her identification out of her purse again to board the plane, her index cards spilled. 'Do you want to play fifty-two card pick-up?' she'd asked her mother once. She'd learned this trick at day care. 'Sure thing,' her mother had said, and then, after Prudie had scattered the cards, she asked if Prudie would be her little helper-elf and pick them up for her.

Prudie dropped to her knees to collect her cards. People stepped over her. Some of these people were impatient, unpleasant. There was no hope of an aisle seat now. By the time she stumbled onto the plane she was crying. Later, over the complimentary Coke, as a Zen exercise to calm herself down, she counted her cards. She'd been preparing for so long she had forty-two of them. She counted them twice to be sure.

She did the crossword in the in-flight magazine for a while. Then she stared out the window at the empty sky. Everything was fine. Her mother was perfectly *sain et sauf*, and Prudie absolutely refused to be sucked into pretending otherwise.

Prudie's dream:

In Prudie's dream, Jane Austen is showing her through the rooms of a large estate. Jane doesn't look anything like her portrait. She looks more like Jocelyn and sometimes she is Jocelyn, but mostly she's Jane. She's blond, neat, modern. Her pants are silk and have wide legs.

They're in a kitchen decorated in the same blue, white, and copper as Jocelyn's kitchen. Jane and Prudie agree that fine cooking can be done only on a gas stove. Jane tells Prudie that she herself is considered a decent French chef. She promises to make something for Prudie later, and even as she says so, Prudie knows she'll forget.

They descend to a wine cellar. A grid frame along a dark wall holds several bottles, but more of the cubbyholes have cats inside.

Their eyes shine in the dark like coins. Prudie almost mentions this, but decides it would be rude.

Without actually ascending a staircase, Prudie finds herself upstairs, alone, in a hall with many doors. She tries a few, but they're all locked. Between the doors are life-sized portraits interspersed with mirrors. The mirrors are arranged so that every portrait is reflected in a mirror across the hall. Prudie can stand in front of these mirrors and position herself so that she appears to be in each portrait along with the original subject.

Jane arrives again. She is in a hurry now, hustling Prudie past many doors until they suddenly stop. 'Here's where we've put your mother,' she says. 'I think you'll see we've made some improvements.'

Prudie hesitates. 'Open the door,' Jane tells her, and Prudie does. Instead of a room, there is a beach, a sailboat and an island in the distance, the ocean as far as Prudie can see.

JUNE

CHAPTER FOUR

in which we read
Northanger Abbey
and gather at Grigg's

Prudie missed our next meeting. Jocelyn brought a card for everyone to sign. She said it was a sympathy card, which we had to take her word for, as it was all in French. The front was sober enough – a seascape, dunes, gulls, and drift. Time and tide or some such cold comfort. 'I was so sad to hear that she had to cancel her trip to France,' Sylvia said, and then looked away, embarrassed, because that was hardly the saddest part.

Jocelyn spoke up quickly. 'You know she's never been.'

We had, most of us, also lost our mothers. We spent a moment missing them. The sun was blooming rosily in the west. The trees were in full leaf. The air was bright and soft and laced with the smells of grass, of coffee, of melted Brie. How our mothers would have loved it!

Allegra leaned over and picked up Sylvia's hand, traced around the fingers, let it go. Sylvia was looking uncommonly elegant tonight. She had cut her hair as short as Allegra's and was dressed in a long skirt with a Chinese-red fitted top. Applied a plummy lipstick and had her eyebrows shaped. We were pleased to see that she'd reached that drop-dead stage of the divorce proceedings. She was on her feet and dressed to kill.

Allegra was, as always, vivid. Jocelyn was classic. Grigg was casual – corduroys and a green rugby shirt. Bernadette had already spilled hummus on her yoga pants.

The pants were spotted with olive and blue flowers, and now there was a hummus-colored spot as well on the ledge of her stomach. You could go a long time without noticing the stain, however. You could go a long time without looking at her pants. This was because she'd broken her glasses sometime after our last meeting and patched them together with a startling great lump of paper clips and masking tape.

It was possible they weren't even broken. It was possible she'd merely lost the little screw.

The meeting was held at Grigg's. Some of us had wondered whether Grigg would ever be hosting us, and some of us had thought he wouldn't be and were already cross about the special arrangements men always expected: how they never made the big meals, the holiday meals, how their wives wrote their thank yous for them and sent out the birthday cards. We were working ourselves into something of a state about it when Grigg said we should have the *Northanger Abbey* meeting at his house, because he was probably the only one in the group who liked *Northanger Abbey* best of all the books so far.

This was not a position we could imagine anyone taking. We hoped Grigg wasn't saying this just because it was provocative. Austen was no occasion for displays of ego.

We'd been curious about Grigg's housekeeping. Most of us hadn't seen a bachelor pad since the seventies. We were picturing mirror balls and Andy Warhol.

We got chili-string lights and Beatrix Potter. Grigg had rented a cozy brick cottage in a pricey part of town. It had a tin roof and a porch overhung with grapevines. Inside was a sleeping loft and the smallest wood-burning stove we'd ever seen. During February, Grigg said, he'd heated the whole place with it, but by the time he'd chopped the logs into the tiny splinters that would fit inside, he didn't need a fire anymore; he'd be sweating like a pig.

There was a rug by the couch that many of us recognized from the Sundance catalogue as something we ourselves had wanted, the one with poppies on the edges. The sun glanced off a row of copper pots in the kitchen window.

Each pot held an African violet, some white, some purple, and you have to admire a man who keeps his houseplants alive, especially when they've been transferred into pots with no holes for drainage. It made us begrudge him the rug less. Of course, the violets could all have been new, bought just to impress us. But then again, who were we that we needed impressing?

The wall along the stairs was lined with built-in book cases, and these were stuffed with books, not just upright, but teepeed across the tops of other books as well. They were mostly paper-backs, and well read. Allegra went to check them out. 'Lots of rocketships in this collection,' she said.

'You like science fiction?' Sylvia asked Grigg. From her tone of voice you might have thought she was interested in science fiction and the people who read it.

Grigg wasn't fooled. 'Always have,' was all he said. He continued to arrange cheese wedges on a plate. They made a sort of picture of a face when he was done, a cheese-wedge smile, two pepper-cracker eyes. We may have just been imagining that, though. He may have been laying out the cheese with no artistic intent.

*

Grigg had grown up in Orange County, the only boy in a family with four children, and the youngest. His oldest sister, Amelia, was eight when he was born, Bianca was seven, and Caty, who was called Catydid when she was little and Cat when she was older, was five.

He was always way too easy to tease. Sometimes they told him not to be such a boy and sometimes not to be such a baby. It didn't seem to leave a whole lot of things for him to be.

If Grigg had been a girl, his name would have been Delia. Instead he was named after his father's father, who'd died just about the time Grigg was born and already no one seemed to remember him very well. 'A man's man,' Grigg's father said, 'a quiet man,' which was a movie Grigg had seen on television and so he always pictured his grandfather as John Wayne.

Even so, it was hard to forgive the name. Every year at school, the first time his new teacher would take attendance, she would call for Harris Grigg instead of Grigg Harris. All year Grigg anticipated the next year's humiliation. And then he found out that his grandfather's real name was Gregory and that his parents had known this all along. Grigg was just a nickname and not a family name, not until Grigg's own parents had made it one. He repeatedly asked them why, but never got an answer he felt settled the question. He told them that from then on he, too, would go by 'Gregory,' but no one ever remembered, even though they could remember to call Caty 'Cat' easily enough.

Grandpa Harris had worked for the electric company as a lineman. It was a dangerous job, Grigg's father told him. Grigg had every hope of having a dangerous job himself someday, though more secret agent than crack utility worker. His own father was a meter reader and had been in the hospital four times with dog bites. He had two shiny scars on the calf of one leg and another scar somewhere no one saw. The Harrises had never owned a dog, and as long as his father was alive they never would. Grigg was five the first time this was explained to him, and he still remembered his reaction, how he thought to himself that his father couldn't live forever.

Grigg was the only one of the children with his own bedroom. This was a continual source of resentment. The room was so tiny the bed barely fit and his chest of drawers had to be put in the hall. Still, it was all his. The ceiling slanted; there was a single window, and wallpaper with yellow rosebuds, which Amelia had picked because the room had been hers until Grigg came along. If he'd been a girl she would have gotten to keep the room.

When the wind blew, a branch tapped against the glass like fingers, but that surely wouldn't have scared Amelia. Grigg would lie in the dark, all by himself, and the tree creaked and tapped. He would hear his sisters laughing down the hall. He knew when it was Amelia laughing and when it was Bianca and when it was Cat, even if he couldn't hear the words. He guessed they were talking about boys, a subject on which they had nothing pleasant to say.

'You girls go to sleep now,' his mother would shout from downstairs. She often played the piano after the children were in bed, and if she could still hear them over her beloved Scott Joplin, then they were too loud. The girls might respond with a temporary silence, or they might not bother. Individually they were governable. As a unit, not so much so.

Grigg's father couldn't stand up to them at all. They hated the smell of his pipe, so he smoked only in his toolshed. They hated sports, so he went out to his car to listen to games on the radio. When they wanted money, they flirted for it, straightening his tie and kissing his cheek until, helpless as a kitten, he pulled his wallet from his back pocket. Once Grigg did the very same thing, blinked his heavy lashes and pouted his lips. Cat laughed so hard she choked on a peanut, which could have killed her. Amelia had heard of that happening to someone, and how would Grigg have felt then?

Grigg was always being laughed at. He'd been the only boy in his first-grade class who could go all the way around the world in jacks, but that, too, turned out to be a social misstep.

One day when he was in the fifth grade, Grigg's father stopped him after breakfast. 'Come out back with me,' he said, in a low voice. 'And don't tell the girls.'

'Out back' meant the little room his father had made for himself in the old toolshed. Out back was strictly invitation-only. There was a lock on the door, and a plaid La-Z-Boy Grigg's mother hated and wouldn't have in the house. There was an old Tupperware dish with an endless supply of Red Hots. Grigg didn't like Red Hots much, but he ate them when they were offered; they were still candy, after all. Grigg was happy to hear that the girls were not invited, were not even to be told. It was not an easy thing, keeping a secret from three older sisters while still making sure everyone knew there was a secret being kept, but Grigg had studied with the masters, who were the girls themselves.

Grigg went to the toolshed. His father was waiting, smoking a cigarette. There was no window in the shed, so it was always dark, even with the lamp on, and the smoke was thick; because no one knew about second-hand smoke then, no one thought anything about it. The lamp had a bendable neck and a glaring bulb, as if someone was about to be interrogated. His father was sitting in the La-Z-Boy with a stack of magazines in his lap.

'This is strictly boy stuff,' his father said. 'Top-secret. Got it?'

Grigg took a seat on an upended apple crate, and his father handed him a magazine. On the cover was the picture of a woman in her underwear. Her black hair flew about her face in long, loose curls. Her eyes were wide. She had enormous breasts, barely contained by a golden bra.

But best of all, unbelievably best, was the thing unhooking the bra. It had eight tentacled arms and a torso shaped like a Coke can. It was blue. The look on its face – what an artist to convey so much emotion on a creature with so few features! – was hungry.

This was the afternoon that made a reader out of Grigg.

Soon he had learned:

From Arthur C. Clarke, that 'art cannot be enjoyed unless it is approached with love.'

From Theodore Sturgeon, that 'sometimes the world's too much to live with and a body sort of has to turn away from it to rest.'

From Philip K. Dick, that 'at least half the famous people in history never existed,' and that 'anything can be faked.'

What Grigg liked best about science fiction was that it seemed to be a place where he was neither alone nor surrounded by girls. He wouldn't have continued to like it as he grew, if it really had been as girl-free a world as he initially thought. His first favorite author was Andrew North. Later he learned that Andrew North was a pen name for Andre Norton. Later still he learned that Andre Norton was a girl.

Grigg didn't tell us any of this, because he thought we wouldn't be interested. 'Those books with rocketships on the spine were the first books I fell in love with,' is what Grigg said. 'You never do get over your first love, do you?'

'No,' said Sylvia. 'You never do.'

'Except for sometimes,' said Bernadette.

'I was at a science fiction convention when I first met Jocelyn,' Grigg told us.

We all turned to look at Jocelyn. Perhaps one or two of us had our mouths open. We would never have guessed she read science fiction. She had certainly never said so. She hadn't gone to any of the new *Star Wars* movies, and she'd never stood in line for any of the old ones.

'Oh, please.' Jocelyn made an impatient brushing motion with her hand. 'As if. I was at the Hound Roundup. Same hotel.'

The evening had hardly begun and already there was a second story we weren't being told.

Almost a year earlier, Jocelyn had gone to Stockton for the annual meeting of the Inland Empire Hound Club. In celebration of a whole weekend free from dog hair (not that Ridgebacks were great shedders: they kept their hair to themselves more than most dogs, this was one of their many attractive features), Jocelyn packed a great many black clothes. She wore a black headed vest under a black cardigan. Black slacks and black socks. She attended panels entitled 'Sight Hounds: What Makes Them Special?' and 'Soothing the Savage Beast: New Modification Techniques for Aggressive Behaviors.' (Which was sad, as the proper quote was about savage breasts. Now that would be a panel!)

On the same weekend and in the same hotel was a science fiction convention known as Westernessecon. In the lower-level conference rooms, science fiction fans were gathering to talk about books and mourn dead or dying TV shows. There were panels on 'Why We Once Loved *Buffy*,' 'The Final Frontier: Manifest Destiny Goes Intergalactic,' and 'Santa Claus: God or Fiend?'

Jocelyn was taking the elevator from the lobby to her room on the seventeenth floor when a man got on. He wasn't young, but he was considerably younger than Jocelyn; that was a rapidly growing category. There was nothing to draw Jocelyn's attention to him, and she paid him no further notice.

A trio of young women came on behind him. All three had chains in their noses, spikes on their wrists. They wore cuffs on their ears as if Fish and Wildlife had tagged and then released them. Their faces were powdered the color of chalk and their arms were crossed over their breasts, wrist spikes on top. The man hit the button for the twelfth floor and one of the women for the eighth.

The elevator stopped again and more people entered. Just as the door was shutting, someone outside clapped it open and more people pushed in. Jocelyn found herself crushed against the back of the elevator. The spikes on one young woman's bracelet caught on Jocelyn's sweater and left a snag. Someone stepped on her foot and didn't seem to realize it; Jocelyn had to wiggle out from under and still there was no apology. The elevator stopped again. 'No room!' someone at the front said loudly, and the door closed.

The chalk-faced woman to Jocelyn's right was wearing the same red dog collar that Sahara sported on dressy occasions. 'I have a collar just like that,' Jocelyn told her. She intended it as a friendly gesture, a hand across the waters. She was trying not to mind being trapped at the back of the elevator. Jocelyn didn't normally suffer from claustrophobia, but she was seldom this squeezed and her breath came fast and shallow.

The woman made no response. Jocelyn waited for one, and then a brief, inconsequential humiliation came over her. What had her crime been? Her age? Her clothes? Her 'Dog is my co-pilot' name tag? Everyone except Jocelyn and the not-young-but-younger-than-Jocelyn man got off at the eighth floor. Jocelyn moved forward, picking at the snag in her sweater, trying to pull it inside, where it wouldn't show. The elevator resumed its ascent.

'She was invisible,' the man said.

Jocelyn turned. 'Excuse me?'

He appeared to be a normal, agreeable man. Lovely, heavy eyelashes, but otherwise quite ordinary. 'It's a game. They're vampires, and when you see one of them holding her arms crossed like that' – the man demonstrated – 'then you should pretend you don't see her. She's invisible. That's why she didn't answer you. Nothing personal.'

This made it sound as if it were all Jocelyn's fault. 'Being a vampire is no excuse for being rude,' Jocelyn told him. 'Ms. Manners says.' Of course Ms. Manners had said no such thing, but wouldn't she probably, if asked?

They'd arrived at the twelfth floor. The elevator hummed and clanged. The man debarked, turned to face her. 'My name is Grigg.'

As if anyone would know whether Grigg was a first or a last name without being told. The door slid shut before Jocelyn could answer. Just as well. 'What a bunch of freaks,' she said. She said it aloud in case there was someone still in the elevator with her. The feelings of invisible people were of no moment to Jocelyn, though Ms. Manners probably wouldn't like that, either; Ms. Manners was a hard woman.

Jocelyn left an unimaginative demonstration by a pet psychic – 'He wants you to know that he's very grateful for the good care you take of him'; 'She says she loves you very much' – and went to her room. She showered, just to use the hotel soap and lotion, shook her hair dry, slipped into her black linen dress, left her name tag on her cardigan on the bed, and took the elevator to the top floor. She stood at the doorway of the hotel bar, looking about for someone she knew. 'I was in Holland and Italy and Australia last year,' an attractive woman at a table near the door was saying, 'and every time I turned on a television, some version of *Star Trek* was on. I'm telling you, it's ubiquitous.'

There was an empty stool at the bar. Jocelyn occupied it and ordered a dirty martini. She couldn't find a familiar face. Usually she didn't mind being out alone; she'd been single too long to care. But here she felt uncomfortable. She felt that her dress was wrong, too tasteful, too expensive. She felt old. Her martini arrived. She drank from it, in a gulp. Another gulp. And another. She'd finish as quickly as possible and leave, look for dog people in the lobby or the restaurant. The bar was headachingly noisy. There were a dozen conversations, high-pitched laughter, a hockey game on the television set, hoses spitting and ice machines crushing.

'All I'm saying is, it would take a thousand years to bring an animal species to full consciousness,' a man near Jocelyn said. 'You suggest otherwise and you lose me.' He was speaking so loudly Jocelyn thought there was no need to pretend she hadn't heard.

She leaned in. 'Actually I would have enjoyed something a bit more lizard-brain,' she said. 'The perfect grammar, the British accent, for God's sake. The boringly endless list of thank yous. As if they aren't all just waiting for the chance to hump your leg.'

Now, that was an inelegant thing to say. Perhaps she was already just a tiny bit drunk. The room did a leisurely spin. Drink in haste, repent at leisure, her mother had always told her. An ad for a poetic sort of running shoe came on the television.

The man had turned toward her. He was a large man with a full beard and a small scotch. He looked like a bear, but good-humored, which real bears never, ever look. Jocelyn was guessing he was a basset breeder; there wasn't a more agreeable group in the world than the basset contingent. She herself had only recently learned to love the bassets, and it was a point of secret shame that it had taken so long. Everyone else seemed to fall in love with them so effortlessly.

'Mostly I was offended by the invertebrates,' the bear man said. 'We are not crustaceans. The same rules do not apply.'

Now Jocelyn was sorry she'd left the demonstration early. How much gratitude could a crustacean express? And if one did, well, she'd certainly want to be there to see it. 'He did a crustacean?' she asked. Wistfully.

'Which of his books have you read?'

'I haven't read his books.'

'Oh my God! You should read his books,' the man told her. 'I complain, sure, but I'm a huge fan. You really should read his books.'

'Well, you're huge. You got that part right.' The voice was tiny, a gnat in Jocelyn's ear. She turned and found Roberta Reinicker's face hovering above her, her brother Tad just behind. The Reinickers had a kennel in Fresno and a coquettish Ridge-back named Beauty in whom Jocelyn was periodically interested. Beauty had good papers and a good confirmation. A sweet if unsteady disposition. She gave her heart to whoever was closest. In a dog, this was a pretty nice trait.

'Scoot over,' Roberta said, taking half of Jocelyn's stool by pressing her hard into the counter. Roberta was a frosted blond in her late thirties. Tad was older and not so pretty. He leaned past Jocelyn to order. 'I have a new car,' he told her. He raised his eyebrows significantly and tried to wait for the punch line. He failed. 'A Lexus. Great mileage. Beautiful seats. The engine – like butter churning.'

'How nice,' Jocelyn said. He was still hovering. If Jocelyn looked straight up she'd see the soft white froglike skin on the bottom of his chin. This wasn't a view one often got, and a very good thing, too.

' "Nice"!' Tad shook his head; his chin went right and left and right and left. 'I hope you can do better than "nice." It's a Lexus.'

'Very nice,' Jocelyn offered. A Lexus was, by all accounts, a very nice car. Jocelyn had never heard otherwise.

'Used, of course. I got a great deal. I could take you for a spin later. You've never had such a smooth ride.'

While he was talking, Roberta's gnat voice came into Jocelyn's ear again, 'What a bunch of freaks,' Roberta said.

Jocelyn did not approve of calling people freaks. Nor did she think the people in the bar looked particularly freakish. There'd been a Klingon, an elf or two down in the lobby, but apparently the aliens weren't drinking. Too bad. A night that began with mind-reading a grateful crustacean and ended with drunken elves would be a night to remember. 'I don't know who you're talking about.'

'Yeah, right,' Roberta said. Conspiratorially.

'So which authors do *you* like?' the bear man asked Roberta.

'Oh!' Roberta said. 'No! I don't read science fiction. Not ever.' And then, into Jocelyn's ear, 'My God! He thinks I'm one of them.'

My God. The bear man was a science fiction fan, not a basset breeder. So what, Jocelyn wondered, had she and he been talking about? How had crustaceans made their way into the conversation?

And surely he couldn't hear Roberta over the other noise in the bar, but he could see the whispering. Jocelyn was mortified by her own mistake and Roberta's bad manners.

'Really?' she asked Roberta, loud enough for the bear man to hear. 'Never? That seems a bit small-minded. I love a good science fiction novel, myself.'

'Whom do you read?' the bear man asked.

Jocelyn took another gulp, set her glass down, crossed her arms. This accomplished nothing. Roberta, Tad, and the bear man watched her intently. She closed her eyes, which did make them disappear, but not usefully so.

Think, she told herself. Surely she knew the name of one science fiction writer. Who was that dinosaur guy? Michael something.

'Ursula Le Guin. Connie Willis? Nancy Kress?' Grigg had come up while she had her eyes closed, was standing just behind Roberta. 'Am I right?' he asked. 'You look like a woman of impeccable taste.'

'I think you must be psychic,' she said.

Tad told them all what a really good book was (nonfiction and with boats – *The Perfect Storm*), and also what wasn't a good book (anything with talking fucking trees like *The Lord of the Rings*). It turned out Tad had never actually read either one. He'd seen the movies. This made the bear man so mad he spilled his scotch into his beard.

Jocelyn went to use the bathroom, and when she came back both Grigg and the bear man were gone. Roberta had saved the bear man's chair for her, and Tad had gotten her a second dirty martini, which was nice of him, though she didn't want it and he might have asked first. And of course, the stool Roberta was on was actually Jocelyn's, not that Jocelyn preferred one to the other. Just that she wouldn't have needed anybody to save her a seat if her own seat hadn't been taken in the first place.

'I managed to get rid of them,' Tad said. He was shouting so as to be heard. 'I told them we were going for a spin in my new Lexus.'

'But not me,' Roberta said. 'I'm exhausted. Honestly, I'm so tired I'm not even sure I can make it to bed.' She illustrated the point by drooping prettily over the bar.

'What made you think I wanted to get rid of them?' Jocelyn asked Tad. Really, what an annoying man! She hated his Lexus. She was beginning to hate Beauty. The prettiest dog you could ever imagine, but did Jocelyn want that 'Chase me, chase me' gene in the Serengeti pool?

'I can tell when you're just being polite,' Tad said, proving, if he only knew it, how much he couldn't. He winked.

Jocelyn told him politely that she had an early panel to get to the next morning and was going to have to call it a night. ('Me too,' Roberta said.) Jocelyn thanked Tad for her untouched drink, insisted on paying for it, and left.

She looked for Grigg and the bear man for a while. She was afraid it might have looked collusive – she disappears to the bathroom; Tad gets rid of the unwelcome guests. However Tad had handled their dismissal, it couldn't have been delicately done. She wanted to say she'd been unaware of it. She wanted to say she'd been enjoying their company. This would be awkward, no doubt, and unpersuasive, but was true; she had that on her side.

She saw a notice in the elevator for a book-launch party on the sixth floor, so she went down and walked by, pretending she had a room on that floor and was about her innocent business there. The party suite was so packed that people had spilled out into the hall. The vampire girls were seated among them. Two of them were visible, drinking red wine and flicking Cheetos at each other. The other had her arms crossed behind the neck of a young man and her tongue in his mouth. He had his hands on her butt, so he was visible, but Jocelyn wasn't sure about the girl. She would have to ask Grigg when she found him: Are you invisible if your arms are crossed but there is a skinny, caped guy inside them, sucking your face?

Jocelyn picked her way through the hall, past the door of the suite. Lights strobed inside; there was music and dancing. The party pulsed. She was surprised to see Roberta, shaking her hair and her ass, moving in the intermittent light from attitude to attitude. Now her hands were on her hips. Now she snaked to one side. Now she did a hip-hop dip. Jocelyn couldn't see her partner, the room was too crowded.

Jocelyn gave up. She went back to her room, called Sylvia and related the whole annoying evening.

'Which one is Tad?' Sylvia asked. 'Is he the one who's always saying "Good girl," to everyone?' But he wasn't, Sylvia was thinking of Burtie Chambers. Sylvia liked the idea that you could disappear by crossing your arms, though. 'God, wouldn't that be great!' she said. 'Daniel will love it. He's always wishing he could disappear.'

Jocelyn didn't see Grigg again until the evening of the next day. 'I was afraid you'd left,' she said, 'and I wanted to apologize for last night.'

He was kind enough to cut her off. 'I got you something in the dealer's room,' he told her. He fished through his convention bag and pulled out two paperbacks – *The Left Hand of Darkness* and *The Lathe of Heaven*. 'Give these a try.'

Jocelyn took the books. She was touched by the gift, though he was also, she thought, making fun of her, because there was Le Guin, the same author she'd claimed, with his guidance, to read and love. Plus, Grigg was a little too eager, obviously excited to have found a reader so utterly ignorant. 'These are classics in the field,' he said. 'And amazing books.'

She thanked him, though she really hadn't planned to begin reading science fiction and still didn't. Perhaps some of this came through. 'I really think you'll love them,' Grigg said. And then, 'I'm perfectly willing to be directed, too. You tell me what I should be reading, and I promise to read it.'

Jocelyn liked nothing so much as telling people what to do. 'I'll make you a list,' she said.

In fact she forgot all about Grigg until he e-mailed her in late January. 'Remember me?' the e-mail asked. 'We met at the convention in Stockton. I'm out of work now and I'm relocating to your neck of the woods. Since you're the only person I know up there, I'm hoping for an insider's view. Where to get my hair cut. Which dentist to see. Could we have a cup of coffee and you make me one of your famous lists?'

If he hadn't had such an odd name Jocelyn probably would have had trouble bringing Grigg to mind. She remembered now how agreeable she'd found him. Hadn't he given her a book or two? She really should dig those out and read them.

She kept his e-mail on the top of her queue for a few days. But a charming, unattached (she assumed) man was too valuable to throw away just because you had no immediate use for him. She e-mailed him back and agreed to coffee.

When she began putting the book club together, she e-mailed him again. 'I remember you as a great reader,' she wrote. 'We'll be doing the completed works of Jane Austen. Are you interested?'

'Count me in,' Grigg answered. 'I've been meaning to read Austen for a long time now.'

'You'll probably be the only boy,' Jocelyn warned him. 'With some fierce older women. I can't promise they won't give you a hard time now and then.'

'Better and better,' Grigg said. 'In fact, I wouldn't be comfortable any other way.'

Jocelyn didn't tell us any of this, because it was none of our business and anyway we were there to discuss Jane Austen. All she did was turn to Sylvia. 'You remember. Stockton. I saw the Reinickers there and they annoyed me so much? I'd agreed to breed Thembe with Beauty and then I backed out?'

'Is Mr Reinicker the one who's always saying "Good girl," to everyone?' Sylvia asked.

Grigg had put the dining room chairs out on the back porch, it being such a perfect evening. There was one papasan chair, with pin-striped cushions, which Jocelyn made Bernadette take. The rest of us sat in a circle around her, the queen and her court.

We could hear the hum of traffic on University Avenue. A large black cat with a small head, very sphinxlike, wound around our legs and then made for Jocelyn's lap. All cats do this, as she is allergic.

'Max,' Grigg told us. 'Short for Maximum Cat.' He hoisted Max with two hands and set him inside, where he paced the windowsill, weaving through the African violets, watching us with his golden eyes, clearly wishing us ill. Of all the cats that come through the pounds, all-black males are the hardest to place, and Jocelyn heartily approved of anyone who had one. Had Jocelyn known about the cat? It might explain Grigg's invitation into the group, something we had ceased to mind, since Grigg was very nice, but we had never settled.

Grigg told us how he'd lost a tech-support job in San Jose when the dot-coms crashed. He'd gotten a severance package and come to the Valley, where housing cost less and his money would last longer. He was working in a temp job at the university, part of the secretarial pool. He was based in the linguistics department.

He'd recently been told that the job was his for as long as he liked. His computer skills had everyone pretty excited. He spent his days recovering lost data, chasing down viruses, creating PowerPoint presentations of this and that. He seldom got to his real work, but no one complained; everyone was relieved to avoid the campus tech support. Apparently the campus group was some sort of elite paramilitary operation in which all information was treated as top-secret, to be doled out grudgingly and only after repeated requests. People came back from the computer lab looking as if they'd made a visit to the Godfather. Grigg's pay was less than it had been, but people were always bringing him cookies.

Plus, he was thinking of writing a roman à clef. The linguists were a pretty weird bunch.

We paused for a moment, all of us wishing that Prudie was there to hear Grigg say 'roman à clef.'

Grigg had laid out a green salad made with dried cranberries and candied walnuts. There were the cheeses and pepper crackers. Several dips, including artichoke. A lovely white wine from the Bonny Doon vineyard. It was a respectable spread, although the cheese plate had a snow scene and was obviously meant to be used only at Christmas and probably for cookies. And the wine-glasses didn't match.

'Why did you say you like *Northanger Abbey* best of all Austen's books?' Jocelyn asked Grigg. She had the tone of someone calling us to order. And also of someone keeping an open mind. Only Jocelyn could have managed to convey both.

'I just love how it's all about reading novels. Who's a heroine, what's an adventure? Austen poses these questions very directly. There's something very pomo going on there.'

The rest of us weren't intimate enough with postmodernism to give it a nickname. We'd heard the word used in sentences, but its definition seemed to change with its context. We weren't troubled by this. Over at the university, people were paid to worry about such things; they'd soon have it well in hand.

'It makes sense that Austen would be asking these questions,' Jocelyn said, 'since *Northanger Abbey* is her first.'

'I thought *Northanger Abbey* was one of her last,' Grigg said. He was rocking on the back legs of his chair, but it was his chair, after all, and none of our business. 'I thought *Sense and Sensibility* was first.'

'First published. But *Northanger Abbey* was the first sold to a publisher.'

Our opinion of the Gramercy edition of the novels sank even further. Was it possible it didn't make this clear? Or had Grigg simply neglected to read the foreword? Surely there was a foreword.

'Austen doesn't always seem to admire reading,' Sylvia said. 'In *Northanger Abbey* she accuses other novelists of denigrating novels in their novels, but isn't she doing the same thing?'

'No, she defends novels. But she's definitely having a go at readers,' Allegra said. 'She makes Catherine quite ridiculous, going on and on about *The Mysteries of Udolpho*. Thinking life is really like that. Not that that's the best part of the book. Actually that part's kind of lame.'

Allegra was always pointing out what wasn't the best part of the book. We were a bit tired of it, truth to tell.

Grigg rocked forward, the front legs of his chair hitting the porch with a smack. 'But she doesn't much care for people who haven't read it, either. Or at least those who pretend not to have read it. And while she makes fun of Catherine for being so influenced by *Udolpho*, you have to say that *Northanger Abbey* is completely under that same influence. Austen's imitated the structure, made all her choices in opposition to that original text. Assumes everyone has read it.'

'You've read *The Mysteries of Udolpho*?' Allegra asked.

'Black veils and Laurentina's skeleton? You bet. Didn't you think it sounded good?'

We had not. We'd thought it sounded overheated, overdone, old-fashionedly lurid. We'd thought it sounded ridiculous.

Actually it hadn't occurred to any of us to read it. Some of us hadn't even realized it was a real book.

The sun had finally set and all the brightness fallen from the air. There was a tiny moon like a fingernail paring. Gauzy clouds floated over it. A jay landed on the sill outside the kitchen and Maximum Cat wept to be let back out. During the bedlam Grigg went and got our dessert.

He'd made a cheesecake. He took it to Bernadette, who cut it and passed the slices around. The crust was obviously store-bought. Good, though. We had all used store-bought crusts ourselves in times of need. Nothing wrong with store-bought.

Bernadette began to give us her opinion on whether Jane Austen admired people who read books or whether she didn't. Eventually we understood that Bernadette didn't have an opinion on this. She felt there was a great deal of conflicting data.

We sat for a bit, pretending to mull over what she'd said. It didn't seem polite to move right on when she'd taken so long to say it. She'd laid her glasses with their great lump of paper clips and masking tape by her plate, and she had that stripped, eye-bagged look people who usually wear glasses get when they take their glasses off.

We talked briefly about moving inside for coffee. The uncushioned chairs weren't comfortable, but Grigg didn't seem to have other chairs; we'd just be taking them with us. It wasn't cold. The city mosquito abatement program had done its work and nothing was eating us. We stayed where we were. A motorcycle coughed and spit its way down University Avenue.

'I think Catherine is a charming character,' said Bernadette. 'Where's the harm in a good heart and an active imagination? And Tilney is a genuine wit. He has more sparkle than Edward in *Sense and Sensibility* or Edmund in *Mansfield Park*. Catherine's not my very favorite of the Austen heroines, but Tilney's my favorite hero.' She directed this at Allegra, who hadn't yet spoken on the subject, but Bernadette was guessing what she thought. And bull's-eye, too.

'She's very, very silly. Implausibly gullible,' Allegra said. 'And Tilney's a bit insufferable.'

'I like them both,' said Sylvia.

'So do I,' said Jocelyn.

'Here's the thing.' The fingernail moon sliced open the clouds. Allegra's eyes were large and dark. Her face had its silent-screen-star expressiveness and a lunar polish, too. She was so very beautiful. 'Austen suggests that *Udolpho* is a dangerous book, because it makes people think life is an adventure,' she said. 'Catherine has fallen completely under its spell. But that's not the kind of book that's really dangerous to people. You might as well argue that Grigg here thinks we're all extraterrestrials, just because he reads science fiction.'

Bernadette made a surprised coughing sound. We all turned to look at her, and she managed an unconvincing smile. She had that great gob of tape and paper clips on her glasses. Her legs were twisted up in her lap in some impossible yoga posture. All our suspicions were suddenly roused. She was fooling no one. She was far too bendable to be human.

But why care? There was no one more benign than Bernadette.

'All the while it's Austen writing the really dangerous books,' Allegra continued. 'Books that people really do believe, even hundreds of years later. How virtue will be recognized and rewarded. How love will prevail. How life is a romance.'

We thought how it was time for Allegra to be getting over Corinne. We thought how hard Sylvia was working to get over Daniel. We thought Allegra could learn something from that. Birdshit landed with a plop on the edge of the porch.

'What should we read next?' Bernadette asked. '*Pride and Prejudice* is my favorite.'

'So let's do that,' Sylvia said.

'Are you sure, dear?' Jocelyn asked.

'I am. It's time. Anyway, *Persuasion* has the dead mother. I don't want to subject Prudie to that now. The mother in *Pride and Prejudice*, on the other hand . . .'

'Don't give anything away,' Grigg said. 'I haven't read it yet.'

Grigg had never read *Pride and Prejudice*.

Grigg had never read *Pride and Prejudice*.

Grigg had read *The Mysteries of Udolpho* and God knows how much science fiction – there were books all over the cottage – but he'd never found the time or the inclination to read *Pride and Prejudice*. We really didn't know what to say.

The phone rang and Grigg went to get it. 'Bianca,' we heard. There was genuine pleasure in his voice, but not that kind of pleasure. Just a friend, we thought. 'Can I call you back? My Jane Austen book club is here.'

But we told him to take the call. We were done with our discussion and could let ourselves out. We carried our plates and our glasses to the kitchen, said good-bye to the cat and tiptoed away. Grigg was talking about his mother as we left; apparently she had a birthday coming up. Not a friend, then, we thought, but a sister.

After we'd gone, Grigg talked to Bianca about us. 'I *think* they like me. They do give me a hard time. They just found out tonight that I read science fiction. That didn't go over well.'

'I could come up,' Bianca offered. 'I'm not scared of Jane Austen-reading women. And nobody picks on my little brother.'

'Except you. And Amelia. And Cat.'

'Were we so awful?' Bianca asked.

'No,' Grigg said. 'You weren't.'

While he was cleaning up, Grigg remembered something. He remembered a day when he'd been playing secret agent and over-heard a conversation his parents were having that was all about him. He was behind a curtain in the dining room and his parents were in the kitchen. He heard his father pull the tab on a can of beer. 'He's more of a girl than any of the girls,' Grigg's father said.

'He's perfectly fine. He's still a baby.'

'He's almost in junior high. Do you have any idea what the life of a girly boy is like in junior high?'

The curtain breathed once, in and out. Grigg's heart was filled with a sudden fear of junior high.

'So teach him to be a man,' his mother said. 'God knows you're the only one here who can.'

The next day at breakfast Grigg was told that he and his dad were going on a camping trip together, no girls allowed. They would hike and they would fish. They would sit around the campfire and tell each other stories, and there would be more stars in the sky than Grigg had ever seen.

Grigg's main image of camping was the little sandwiches you made with graham crackers, Hershey bars, and marshmallows roasted on sticks that you'd peeled with sharp and dangerous hunting knives. Naturally he was excited. Bianca and Cat said how glad they were not to be going. Even though they were hard-core outdoorswomen who had no trouble putting hooks right through worms so that their guts spilled out, and Bianca had once shot a Coke can off a fence with a BB gun. Even though Grigg would probably have nightmares like a baby and have to come home. Amelia had started a program to become an X-ray technician and was too grown-up to care who got to go camping and who didn't.

This was the seventies. Grigg's father had developed an obsession with the Heinlein book *Stranger in a Strange Land*. He took it out of the library and then told the librarian he'd lost it. For a couple of months now, it had been the only thing he read. When he wasn't reading it, he was hiding it somewhere. Grigg would have liked to take a look, but he couldn't find it. The library wouldn't allow him to check it out, even when they had a copy, which now they didn't.

The Harris men loaded the car with sleeping bags and groceries and headed north along 99 for Yosemite. Three hours later they picked up two girls at a gas station. 'How far are you going?' Grigg's father asked them, and they said they were on their way to Bel Air, which was, of course, the wrong way and farther the wrong way than simply going back home would have been. So Grigg was astonished to hear his father agree to take them. What about no girls allowed?

Grigg's father was very chatty, and his language changed, so that suddenly he was using words like 'far out' and 'heavy.' 'Your old man's pretty cool,' one of the girls told Grigg. She had a bandanna tied over her hair and a sunburnt nose. The other girl's hair was clipped close to her head – you could see the shape of her skull, and you could also see the shape of her breasts through the thin cotton of her blouse. She was black-skinned, but light, and with freckles. They were headed for a very mellow scene, they said, one that Grigg and his dad would probably dig.

'We're going camping,' Grigg told them.

His father frowned and dropped his voice so that only Grigg would hear. It wouldn't be cool to leave two pretty girls hitching, he said. Someone not right might pick them up next. Grigg wouldn't want to read that in the papers the next day! Suppose it was Bianca and Cat? Wouldn't Grigg want someone to take care of them? A real man looked out for women. Besides, if they got to Yosemite a day late, what was the big deal with that?

By the time his father had finished, Grigg felt small and selfish. At the next stop his father bought dinner for everybody. Afterward Grigg found himself in the backseat with the girl with the bandanna. Her name was Hillary. The girl with the breasts was in the front. Her name was Roxanne.

There were some cosmic forces coming together, Hillary told them. The car windows were open; she had to talk very loud.

Grigg watched the landscape pass. He saw straight rows of almond trees that seemed to curve as they went by, roadside stands selling lemons and avocadoes. It had been a long time since the last rain. Little clouds of dust spun above the fields. 'He Is Coming,' one billboard announced. 'Are You Ready?'

Grigg pretended he was running alongside the car, leaping the drainage ditches and overpasses. He was as fast as the car, and as tireless. He swung arm over arm down the telephone wires.

If you knew anything about ancient texts, Hillary said, Nostradama and the like, then you knew some major karma was coming due. It was going to be intense, but it was going to be beautiful.

Grigg's dad said he'd suspected as much.

Roxanne changed the radio station from the one they'd been listening to.

They stopped often at gas stations so the girls could pee. Grigg's sisters never asked to stop the car to pee.

By the time they made it to the Grapevine, the sky was dark. The freeway was crowded. A river of red lights flowed in one direction, one of white in the other. Cat had once made up a game called Ghosts and Demons, based on car lights, but you couldn't play it when there were so many of them. Anyway, Cat was the only one who could make it fun; without her it was a pretty boring game.

It was around nine o'clock when they drove through the gates to Bel Air. Hillary directed them to a massive house with a wrought-iron fence of metal leaves and vines on which actual leaves and vines had been trained. Grigg's father said he needed a rest from the driving, so they all went inside.

The house was enormous. The entryway was mirrored and marbled, and opened into a dining room whose glass-topped table had chairs for ten. Hillary showed them how there was a button on the floor beneath the table so the hostess could summon the help without leaving her seat. This seemed unnecessary to Grigg, as the room where the bell would ring, the kitchen, was only a few steps away. The house belonged to some friends of hers, Hillary said, but they were out of town.

The dining room ran into the kitchen, and across the back of both rooms was an atrium with a palm tree and three shelves of orchids. Past the glass of the atrium, Grigg could see the neon-blue water of a swimming pool, lit up and filled with people. Later, when he tried to remember this, Grigg asked himself how old these people had been. About Amelia's age. Maybe Bianca's. Certainly not his dad's.

In the kitchen, three kids were seated at the counter. Hillary got Grigg's dad a beer from the refrigerator. There was the smell of pot in the air. Grigg could recognize the smell of pot. He'd seen *2001: A Space Odyssey* six times, and two of those screenings had been on a university campus.

His dad began talking to a young man with long hair and a messianic face. His dad asked the young man whether he'd ever read Heinlein (he hadn't) and the young man asked whether Grigg's dad had ever read Hesse (he hadn't). Things were changing, they assured each other. The world was in spin. 'It's a great time to be young,' Grigg's dad said, which he clearly wasn't, Grigg hoped he knew.

Something about his dad's part of the conversation embarrassed Grigg. He excused himself to the bathroom (as if he would ever really need to go again! – all those stops on the road) and went to explore the house. He thought he might be running a slight fever. He had that magical, made-of-glass feeling and he moved through room after room, bedrooms and studies and libraries and TV rooms, as if in a dream. The house had rooms with floor-to-ceiling mirrors, a billiard table, and a wet bar. There was a girl's bedroom with a canopy bed and a Princess phone. Cat would die for a phone like that. Grigg made a collect call home.

Amelia answered. 'How's the camping?' she said. 'I didn't know there were phones in the high country.'

'We're not camping. We're in Bel Air.'

'This is costing a fortune. Give me your number and we'll call you right back,' Amelia said.

Grigg read the number off the dial. He lay on the bed under the canopy, pretending it was the jungle, mosquito nets, tribal drums, until the phone rang. 'Hey there.' It was his mother. 'How's the camping?'

'We're in a house in Bel Air,' Grigg said. 'We're not going camping until tomorrow.'

'Okay,' his mother said. 'Are you having a good time? Are you enjoying being with your dad?'

'I guess.'

'Thanks for calling,' his mom said. And then she hung up. She was going with the girls to a movie. Nothing he would like, she had assured him. Something girly.

Grigg went to open the girl's closet. He wasn't allowed in the girls' closets at home. There were scrapbooks in there, and shoe boxes full of secret shit. Once he'd opened Cat's secret-shit shoe box, and she screamed at him for half an hour even though all he'd seen was some inexplicable buckeye nuts in a little plastic candy dish she'd lined with red velvet.

The only shoe boxes in this girl's closet had shoes in them. She also had a shoe tree. She had, in fact, more shoes than his three sisters put together.

Another place for secrets was under the folded clothes in the bureau. Grigg looked but again came up empty. There was a vanity table with a locked drawer, which he worked on for a while, but he needed fingernails or a credit card. Or a key. He found some keys on a chain slung over the bedpost. None of them fit.

A boy and a girl came into the bedroom. They were halfway out of their clothes before they even saw Grigg. The boy's penis bloomed through the slit in his shorts like a mushroom after a rain. Grigg put the keys on the vanity. The girl screamed when he moved, then laughed. 'Do you mind, man?' the boy asked. 'We'll only be a minute.' The girl laughed again and hit him in the arm.

Grigg went back to the kitchen. His dad was still talking to the messiah. Grigg hovered in the doorway at just that spot where the sounds from the pool were as loud as his father's voice. 'You go the same places, see the same people. Have the same conversations. It takes like half your brain. Less,' Grigg's dad said.

'Jeez,' the boy said.

'Half a life.'

'Jeez.'

'It's like a cage and you don't even know when the door closed.'

The boy became more animated. 'Feel around you.' He demonstrated. 'No bars, man. No cage. You're just as free as you think you are. Nobody makes you do it, man. Nobody makes you set the alarm, get up in the morning. Nobody but you.'

Grigg went outside to the pool. Someone threw a towel at him. It was Hillary, and she was wearing nothing but the rubber bands in her braids. She laughed when she saw that he was looking at her. 'You're not such a little boy, after all,' she said. 'But no clothes allowed out here. You want to look, you got to be looked at. Them's the rules. Otherwise' – she leaned in and her breasts swung toward him – 'we'll think you're a little pervert.'

Grigg went back inside. His face was burning, and the most familiar part of the strange stew of things he was feeling was humiliation. He focused his attention on that part simply because he recognized it. In the study he found another phone and called home again. He didn't expect anyone to answer – he thought they'd all be at the movies – but Amelia picked up. She told the operator she wouldn't accept the charges, and then, less than a minute after he had hung up, the phone rang and it was Grigg's mom again.

'We're on the way out the door,' she said. She sounded cross. 'What *is* it?'

'I want to come home,' Grigg said.

'You always want to come home early. Cub Scout camp? Every
sleepover since you were three? I always have to make you stay, and you
always end up having a fabulous time. You have *got* to toughen up.' Her
voice was louder. 'I'm coming,' she called. And then, to Grigg again, 'Be
fair to your dad. He's been really looking forward to this time with you.'

Grigg put the receiver down and went to the kitchen. 'I'm so unhappy,'
his father was saying. He passed a hand over his eyes as if he might have
been crying.

Grigg would rather have taken all his clothes off and stayed at the
pool to be laughed at than hear his father say this. He tried to figure out
ways to make his father happy. He tried to figure out the ways he was
making his father unhappy.

He made up his mind to leave. If his father wouldn't take him, he'd
go alone. He'd walk. The days would pass; he'd eat oranges off the trees.
Maybe find a dog to walk with him, keep him company. Nobody would
force him to get rid of a dog that had brought him all the way home.
Maybe he'd hitch and maybe someone not right would pick him up and
that would be the end of that. He heard the sound of breaking glass and
laughter from the pool. Doors slamming. The phone ringing, deep in the
house. I'm so unhappy, he thought. He went to the room with the canopy
bed and fell asleep.

He woke to the sound of rain. It took him a moment to remember
where he was. Los Angeles. Not rain, then – he was hearing the sound
of sprinklers on the lawn. The white curtains swelled and dropped at the
open window. He'd drooled on the bedspread. He tried to dry it with
his hand.

He went looking for his father again to ask when they were going
camping. The kitchen was empty. The door to the pool stood open and
Grigg went to close it. He was careful not to look out. He smelled
chlorine and beer and maybe vomit.

Grigg sat on his father's stool at the kitchen counter with his back to
the door. He put his hands tight over his ears and listened to his heart
beating. He pressed on his eyelids until colors appeared like fireworks.

The doorbell rang. It rang again and again and again, as if someone
were leaning on it with an elbow, and then stopped. There were noises
in the hall, someone was making a commotion. Someone tapped him on
his shoulder. Amelia was standing behind him; Bianca was behind her,
and behind Bianca was Cat. Each of them wore an expression Grigg
knew well, as though someone had tried to mess with them and no one
was going to make that mistake again.

'We're here to take you home,' Amelia said.

Grigg burst into racking, snot-producing sobs, and she put her arms around him. 'It's okay,' she said. 'I'll just get Dad. Where is he?'

Grigg pointed toward the pool.

Amelia went out. Bianca moved into her place beside him.

'Mom said I had to stay,' Grigg told her. There was no harm in saying so. Obviously Mom had been overruled.

Bianca shook her head. 'Amelia called back here and asked for Grigg, and no one knew who that was or would even try to find out, they thought Grigg was such a funny name. But they gave her the address and she told Mom we were coming whether Mom liked it or not. She said you sounded weird on the phone.'

Amelia came back inside. Her face was grim. 'Dad's not ready to leave yet.' She put her arm around Grigg, and her hair fell on his neck. His sisters used White Rain shampoo, because it was cheap, but Grigg thought it had a romantic name. He could take the cap off the bottle in the shower and smell Amelia's hair, and also Bianca's, and also Cat's. For a while he drew a comic with a superwoman in it named White Rain. She controlled weather systems, which was something he'd made up all by himself, but he later learned that someone else had had the idea first.

As Grigg stood in the kitchen of that Bel Air mansion with his sisters around him, he knew that his whole life, whenever he needed rescuing, he could call them and they would come. Junior high school held no more terrors. In fact, Grigg felt sorry for all the boys and girls who were going to tease him once he got there.

'Let's go, then,' said Amelia.

'As if you don't always sound weird,' said Cat.

The saddest thing of all was that when Grigg finally read *Stranger in a Strange Land*, he thought it was kind of silly. He was in his late twenties at the time, because he'd promised his mother never to read it and he kept the promise as long as he could. There was a lot of sex in the book, for sure. But a leering sort of sex that was painful to associate with his father. Grigg read *The Fountainhead* next, which he'd promised Amelia never to read, and that turned out to be kind of a silly book, too.

This was the third story we didn't hear. Grigg didn't tell it to us because we'd already gone home by the time he remembered it, and anyway none of us had read *Stranger in a Strange Land* and we were way too snotty about science fiction for him to criticize Heinlein in our chilly company. Nor did he want to describe the sex to us.

But this was a story we would have liked, especially the rescue at the
end. We would have been sad for Grigg's father, but we would have
liked the White Rain girls. From the sound of it, no one who'd known
Grigg since infancy could have doubted he was born to be a heroine.

From The Mysteries of Udolpho,
by Ann Radcliffe

*'Bring the light forward,' said Emily, 'we may possibly find our way through
these rooms.'*

*Annette stood at the door, in an attitude of hesitation, with the light held
up to show the chamber, but the feeble rays spread through not half of it.
'Why do you hesitate?' said Emily, 'let me see whither this room leads.'*

*Annette advanced reluctantly. It opened into a suit of spacious and ancient
apartments, some of which were hung with tapestry, and others wainscoted
with cedar and black larch-wood. What furniture there was, seemed to be
almost as old as the rooms, and retained an appearance of grandeur, though
covered with dust, and dropping to pieces with the damps, and with age.*

*'How cold these rooms are, Ma'amselle!' said Annette: 'nobody has lived
in them for many, many years, they say. Do let us go.'*

*'They may open upon the great staircase, perhaps,' said Emily, passing on
till she came to a chamber, hung with pictures, and took the light to examine
that of a soldier on horse-back in a field of battle. – He was darting his
spear upon a man, who lay under the feet of the horse, and who held up one
hand in a supplicating attitude. The soldier, whose beaver was up, regarded
him with a look of vengeance; and the countenance, with that expression,
struck Emily as resembling Montoni. She shuddered, and turned from it.
Passing the light hastily over several other pictures, she came to one concealed
by a veil of black silk. The singularity of the circumstance struck her, and
she stopped before it, wishing to remove the veil, and examine what could thus
carefully be concealed, but somewhat wanting courage. 'Holy Virgin! what
can this mean?' exclaimed Annette. 'This is surely the picture they told me
of at Venice.'*

*'What picture?' said Emily. 'Why a picture,' replied Annette, hesitatingly
– 'but I never could make out exactly what it was about, either.'*

'Remove the veil, Annette.'

*'What! I, Ma'amselle! – I! not for the world!' Emily, turning round, saw
Annette's countenance grow pale. 'And pray what have you heard of this
picture, to terrify you so, my good girl?' said she. 'Nothing, Ma'amselle. I
have heard nothing, only let us find our way out.'*

'Certainly: but I wish first to examine the picture; take the light, Annette,

while I lift the veil.' Annette took the light, and immediately walked away with it, disregarding Emily's calls to stay, who, not choosing to be left alone in the dark chamber, at length followed her. 'What is the reason of this, Annette?' said Emily, when she overtook her; 'what have you heard concerning that picture, which makes you so unwilling to stay when I bid you?'

'I don't know what is the reason, Ma'amselle,' replied Annette, 'nor any thing about the picture, only I have heard there is something very dreadful belonging to it – and that it has been covered up in black ever since – and that nobody has looked at it for a great many years – and it somehow has to do with the owner of this castle before Signor Montoni came to the possession of it – and –'

'Well, Annette,' said Emily, smiling, 'I perceive it is as you say – that you know nothing about the picture.'

'No, nothing, indeed, Ma'amselle, for they made me promise never to tell: – but –'

'Well,' rejoined Emily, who observed that she was struggling between her inclination to reveal a secret, and her apprehension for the consequence, 'I will inquire no further –'

'No, pray, Ma'am, do not.'

'Lest you should tell all,' interrupted Emily.

JULY

CHAPTER FIVE

in which we read
Pride and Prejudice
and listen to Bernadette

Sylvia's first impression of Allegra was that no one had ever before had such a beautiful baby.

Jocelyn's first impression of Grigg was that he had nice eyelashes and a funny name, and didn't interest her in the slightest.

Prudie's first impression of Bernadette was that she was startling to look at and dull if you listened, which you hardly ever had to do.

Bernadette's first impression of Prudie was that, in all her long years, she had rarely seen such a frightened young woman.

Grigg's first impression of Jocelyn was that she appeared to think sharing an elevator with him for a few floors was some sort of punishment.

Allegra's first impression of Sylvia was blurred with her first impression of the larger world. For me? she'd asked herself, back when she had no words and no way to even know she was asking. And then, when Sylvia, and then, when Daniel had first looked into her eyes – More for me?

In Austen's day, a traditional ball still opened with the minuet. The minuet was originally danced by one couple at a time alone on the floor.

'Everyone knows,' Prudie said, 'that a rich man is eventually going to want a new wife.' She was seated with Bernadette at a large round table at the annual fund-raiser for the Sacramento Public Library. Rich men were all around them, thick on the floor as salt on a pretzel.

At the far end of the hall, in front of the huge arched window, a jazz band played the opening notes to 'Love Walked In.' You could look up five stories, sighting along massive stone columns past four rows of balconies, each railed in wrought iron, to the dome of the Tsakopoulos Library Galleria. Great rings of glass hung suspended above.

Prudie had never been inside the Library Galleria before, though one of the teachers at the high school had had her wedding here. Somewhere on the balconies were little bronze fox faces. Prudie couldn't see them from where she was sitting, but it was sweet to know they were there.

This was a romantic space. You could imagine serenading a lover on one of those balconies, or assassinating a president if that was the sick way your imagination ran.

So Prudie was disappointed that, simply because they'd both arrived before anyone else, she would now spend the evening seated by and talking to Bernadette. Dean on the other side, of course, but when couldn't she talk to Dean?

In point of fact, Prudie would not be talking to Bernadette so much as Bernadette would be talking to Prudie. Bernadette talked way too much. She meandered around her point, which, when gotten to, was seldom worth the journey. A housewife in the fifties, and, Prudie reminded herself, poor Bernadette, because they actually did expect you to keep your house clean back then. The women's movement arriving at last, but too late to save Bernadette from the tedium of it all. And now an old lady of little interest to anyone. *Peu de gens savent être vieux.*

Both Prudie and Bernadette were here at some expense – tickets were one hundred twenty dollars apiece – to provide Sylvia with moral support. It was a dinner; it was a dance; local writers had been promised as entertainment, one to each table – Prudie was looking forward to that – but Sylvia was why she'd come. Sylvia had to attend, because it was for the library. And Allegra had said that Daniel was coming, too, *and* bringing a date – that family practice lawyer, Pam, he was so in love with.

While all Sylvia had was the Jane Austen book club. They weren't much, they couldn't even the score, but they could at least show up.

Everywhere Prudie looked she saw the signs of wealth. She tried for the fun of it to view the scene as a Jane Austen character would. A young woman with no money and no prospects, here, in the way of all these rich men. Would she feel determined? Would she feel desperate? Would there be any point in looking about, making a secret selection, when you could only sit and wait for someone to come to you? Prudie decided she would rather teach French at the high school than marry for money. It was a decision quickly made, but she could always revisit it.

Dean had gone off to check Prudie's coat and get himself a drink, or he might have objected to her comment about rich men and their new wives. Dean was not a rich man, but he was the faithful sort. He might have said that money wouldn't change him. He might have said that Prudie was the wife he would want, for richer or poorer. He might have said that he never would be rich, and wasn't Prudie the lucky wife, then?

Prudie wouldn't have made the comment in Sylvia's hearing, either, but neither Sylvia nor Allegra had arrived yet. So far it was only Prudie and Bernadette, and Prudie didn't know Bernadette all that well, so Sylvia's divorce was one of the few topics of conversation they had in common. Jane Austen, too, of course, but the meeting on *Pride and Prejudice* was still a week away; Prudie didn't want to spoil it with premature articulation.

Bernadette had set aside her no-effort dress policy in honor of the black-tie occasion and was *très magnifique* in a silver shirt and pants, with her silver hair moussed up from her forehead. Her glasses had been repaired and the lenses cleaned. She was wearing screw-on chunks of amber on her ears. They looked like something Allegra might have made. Bernadette's earlobes were very large, like a Buddha's; the earrings elongated them even further. There was a slight scent of lavender perfume and maybe a green-apple shampoo, the zinnias in the centerpiece, and some hardworking air-conditioning. Prudie had a good nose.

Bernadette had been responding to Prudie's statement for quite some time and still hadn't finished. Prudie had missed much of it, but Bernadette usually closed with a recap. Prudie waited until she appeared to be winding down to listen. 'Being rich doesn't effect the wanting,' Bernadette was saying. 'So much as the having. You can't possibly know all your husband's failings until you've been married awhile. Happiness in marriage is mostly a matter of chance.'

Clearly Bernadette didn't understand that they were speaking of Sylvia. Her opinions, while reasonable in some other context, were inappropriate in this one, and it was a good thing Jocelyn wasn't there to hear them.

Prudie gave her a hint. 'Daniel is such a cliché.'

'Someone has to be,' said Bernadette, 'or what would the word mean?'

Subtlety was getting Prudie nowhere. She abandoned it. 'Still, it's a shame about Sylvia and Daniel.'

'Oh, yes. Capital crime.' Bernadette smiled, and it was the kind of smile that made Prudie think she'd maybe understood what they were talking about all along.

The band switched to 'Someone to Watch over Me.' The song caught in Prudie's throat. Her mother had been such a Gershwin fan.

An elegant black woman in a mink stole (in this heat!) sat down next to Prudie, who was forced to tell her that the whole table was taken. 'So I see,' she said coolly. Her mink brushed over Prudie's hair as she rose and left. Prudie worried that the woman might have thought she was some sort of racist, which she certainly wasn't, anyone who knew Prudie could tell you that. She would have liked nothing better than to share the table with such an elegant woman. Where the hell was Jocelyn?

'It's hard to choose a person to spend your life with,' Bernadette said.

'Lots of people don't get it right the first time out. I certainly didn't get it right the first time out.'

Prudie wasn't surprised to learn that Bernadette had been married more than once. Hadn't Allegra complained to her that Bernadette always did repeat herself? (Hadn't Allegra said this more than once?)

Allegra was lying across the bed in the room where Sylvia now slept alone. Sylvia was trying on dresses and Allegra was advising. None of the mirrors in the house showed your whole figure down to the shoes, so an advisor was advisable. And Allegra had an artist's eye. Even when Allegra was little, Sylvia had trusted her judgment. 'Are you going out like that?' Allegra would ask, and Sylvia would answer no, no, of course she wasn't, and go back to her room to try again.

They were running a bit late, but since Sylvia was dreading the whole evening anyway, running late seemed desirable. She would have liked a glass of wine, and maybe more than a glass, but she would be driving. Allegra was drinking a chilled Chardonnay and hadn't even started to dress yet. She would throw something on in two minutes and be breath-taking. Sylvia would never tire of looking at her.

It was too hot to have the blinds open, but Allegra had said she couldn't see Sylvia well enough with them closed. Sunlight streaked the bedroom wall, cut to ribbons by the slats of the blinds. Half the family portrait was illuminated – Allegra and Daniel were bright and golden, Sylvia and the boys were in the shade. In a book, that would mean something. In a book, you wouldn't feel good about what was coming for Sylvia and the boys.

'There won't be anyone there my age tonight,' Allegra said. Sylvia recognized it as a question, even though Allegra hadn't inflected it as one. Allegra did this whenever she thought she already knew the answer.

'Prudie,' Sylvia reminded her.

Allegra gave Sylvia the look Sylvia had been getting ever since Allegra turned ten. She said nothing out loud, because Prudie had recently lost her mother and should be treated with kindness. But Allegra had no patience for Prudie's French. She herself didn't speak Spanish to people who wouldn't understand it. When you shared a mother tongue, why not use it?

'What's the point of having dancing at these events, anyway?' Allegra asked. 'I'm not just speaking on behalf of the lesbians here. This is for us all. A dance is about who you'll dance with. Who will ask you? Who will say yes, if you ask? Who you'll be forced to say yes to. A dance is about its enormous potential for joy or disaster.

'You remove all that – you provide a band at an event where husbands just dance with their wives – and the only part of a dance you've got is the dancing.'

'Don't you like to dance?' Sylvia asked.

'Only as an extreme sport,' Allegra answered. 'With the terror removed, not so much.'

Grigg had suggested that he drive Jocelyn into Sacramento because he was still new to the area, while she had been to the Galleria on other occasions. As Jocelyn had dressed for the evening she'd found herself filled with affection for him. Really, he hardly knew Sylvia, plus his income was not what it had been. Yet here he was, buying a pricey ticket, putting on a gray suit in the dreadful summer heat, and spending a whole evening with a bunch of old women, and married women, and lesbians, just from the goodness of his heart. What a good heart that was!

She finished her makeup and then there was nothing more to be done, except to brush the dog hair off, and absolutely no point in doing that until she was out the door. Jocelyn was ready to go at the exact moment they should have been going.

But there was no sign of Grigg, and in the twenty minutes she waited, her affection began to fade. Jocelyn was a punctual person. This was, she believed, a matter of simple courtesy. Arriving late was a way of saying that your own time was more valuable than the time of the person who waited for you.

Waiting gave Jocelyn too much time to think about the evening ahead. She'd hardly seen Daniel since he moved. She could look around her own house, and there was the stereo system he'd helped her pick out, the dryer he'd helped her hook up. All those times over all those years, Daniel had dropped by with a movie he and Sylvia had rented and thought Jocelyn would like, or Chinese food when they knew she'd be getting back from a show too tired to eat unless she was made to. Once when she had had a nasty flu, Daniel came over and cleaned her bathroom, because he suspected the toothpaste on the mirror was preying on her mind and interfering with her recovery.

Hating Daniel was such terribly hard work that in his absence Jocelyn had allowed herself to stop. Although she would have said this to no one, tonight would be hard on her as well as Sylvia. She had no desire to see Daniel's new girlfriend and no desire to look closely at why that should be. She resented Grigg for the delay in getting it over with.

Then, when Grigg did arrive, there were no excuses, no apologies. He seemed, in fact, to be totally unaware that he was late. Sahara was wild and welcoming. She seized a ball in her mouth and raced between the chairs and over the couch, oblivious of the heartbreak that lay just ahead. This diverted attention from Jocelyn's cooler reception. 'Nice dress!' Grigg said, which in no way soothed her, but made it hard to be snappish in return.

'Let's go,' she told him. She was careful not to make it sound like an order and not to make it sound like a complaint.

She added a request, in case her tone had been off in spite of the effort. Since it was Jocelyn, her request might have sounded to the uninitiated, something like an order. 'You need to dance with Sylvia tonight.' By which she meant: Daniel needs to see you dancing with Sylvia tonight. Jocelyn stopped and looked Grigg over, more thoroughly than she'd ever done before. He was quite a nice-looking man in his own un-eye-catching way. He'd do.

Unless he was a goofy-looking dancer. 'You do know how to dance?' she asked.

'Yes,' he said, which didn't mean anything, lots of people who couldn't dance thought they could.

'You don't look like a dancer.' Jocelyn hated to press, but this was important.

'What do I look like?'

Who could say? He looked like a country-western singer. A college professor. A plumber. A spy. He had no distinctive look. 'You look like someone who reads science fiction,' Jocelyn guessed, but apparently it was the wrong answer, even though he claimed to love those books so.

'I have three older sisters. I can dance,' Grigg said, and he sounded really, really annoyed.

> *On country dancing:*
> *The Beauty of this agreeable Exercise (I mean when perform'd in the*
> *Genteel Character) is very much eclipsed and destroyed by certain Faults*
> *... One or two Couples either by Carelessness or Want of better*
> *Instruction will put the whole Set in Disorder.*
> — KELLOM TOMLINSON, Dancing Master

'Prudie and I went to the Scottish games at the Yolo County Fair-grounds last weekend,' Dean told Bernadette. 'Suddenly she's craving the Highlands. Have you ever been?'

'Not to the games,' Bernadette said. 'But to the fairgrounds, Lord yes. When I was young I danced all over the state every single summer. Of course, county fairs were much tinier then. They were so small they'd fit in your pocket.' She waited to see whether anyone wanted to hear more. No one told her to go on. No one changed the subject, either. Dean was smiling at her. Prudie was stirring her drink with her celery. The data was unclear.

But Dean and Prudie were both so very young. Bernadette could see that if anything interesting was to be said tonight, it fell to her to say it. 'I was in a group called the Five Little Peppers,' she continued. 'My mother thought tap dancing was the ticket to Hollywood. She was real ambitious for me. And real out-of-date. Even then, late forties, early fifties, tap dancing was – what do the kids say now? Played?'

'Okay,' said Prudie. Her pale face had frozen over at the word 'mother.' Bernadette felt so sorry for her.

'Were you and your mother close?' Prudie asked.

'I liked my father better,' Bernadette said. 'My mother was sort of a pill.'

We lived in Torrance then, so we were close to Hollywood, but not as close as Torrance is to Hollywood now, seeing as the roads and the cars are all different. I took tap and ballet at Miss Olive's. I was the best dancer there, which didn't mean squat, but gave Mother ideas. Dad was a dentist with an office in the back of our house, and one day he worked on someone who knew someone who knew someone in pictures. Mother pushed and prodded and coaxed and sulked until Dad got us introduced to someone somewhere in that chain of someones.

Mother paid Miss Olive to choreograph a special number just for me – 'The Little Dutch Girl.' I had this lace apron to pull over my face and peek out from, and I had to learn to tap in those big wooden shoes. Over we drove. And then I never even got to dance. That Hollywood muckety-muck took one look at me. 'Not pretty enough,' he said, and that was the end of that, except that Dad made it clear he thought he'd humiliated himself for nothing and he wasn't doing it again.

I didn't really care. I always had a lot of self-confidence and the studio guy just seemed like a horrid man. Mother was the one hurt by it. She said how we wouldn't ever go to any picture he produced, so I never did get to see *Easter Parade* until it was on television, even though everyone said Judy Garland and Fred Astaire were so great together.

Anyway, Miss Olive told Mother about this group called the Five Little Peppers and how they were looking to replace one of their girls. I auditioned in my silly wooden shoes, because Mother had paid for the choreography and wanted a return on that investment. You couldn't do a heel roll in those shoes to save your life. But the Peppers took me because I was the right height.

It was a stair-step group. I was taken on as the first stair, which meant I was the tallest. I was eleven then, the fifth stair was only five.

The thing about a stair-step group is that the littlest stair gets a lot of attention simply for being little. The littlest is pretty much always a spoiled little apple. The first stair gets a lot of attention if she's pretty, which, never mind what *some* people said, I was okay to look at.

Being first stair actually made me a better person. Kinder, more tolerant. All that attention turned me good. It didn't last. I didn't grow and the second stair did, and the next summer we switched places. I learned that the girls in between the first stair and the last stair, well, they're just the girls in between.

Especially the tallest of the girls in between. I was the nicest girl in the Peppers when I was first stair, but when I wasn't, then the new first stair was the nicest. Funny how that worked.

Our manager was this tyrannical old woman we were made to call Madame Dubois. Emphasis on the second syllable like that. Ma*dame*. We called her other things when we were on our own. Madame Dubois was our manager, our micro-manager. She told us how to do our makeup, how to pack our suitcases, what books we should read, what foods we should eat, and who our friends should be. Nothing was too large or too small to be left in our incapable hands. She gave us notes after every performance, even though she wasn't a dancer and never had been. My notes were always about how I should practice. 'You'll never be really good unless you practice,' she said. And fair enough. I never really did and I never really was.

Our bookings were handled by an oily guy named. Lloyd Hucksley. He had spent the war as a supply sergeant and now was scuttling around doing whatever Madame Dubois got into her head he should do.

I danced with the Peppers for eight years. Other girls came and left. For a couple of seasons my best friend was the third stair. Mattie Murphy. But then she started getting taller and I didn't and then she stopped getting taller, so we were the same height. We knew one of us would have to leave. It was awful to feel that coming and not be able to do a blessed thing about it. Mattie was a better dancer, but I was the better-looking. I knew how it would be. I asked Mother to let me quit so Mattie wouldn't have to. And also because Lloyd Hucksley seemed like he was getting sweet on me, now that I was older.

Oh, I had my reasons for wanting to go, but Mother wouldn't hear of it. What would happen to my motion picture career if I up and left the Peppers? When Mattie and Lloyd got married, you could have knocked me over with a feather.

After Mattie left I was the third stair. You'd think I would have met a lot of people; we traveled so much. You'd think it was a real exciting life. You'd be surprised what a steady set entertains at the county fairs. Everywhere we went it was the same faces, the same conversations. I was always wishing for more of an assortment. That's when I got so into books.

Mother was turning desperate. She made me perform everywhere, family gatherings, cocktail parties. She even made me dance for Dad's patients, because, she said, you just never know who's going to turn out to *be* someone. Can you imagine? You go to have a tooth pulled and there's a top-hat-and-cane number thrown in? Dad finally put a stop to it, thank the Lord. Though some of those patients were very appreciative. People will sit through anything if it puts off a tooth extraction.

Sylvia was standing in the walk-in closet, looking at the empty clothes-rod where Daniel's suits and shirts used to hang. Perhaps it was time for her clothes to spread out a bit, enjoy the open space.

'I've been thinking about Charlotte,' Allegra said. She was still in the bedroom, sprawled on the bed. 'In *Pride and Prejudice*. Lizzie's friend who marries the tedious Mr Collins. I've been thinking about why she married him.'

'Oh, yes,' Sylvia answered. 'The troubling case of Charlotte Lucas.'

The only sign of Daniel left in the closet was years and years of paperwork – taxes filed jointly, warranties for appliances picked out together, smog tests passed, mortgage payments paid. And on the top shelf, letters written during the summer of 1970, when Daniel drove to the East Coast and back with a college friend. Someday soon Sylvia would get those letters down, re-read them. In thirty-two years of marriage she and Daniel had spent very little time apart. She'd no memory of what they'd written to each other during that early separation. There might be something in the letters that would be useful now, some sort of clue about what had happened and why. Some guidance for living alone.

Some guidance for living alone as long as Daniel was coming back. Until tonight Sylvia had been able to behave as if he were just away somewhere, on another trip. She hadn't even tried to pretend this; it pretended itself. Tonight, when she would see Daniel with Pam for the first time – Allegra had met Pam, Sylvia hadn't – tonight he would really be gone.

She put her game face on and walked back into the bedroom. 'I like Charlotte a ton,' Sylvia said. 'I admire her. Jocelyn doesn't. Jocelyn has very high standards. Jocelyn has contempt for people who settle. Jocelyn, you'll note, is not married and never has been. But Charlotte has no options. She sees one chance for herself and she makes it happen. I find that moving.'

'Sexy,' Allegra said. She was referring to Sylvia's dress, a thin, clingy knit with a low neckline.

'It's too hot for a knit,' Sylvia said. She wasn't sure that sexy was the look she was going for. She didn't want Daniel to think she'd tried too hard, cared too much. She skinned out of it, went back to the closet.

'Does Charlotte really have fewer options than Lizzie?' Allegra asked. 'Lizzie's already in her twenties. No one's proposed to her yet. She has no money and lives in a small, confined society. But she won't settle for Collins. Why should Charlotte?'

'Lizzie is pretty. It makes all the difference in the world.' Sylvia zipped herself into her linen sheath and came out again. 'What do you think? Too casual?'

'You can always dress something like that up,' Allegra said. 'The right shoes. Jewelry. You should iron it.'

Too hot for ironing. Sylvia took the dress off. 'It does bother me that Austen wouldn't make up a good man who finds Charlotte worth having. The Brontës would have told her story very differently.'

'Charlotte on Charlotte,' Allegra said. 'I will always love the Brontës best. But that's just me – I like a book with storms in it. What I was thinking was that Charlotte Lucas might be gay. Remember when she says she's not romantic like Lizzie? Maybe that's what she means. Maybe that's why there's no point in holding out for a better offer.' Allegra rolled onto her back and propped her wineglass onto her face so as to get the last drops. Sylvia could see her nose through the curved glass. Even this, on Allegra, was a flattering look.

'Are you saying Austen meant her to be gay?' Sylvia asked. 'Or that she's gay and Austen doesn't know it?'

Sylvia preferred the latter. There was something appealing in thinking of a character with a secret life that her author knew nothing about. Slipping off while the author's back was turned, to find love in her own way. Showing up just in time to deliver the next bit of dialogue with an innocent face. If Sylvia were a character in a book, that's the kind of character she'd want to be.

But wouldn't.

Grigg and Jocelyn found themselves behind a tractor on the way to the freeway. Grigg edged out a couple of times, only to fall back, when he probably would have made it past just fine if he'd really hit the gas.

That's what Jocelyn would have done. The air-conditioning in his car was too feeble for the Valley summer. She could feel her makeup melting into her mandarin collar.

There was dust on the dashboard, and a large collection of cups and wrappers from various snacks and meals around her feet. Jocelyn hadn't offered to drive her own car, because it had been five whole days since she'd vacuumed it. The passenger-side window was streaked with dog spit and nose prints. She hadn't wanted to ask Grigg, all dressed up as he would be, to deal with dog hair and dirt. Evidently he'd had no similar compunction.

'Say,' Grigg said. They'd made it onto the freeway, and the tractor disappeared behind them in a stink of exhaust. Sacramento had some of the worst air quality in the country.

Grigg was driving exactly the legal limit; Jocelyn could see the speedometer. Daniel was the only other driver she knew who did that. In the whole world. 'Say,' Grigg repeated. 'Did you ever read those books I bought for you? The Le Guins?'

'Not yet.' Jocelyn felt a tiny sting of conscience. Feeling guilty did not improve her mood. Book-giving became a pushy, intrusive action when it was followed by 'So how did you like those books?' Jocelyn gave many, many books away and never asked whether anyone had liked them.

Why should she apologize over not reading two books she'd never asked for? She didn't have to actually read science fiction to know what she thought of it. She'd seen *Star Wars*. When would Grigg get off her case about those damn books?

In all fairness, she reminded herself, this was the first time he'd mentioned them. But she'd felt his not mentioning them on other occasions. So there was no need; her conscience was clear, yet she seemed compelled to defend herself. She tried to do this without sounding defensive. She turned to face Grigg and he was looking directly back at her. She hadn't expected that, hadn't expected to see straight through his eyes to – whatever. It gave her a sudden squeezed feeling in her chest; a sudden heat spread over her neck and face. She hadn't felt that squeeze, that heat for a long time. She had no intention of feeling it now. What had they been talking about? 'I like books about real people,' Jocelyn said.

'I don't understand the distinction.' Grigg's eyes had returned to the road. 'Elizabeth Bennet is a real person, but the people in science fiction books aren't?'

'Science fiction books have people in them, but they're not about the people. Real people are really complicated.'

'There's all kinds of science fiction,' Grigg said. 'When you've read some I'll be interested in your opinion.'

In just the time it took for Grigg to finish that sentence Jocelyn recovered her composure. He'd kept his tone neutral, but really, how rude. If he weren't being so unpleasant she would have pointed out the exit where she sometimes took the dogs to run. In the other direction was a bird sanctuary, which, in cooler weather, was also a nice hike. She would have told him how, in the winter, all the brown, dry fields here flooded. You could look across a tabletop of water and see the tallest branches of the trees. She might have said that only a native could love the summer landscape of the Valley, with the grasses all dead and the oaks parched and gray. She might have found herself saying something poetic, and God knows nothing good ever comes of that. No danger of it now, though.

A truck loaded with tomatoes passed them on the right. Jocelyn could smell it going by. Several tomatoes bounced off and hit the pavement when the truck swerved back into their lane. How could they possibly be traveling more slowly than a tomato truck?

Grigg switched on the radio, and some group Jocelyn was too old to know or like came out of it. Grigg didn't ask whether she was okay with the music or the volume or anything. Then, before she knew what was happening, he had taken the Jefferson Boulevard/Downtown exit. 'I-5 is quicker,' Jocelyn said, but it was too late.

'I like the Tower Bridge,' Grigg told her. 'I like to see the river,' which, in fairness, you could do from the bridge, but it wasn't much of a view. I like to sit in the baseball traffic, he might as well have said. I like to be on the surface streets as long as possible, waiting at the stoplights. I like to be as late as I can manage to be. Hadn't the whole point of driving together been that Jocelyn would tell Grigg how to go and he would go the way she said? She liked nothing about Grigg this evening.

And she was not, had never been, the sort of stupid woman who suddenly liked a man simply because she didn't like him. Thank God.

The car vibrated on the bridge and Grigg's voice took on an odd tremble as a result. A cartoon voice, young Elmer Fudd. 'I wonder which writer will eat with us? I hope you don't have to deal with anything, you know, too genre.'

The Capitol dome appeared in the distance, rising into the golden dusk dead ahead. Grigg stopped at another red light when he could have sneaked through on the yellow. 'By the time we get there the whole thing will be over,' Jocelyn said.

The light turned green. Grigg was slow changing gear; the car made a peevish noise. They passed the dandelion fountain, a sad sight when there was no water in it, heat braiding the air above the metal spikes. Around the K Street Mall the car made a strange coughing sound – three times in rapid succession. Then it died.

> *For, if they should happen to begin out of Time, it is a thousand to one if they recover it throughout the Dance. But on the other Hand, had they waited a remarkable Place of the Tune, and taken the Time at Beginning, they might have come off with Reputation and Applause.*
> — KELLOM TOMLINSON, Dancing Master

Grigg was out of gas. He was just able to coast to the curb, leave the car almost parked. Jocelyn had Triple A, but she'd left her card behind in her usual purse. She was carrying a tiny clutch bag with nothing much in it. Hadn't brought her cell phone, or she would have called Sylvia half an hour earlier to say they were going to be late. Poor Sylvia would be wondering where they were, why Jocelyn had left her to deal with Daniel and Pam all alone. Sylvia would never have left the house so ill prepared for disaster.

Grigg didn't have Triple A. 'Is there a gas station nearby?' he asked.

'Not for miles.'

'God, I'm sorry,' he said. He unbelted his seat belt. 'Why don't you wait here? I'll find a phone.'

'I'm going to walk the rest of the way,' Jocelyn told him. 'While you're getting the gas.' She didn't think this was an unreasonable decision, but if it was, she didn't care. She was proud of how calm she was being. She had been kept waiting, insulted, and stranded. All this, with impeccable, icy self-possession. Who wouldn't be proud?

'How far is it?'

'Ten, twelve blocks.'

There was a vagrant across the street. He wore a Bay to Breakers T-shirt, the really classic one with the fish that looked like a shoe. Jocelyn had that same shirt, but his had Rorschach blots of grime down the front and he'd tied a bandanna around one of his biceps, as if he were in some kind of paisley mourning. He was watching them with a great deal of interest. He called out something, but not something she could decipher. 'True bread' was the closest she could come.

'It's too hot to walk that far,' Grigg said. 'And not necessary. I'll find a phone and call a cab. I really am *so* sorry. I had the car in the shop just last week, because the gas gauge was screwy. I guess they didn't fix it.'

'It doesn't matter. I just want to be with Sylvia. I don't mind walking.'

'True bread,' the man across the street called out, more insistent now.

'I'm not staying here,' said Jocelyn.

What was ten or twelve blocks to a man in flat shoes? Grigg said that he would come then, too. They started off. This was not the best part of town. They crossed street after street at a quick pace, stepping over cans, flyers, and one plate of vomit. Jocelyn wiped her face and rubbed her mascara into her eyes. She couldn't imagine how she must look. Her hair was flat with sweat about her temples. Her skirt was sticking to her legs.

While Grigg looked fine. No jacket – he'd left that in the car – but no real wear and tear, either. It was more irritating to Jocelyn than anything else he'd done the whole evening. It was also sort of impressive. 'What do you think of Sylvia?' she asked.

'She seems very nice,' Grigg said. 'Why?'

'She's more than nice. She's smart and funny. Nobody kinder.'

'Sylvia is in love with Daniel,' Grigg said, as if he knew what she was up to, which, of course, she was and he did.

'There's no percentage in that.'

'But see, it's not for you to say. It's not for you to decide who she loves. You should stop interfering and let her work out her own happiness.'

Jocelyn went rigid beside him. 'You call it interfering?' Her voice was both incredulous and deadly. It contained all the fury of finding herself walking fifteen, sixteen, seventeen blocks in the Valley heat because someone had neglected to fill the gas tank, of trying to be a good sport about it only to find herself insulted by this same someone. 'To wish my friends happy? Where Sylvia is involved I hope I never do stop interfering,' Jocelyn said. 'I won't ever apologize to anyone for that.'

Would you mind if I didn't go tonight?' Allegra asked.

All the air went out of Sylvia's lungs. Of course I mind, she said, but not out loud, she was still Sylvia. How can you be so selfish? How can you even think of sending me off to face your father alone? How can you not know what this night is doing to me? (Why did we buy you a hundred-twenty-dollar ticket?) Please, please come.

The phone rang before Sylvia managed a word. She guessed it was Jocelyn wondering where they were, but Allegra picked up the receiver, checked the caller ID, and set the receiver back in the cradle. She rolled onto her side so that Sylvia couldn't see her face.

'*You've reached the Hunters*',' Daniel said. Sylvia hadn't changed the message, on the grounds that it was good for unknown callers to get a man. She'd neglected to factor in the impact of Daniel's voice on her, because usually, if the message ran, it meant she wasn't there to hear it. '*We're not home. You know what to do.*'

'Allegra?' Sylvia recognized Corinne's voice. She sounded sad and possibly drunk. 'We have to talk. When are you going to talk to me?

'I saw Paco today. He told me I've done two unforgivable things. *You* should have been the one to tell me this. You should have let me defend myself. I think even you'll agree that's only fair.'

Corinne was obviously just getting started. Sylvia had recently cleared the tape, so there was plenty of empty time. She felt awkward overhearing this private message; Allegra, so open about the broad outlines of her sex life, was secretive about the details.

Maybe she'd talked to Daniel. Sylvia wished she could ask him whether he knew what Corinne had done. Sylvia needed Daniel's help to deal with Allegra. Sylvia needed Allegra's help to deal with Daniel. No one was being any help at all.

Sylvia picked up Allegra's wineglass and took it to the kitchen. She stood at the sink in nothing but her slip and waited for Corinne to finish. She could still hear her voice like a stream of water in the distance, no words, just a rise and fall. Sylvia washed and dried the glass by hand, the way Jocelyn was always telling her she should.

She was angrier and angrier with Allegra. Whatever had happened, whatever Corinne had done, Allegra was the one who'd left. You didn't walk out on someone you loved. You didn't sit silent while they poured their drunken hearts into your phone machine, as if you didn't even hear them. People in love found the one way to stay together.

She thought of Allegra's drawn face and reddened eyes. She thought of how hard Allegra was finding it to get to sleep at night, how at midnight and one and two, she herself would wake to hear some movie playing on the DVD player. Allegra had even talked of getting a pirated *Fellowship of the Ring*, although she thoroughly disapproved of pirating, although when they'd seen it in the theater she'd complained and complained about the way Gimli was being played for cheap laughs.

Sylvia thought how all parents wanted an impossible life for their children – happy beginning, happy middle, happy ending. No plot of any kind. What uninteresting people would result if parents got their way. Allegra had always been plenty interesting enough. Time for her to be happy.

How dare you, she said, standing in the kitchen, to Allegra in the bedroom. How dare you hurt my daughter so much. You pick up that phone right now, young lady – you let Corinne apologize. You let her

atone for whatever it was, those two unforgivable things that she did.
You let Allegra be happy now. You let Allegra be loved.

The band was taking a break. Bernadette, Dean, and Prudie were joined
at the table by a writer named Mo Bellington. Mr Bellington had too
much hair and not enough neck. Nice teeth, though. Bernadette noticed
people's teeth. Everyone did, but not everyone knew that they noticed.
Bernadette's father had worked on Bernadette's teeth himself, with the
result that, though she was now well along in her sixties, she had never
lost a filling.

According to promotional materials on the table, Mo Bellington wrote
mysteries that took place in the tiny town of Knight's Landing. His
detective was a cynical sugar-beet farmer who unearthed femurs and
knucklebones almost every time he rototilled. On the table was a postcard
of the jacket of Bellington's most recent book. The title was *Last Harvest*.
The two final *t*'s were knives, blood dripping down the blades into a
field below. Bernadette was pretty sure she'd seen covers like that before.
Nor did the title seem original. But if the artwork wasn't wholly new,
still she thought it reasonably well achieved.

'I guess you're my group,' Mr Bellington said, looking with obvious
disappointment at the empty chairs. There was loud laughter at a nearby
table. At another, someone tapped a wine-glass with a fork, preparing to
give a toast. Clearly there was livelier company elsewhere.

'More of us are coming,' Bernadette assured him. 'I can't imagine
where everyone is Jocelyn is the most punctual person alive. I've never
known her to be late. Sylvia, not so much so. And Allegra. Don't ask!'

Mr Bellington made no answer and looked neither reassured nor
entertained. He was a very young man to be writing books already.
Bernadette could tell right off that he hadn't lived long enough to have
much to say. His sugar-beet farmer would be thinly drawn.

He walked around the table to sit next to Dean. This put his back to
the rest of the room. Bernadette would have thought a writer would
want to see what was going on.

If he'd taken the empty seat next to Bernadette, he'd have had his
back to one of the huge columns and been able to see the dance floor
and the podium *and* the band. Bernadette could see fully three other
tables of people. But she had herself become invisible, especially to
younger men. This had begun back in her fifties, so she was used to it
by now. She'd become more audible to compensate.

'This whole event puts me in mind of my first husband,' she said.
'John was a politician, so I know from fund-raisers! Comb your hair,

dear, wash your face, and here's a list of things you can say if anyone tries to talk with you:

'One: What a lovely event this is.

'Two: Isn't the food delicious?

'Three: Aren't the flowers beautiful?

'Four: Isn't my husband the best man for the job? Let's all be quiet now and listen to him talk! I myself am going to smile like an idiot the whole time he's speaking.'

Even without music the room was noisy enough, the table big enough to make conversation across it difficult. Bernadette could see that Mr Bellington wasn't planning to try. He spoke to Dean. 'If you have any questions about my books,' he said, 'that's what I'm here for. Content? Process? Where do I get my ideas? The word "last" in *Last Harvest* is kind of a pun. "Last" as in "final," but also "last" as in "most recent." Ask me anything.'

There was something pompous, self-important in his delivery. Bernadette had just met him and already she was liking him less. The first course arrived, a lovely mushroom soup with maybe a dash of sherry.

'This is delicious,' Mr Bellington said. 'Well done.'

He directed his words toward Bernadette. What was that about? Did he think she'd made the soup?

'Do you love Jane Austen?' she asked. There was only one possible answer to the question. She would like to think that any man who wrote would get it right. She spoke loudly to lessen the risk of being ignored, and repeated her question just in case. 'What do you think of Jane Austen, Mr Bellington?'

'Great marketing. I envy her the movie deals. Call me Mo.'

'Which of her books is your favorite?' Prudie smiled in that unhappy way that made her lips disappear.

'I liked the movie with Elizabeth Taylor.'

Prudie's hand had become unsteady. Bernadette saw the tremor in her Bloody Mary. 'Your favorite Jane Austen is *National Velvet*?'

Prudie was being mean. Bernadette resolved to stop her. Soon. Meanwhile, it was good to see her putting up a fight. Not five minutes earlier her mother's death had been painted across her face like one of those shattered women Picasso was so fond of. Now she looked dangerous. Now Picasso would be excusing himself, recollecting a previous engagement, backing away, leaving the building.

Dean coughed helpfully. Somewhere in the cough was the word 'persuasion.' He was throwing Mo a lifeline.

Mo preferred to go down. 'I haven't actually read any Austen. I'm

more into mysteries, crime fiction, courtroom stuff.' This was dis-
appointing, but not damning. On the one hand it was a failing; on the
other, manfully owned up to. If only Mo had stopped there.

'I don't read much women's stuff. I like a good plot,' he said.

Prudie finished her drink and set the glass down so hard you could
hear it hit. 'Austen can plot like a son of a bitch,' she said. 'Bernadette,
I believe you were telling us about your first husband.'

'I could start with my second. Or the one after that,' Bernadette
offered. Down with plot! Down with Mo!

*Dancing master Wilson complained about certain figures, such as 'lead
down the middle and up again' or 'lead out to the wall and back,' noting
that they were angular and dull. 'Straight lines,' he said, 'are useful, but not
elegant; and, when applied to the Human Figure, are productive of an
extremely ungraceful effect.'*

'Start with the politician,' Prudie said. 'We'll get to the others. We have
the whole evening.'

Bernadette loved to be asked to tell a story. She settled in for a long
one. Anything for Prudie. 'His name was John Andretti. He grew up in
Atherton.'

John made the best first impression. He had an instant charm; you
were the most fascinating person in the room. Until someone else caught
his eye.

I met him up at Clear Lake, where we were tapping on the Fourth of
July. It was my last year with the Peppers and we weren't the Little
Peppers anymore, because we were kind of grown-up for that. We were
the Red-Hot Peppers by then. And I was the shortest. I was the last stair,
even though I was nineteen years old.

My family was supposed to go to Hawaii for three whole weeks that
summer. I was so looking forward to it. But my father felt he couldn't
leave his patients for that long, and so it was a trailer instead of a
bungalow, a lake instead of the ocean. One damn tap dance after another.
Madame Dubois had us all in polka dots that year. There was a flamenco
craze. Going on in her brain.

Dad came with us, because he loved to fish. There was mercury in
Clear Lake, from the old mines, but we didn't think about that at all
then. Now they tell you to only eat one fish from that lake a month, and
this after years of cleanup. I didn't like fish, so I would pick at my plate,
even though Mother was always nagging us to eat it. She used to call fish
'brain food,' which is what we all thought back then. Now I read how

they're putting warning labels on tuna. But eggs are good again. You have your good fats and your bad fats.

I once bit the end off a thermometer just to see if I could. Turned out to be dead easy. I spit the mercury right out, but Mother was so upset she gave me ipecac anyway. Then there she was all those years later, trying to get me to eat those fish.

I went swimming a lot, which was probably no better for me. I'd just learned to water-ski. So I was out on the lake one day, and John cut too close with his boat and upended me in his wake. Steered round to apologize and picked me up, shouting to my father how he'd take me in to shore. He used to say that he'd landed me like a fish. You're the littlest thing I ever pulled out of the water, he used to tell me. I should have been made to throw you back.

He was a good politician, at least as far as the getting elected went. He remembered people's names, and not just their names, but the names of their wives, husbands, children. He had a narrative line.

Bernadette nodded politely to Mo. 'People don't always realize how important that is in running an election. The voting public likes a good plot. Something simple.'

John's was a classic. Or else it was a cliché. He was born real poor, and he made sure you knew that straight off. His speeches were all about his hardscrabble background – the obstacles over-come, the disappointments survived. The pledges he'd made to himself when discouraged. As God is my witness, I'll never be hungry again. Brave stuff.

With just a hint of some old betrayal. This was the genius part. Nothing too specific, but the clear implication that he was too good to give you the details. Not one to tell tales and all. Not one to hold a grudge. You had to admire him for his generosity as well as his determination.

In truth he was the angriest man alive. He kept a list of insults. I mean an actual list, and there were items on it that went back twenty years. There was this boy named Ben Weinberg. They'd gone to school together; John's father worked for Ben's father. Ben had brains, friends, athletic ability, and lots of old money. The best of everything. John had to struggle so to get one-tenth of what was just handed to Ben. In the story of John's life according to John, John was Oliver Twist and Ben was Little Lord Fauntleroy.

One day when John was sixteen Ben called him a nasty little climber, and there it was, twenty years later, number three on John's list. His mother had places one and two.

'So easy not to be a climber when you're born on top,' John said. We were married by then, and I was starting to get a clue. Before that I bought it all. I didn't see the list until I made my first appearance on it. I was certainly no judge of character back then.

I hope I've learned a thing or two since. No one with real integrity tries to sell their integrity to you. People with real integrity hardly notice they have it. You see a campaign that focuses on character, rectitude, probity, and that's exactly when you should start asking yourself, What's this guy trying to hide?

But, there you go. Hindsight is twenty-twenty, just as they say.

'*Tout le monde est sage après le coup,*' Prudie said.
'Yes, dear,' Bernadette answered.

After Lloyd and Mattie left to get married, Madame Dubois said we couldn't any of us date anymore, as it was bad for the act if we got reputations. We were to remember we were ladies. So John and I snuck around, and finally I left my dancing shoes behind and we ran off and got married in Vegas at the Wee Kirk o' the Heather. There was the nicest woman working there, Cynthia something-or-other. I remember she said she'd been a clerk at Woolworth before this job, and she missed the free fabric ends she used to get. Isn't it funny, the things you remember? The chapel had some dresses, and I tried them all on, but they were too big for me. I really was the tiniest thing back then, couldn't fit into anything off the rack.

So Cynthia altered a skirt for me right on the spot, and she combed my hair and did my makeup. There were a few couples ahead of us; we had a bit of a wait. She gave me a cigarette. I never smoked in my life but just this one time – the occasion seemed to call for it. Cynthia pointed out how now I was going to be Nettie Andretti; I'd never even thought of that. I was going by Nettie then. That's the day I began using my full name, Bernadette.

While she did my hair, Cynthia told me this story – how there was a curse on her family because her grandpa had once hit a pure white cat with his car. He said it was an accident, but it probably wasn't, because ever since, whenever anyone in the family was about to die, they saw a white cat. Her uncle saw a white cat from his bedroom window when he was only twenty-six. It streaked through the yard, grabbed one of his socks from the clothesline, and made off over the fence with it. And then he went out that very night with some friends and got killed in a bar fight by someone who thought he was someone else. They never did find that sock.

Cynthia was in the middle of telling me this. She had just said how her mother said she didn't believe in any of that nonsense and to prove it went out and bought herself a white cat. I know something weird happened next, because of the way Cynthia was telling it, but I never heard what. John and I were called just then and I had to go get married. I was in a bad mood when I said my vows, because I wanted to hear the end of the white cat story. I've always wondered how that ended.

The year before I met John, Mattie had begged me to come and visit her and Lloyd. He'd gotten religion, and they were living in a commune on this ranch in Colorado. Mother was so angry to think I might have married Lloyd with just a little effort, since he really had been sweet on me first. And now he'd turned out so spiritual. Really, she was very middle-class. She should have known there'd be nothing respectable about the truly righteous. She packed my clothes like I was off for four weeks of Bible study.

The commune was run by a Reverend Watson. I thought he was a megalomaniac. Lloyd thought he was attentive. Lloyd always had liked being told what to do.

I don't think Reverend Watson had any religious training at all. His inspiration was the Latter Rain sect, but he cut and pasted as suited him. He preached that the trappings of the occult – things like zodiac signs and numerology – had been stolen from God by the devil and it was up to him to wrest them away, put them back to their holy purposes. And there was something about extraterrestrials, too; I forget exactly what. They were coming to get us, or they'd already been and left us behind. One of those two.

While I was visiting, he had them all reading a book called *Atomic Power with God, Through Fasting and Prayer*, which said that if you could learn to control your appetites you'd gain supernatural powers. You'd be released from gravity. You'd be immortal. So Reverend Watson said we were all to fast and be celibate. They mostly served boxty, because it was cheap, so the fasting was sort of redundant, and the celibacy was nothing to me, but Mattie minded. No one in the community drew a steady paycheck. God was to provide. I would have called my parents to come and get me, but the phones had all been turned off.

The minute Lloyd heard immortality was possible, then immortality was what he wanted. Every day that passed without him floating up to heaven was a great disappointment to him. To Reverend Watson, too, and Lloyd minded the reverend's disappointment more than he minded his own.

They were all trying to pull me in, even Mattie. I didn't blame her;

I just thought she needed rescuing. One day Lloyd asked me to work the Ouija board with him. He was so disheartened. He still couldn't fly and the spirits weren't talking to him, though they were quick enough to send messages to the rest of the congregation. I was sorry to see him so down, and fed up with things in general. I mean, my father was in the Masons and I was queen of Job's Daughters one year. We went to church. I sang in the choir. But I hadn't lost my mind over it.

So I pushed the planchette. *Leave Watson*, I made it say. Lloyd leapt up so fast he knocked his own chair over. He went straight to Reverend Watson and told him Satan was striding amongst us, and Reverend Watson came right back to cast him out. There was a tremendous to-do and I was sort of pleased, because things were less boring than before, but Reverend Watson's eye fell on me then and it was a suspicious eye.

There were only four women in his congregation, and we began to hear a lot about Eve. None of it good. Reverend Watson believed that Eve had done a whole lot more than speak to the serpent in Eden. He believed she'd slept with it. True believers were descended from Adam and Eve, he told us, and then, looking straight at me, unbelievers from Eve and the snake. And since Adam's downfall was to listen to Eve, the women were now forbidden to speak. All the evil in the world, Reverend Watson said, came from listening to a woman's voice.

Mattie was afraid to go against Reverend Watson. There I was, her guest for four weeks and I could only talk if there was no one to hear me, which certainly misses some of the point of talking. But then Reverend Watson went to a conference in Boston, and when he came back, we were allowed to speak again, as he had a new plan for transcending the mundane plane of our earthly lives. The new plan involved psychotomimetics. Latter Rain with LSD. Acid Rain.

Lloyd was high for days. He finally had some visions of his own. He saw that he *could* fly, but just didn't want to. What do I have to prove? he asked. I took it myself. It made me so happy. Everything around me danced. Pots. Fenceposts. Goats.

I saw it all from somewhere above, as if life were one big Busby Berkeley number. We were on the ranch, very isolated from the outside world. It was winter. Hundreds of crows gathered in the trees outside the kitchen. There were so many it looked as if the trees had leafed all in black. I went outside and they swam up in elaborate patterns, like words inked on the air. They settled down again, cawing at me. 'Go,' they said. 'Go. Go. Go.'

*

'I just love crows.' Bernadette looked at Mo. 'I hope you put lots of crows in your books. I bet they flock around the sugar-beet fields. Especially when bodies are being unearthed. You could have crows who find clues. There's a bunch now, nesting in the parking lot of the University Mall. I see them when I go to get my hair cut.'

'I sort of do that, only with magpies,' Mo said. 'Magpies really represent the Valley to me. One reviewer said I had a magpie motif. I use them for portent as well as theme. I could explain how I do that.'

'If only we were talking about magpies,' Prudie said firmly. 'Go on, Bernadette.'

Well, it seemed to me if a crow told you to do something you should do it. I left without even changing my clothes. I walked right off the ranch. It was miles and miles to a road with any traffic, and it rained before I was halfway there. Great gobs of rain, so thick I could hardly see through.

My shoes were covered with mud, as if I was wearing shoes on my shoes. I remember thinking that was a real profound thing to think. The mud would break apart and re-form while I walked. Made my feet so heavy, it seemed like I was walking forever. Of course I probably didn't go in a straight line. Not as the crow flies.

By the time I finally reached the highway I'd sobered up. Hitched a ride with a man about my father's age. Mr Tybald Parker. He was shocked by my appearance. And he scolded me for hitching, said it was a dangerous thing for a woman to do. He gave me his handkerchief.

I told him everything – not just Mattie and Lloyd and Reverend Watson, but everything I could think of. The Peppers. Dad's dental practice. It was so nice to talk freely again; I never stopped to think what I should say and what I shouldn't. It was such relief.

He got me a hotel room so I could shower and sleep, and he bought me a meal with no potatoes in it and helped me call my parents to wire me some money so I could get the bus home. 'Don't take any wooden nickels,' he told me just before he left. It was the first time since I'd gone to visit Mattie that I felt God's presence in my life.

I got a Christmas letter from Mr Parker every year for more than twenty years, until he died. They were wonderful letters, all about people I didn't know, getting degrees, getting married, going on cruises, having babies. I remember how his grandson went to UCLA on a baseball scholarship.

So, all the while I was learning about John and his temper and his grudge list, he was learning about me. Drugs, cults. Visionary crows. He was quite frantic; it was very bad for the campaign. He told me I must never say anything about anything to anyone. I was so tired of being told to shut up. But I stayed quiet. Got pregnant, which John said was a sure vote-getter. Smiled, smiled, smiled, and secretly hoped he'd lose, so I'd be allowed to talk again.

One day he had a debate scheduled, all five candidates meeting the press. I fixed his tie. 'How do I look?' he asked, and I told him he looked good. He was a handsome man. Turned out there was a pair of my underpants stuck to the back of his jacket. They'd been in the dryer; I suppose there was static electricity. They were huge because I was pregnant, but at least they were clean.

I don't know how they got on his jacket. He said I must have put them there when I hugged him. As if I wanted the voters and the press and everyone to see my underpants! I showed up on his list again; by now no one had more appearances there than I did. *Bernadette has destroyed me*, is how the item read.

As if he needed me for that. John turned out to have a past, too, a little bywater off the public narrative. Gambling debts and an arrest record. Aggravated assault.

He ran off with my little sister without even divorcing me. Dad had to go looking all over the state for them to bring my sister home. Because of who John was, it made the papers. Our family didn't look so good, either. The drugs came out then. The cult. One of the Peppers told me they had an opening, but when I went to talk with Madame Dubois she wouldn't take me back now that I was a mother, and notorious to boot. Madame Dubois said that *some* standards had to be maintained. She said that I'd pollute the Peppers.

She told me no one would ever marry me again, or my sister either, but that turned out not to be a problem.

If a fine Picture, beautiful Fields, crystal Streams, green Trees and imbroider'd Meadows in Landscape or Nature itself will afford such delightful Prospects, how much more must so many well-shap'd Gentlemen and Ladies, richly dress'd, in the exact Performance of this Exercise, please the Beholders.

— KELLOM TOMLINSON, Dancing Master

Sylvia decided to speak frankly with Allegra. I really need you tonight, she was going to say. I don't think it's all that much to ask. For one evening, try to think about me.

She met Allegra in the hallway, wearing Sylvia's knit dress. 'Okay?' Allegra asked.

Sylvia felt a wash of relief, partly that Allegra was coming, partly that Sylvia hadn't told her she had to. Confrontation with Allegra rarely turned out the way you planned. 'Sexy,' Sylvia said.

Allegra's mood had improved. She had a lighter step, a straighter back. She was carrying Sylvia's midnight-blue dress with the sunburst stitching at the shoulder. 'Wear this.' Sylvia put it on. Allegra picked out earrings and a necklace for her. Brushed Sylvia's hair to one side and pinned it. Applied eye shadow and lipstick, gave her a tissue to blot with. '*Pues. Vámonos, vámonos, mamá*,' she said. 'How did we get so late?'

Sylvia took Allegra's hand as they went outside, squeezed it once, let it go. Beeped open the car and slid into a long, hot night.

The entrée arrived, salmon and string beans, served with a local Zinfandel. An extremely successful mystery writer delivered the keynote while everyone else ate. Initially there were problems with the microphone, some rasping, squealing feedback, but this was quickly solved. The keynoter was brief and charming; he was perfect.

After he finished, Mo told Dean that the legal procedures in the extremely successful mystery writer's books were all screwed up. 'Lots of people don't care,' Mo said. 'I'm kind of a stickler for accuracy myself.' He began to take Dean through the errors of the other writer's most recent book, point by point. 'Lots of people don't understand how the discovery phase works,' he said. He was prepared to explain.

Bernadette leaned in to Prudie and spoke quietly. 'I may have shaded a few things. I didn't know Mo was a stickler for accuracy. I thought he just liked plot. So I added some bits. Sports. Lingerie. Sexy little sisters. Guy stuff.'

'Drugs. Talking animals,' Prudie said.

'Oh, I didn't make up the crows.'

Prudie found she felt no immediate need to know which parts were true and which weren't. Maybe later she would. But Bernadette was not her mother; maybe she'd never care.

'My husbands weren't any of them bad men. I was the problem. Marriage seemed like such a small space whenever I was in it. I liked the getting married. Courtship has a plotline. But there's no plot to being married. Just the same things over and over again. Same fights, same friends, same things you do on a Saturday. The repetition would start to get to me.

'And then I couldn't fit my whole self into a marriage, no matter who my husband was. There were parts of me that John liked, and different parts for the others, but no one could deal with all of me. So I'd lop some part off, but then I'd start missing it, wanting it back. I didn't really fall in love until I had that first child.'

The music resumed. Prudie could see the black woman, sans mink, dancing. She'd taken her shoes off as well as her stole. Her partner was a stout, bald white man. Three other couples were on the floor, but this pair drew your eye. There was something deeply incongruous about wearing formal clothes and boogying on down. It took a good dancer to make you overlook this. Prudie wondered whether they were married. Was she his first wife? Had she lopped off some part of herself to make him fit? If so, she looked pretty happy without it.

Now there were eight couples on the dance floor. Half of these, by Prudie's calculation, were rich men with their second wives. She based her identifications on the differential between the woman's youth and attractiveness and the man's, and on Sylvia's behalf, she disapproved. She had herself married a man much better-looking than she deserved, which seemed to her the way it ought to be done.

Dean saw Prudie watching the dance floor. 'Dance with me, baby,' he said. It was an obvious plea to miss the detailed explanation of search and seizure.

Prudie hadn't danced, even alone in the living room to Smokey Bill Robinson, since her mother died. Her mother was a huge fan of Smokey Robinson's. But Prudie thought she could do this for Dean. It wasn't a lot to ask. 'Okay,' she said. She realized she couldn't. 'In a minute. Maybe later.'

'How about you, Bernadette?'

Bernadette took off her earrings and set them by her plate. 'They'd weigh me down,' she said, and followed Dean off.

A shadow fell over Prudie. This turned out to be Jocelyn arriving at last, stooping down to kiss her cheek. 'You hanging in there?' Jocelyn asked. She smelled of sweat and soap-dispenser soap. Her hair was wet and spiked around the edges of her face. Her makeup had been partially and patchily removed. She fell into the chair next to Prudie, bent down, removed one shoe and massaged the arch of her foot.

'You missed the soup and the keynote. I was worried,' Prudie said. She actually hadn't been, but that was only because Bernadette had distracted her and no thanks to Jocelyn. Prudie *should* have been worried. Jocelyn could be deliberately rude, but she was never thoughtless. Jocelyn was never late. Jocelyn was never – unkempt. How weird was this, that Bernadette would look better than Jocelyn? 'No sign of Sylvia,' Prudie told her. 'No sign of Daniel, either. What do you think that means?'

'I'll go phone her,' Jocelyn said. She put her shoe back on. 'I'm surprised about Daniel. Allegra said he'd be here for sure.'

' "Scenes might arise unpleasant to more than myself"?' Prudie suggested.

'Sylvia would never make a scene.'

'You would.'

Jocelyn left. Grigg took the seat by Mo. There were several empty chairs between Grigg's and Jocelyn's. Your love is lifting me higher, the band played. Only without any words. 'Can you give Jocelyn a ride home?' he asked Prudie. 'Later? After the dancing? I ran out of gas.'

'Sure,' Prudie said. 'But Dean will take you to get gas. Whenever you want.'

Jocelyn returned to the table. 'They're five minutes away,' she said. 'Almost here.'

Grigg busied himself with his dinner. He turned his chair to face Mo. 'So. Mysteries. I love mysteries. Even when they're formulaic, I just love the formula.'

'Mine aren't formulaic,' Mo said. 'One time I didn't even have a murder until right at the end.'

Who didn't love mysteries? 'How do you know Bernadette?' Prudie asked Jocelyn.

'She was married to my godfather.'

'What did she do?'

'Job-wise? Ask her.'

'That would take too long,' Prudie said.

'I don't know that I can do it short, either. She never finished school, so she was always picking up this or that. Teacher's aide. Manicurist. I remember she told me she worked a carnival once, getting people to throw rings around stacks of dishes. She was one of the Snow Whites at Disneyland for a while. Pet sitter. Mostly she married. Very Austen like, except that there were so many of them. I don't mean that to sound mercenary. You know how cheerful she is; she always thought this was the one that would last. I used to worry about her kids, but just on principle. They always seemed fine, and they turned out great.

'She was my favorite of all Ben's wives. They lived in this big old house in Beverly Hills with a beautiful garden and a wrap-around porch. There was a pond with goldfish and a wooden bridge. It was the greatest place.'

'Not Ben Weinberg.'

'Have you heard of him? He was a Hollywood bigwig for a while. He worked on a lot of Fred Astaire pictures.'

Easter Parade. 'Oh my God,' said Prudie. 'Too much plot!'

She turned to look at the dance floor. It was night behind the five-story arch of glass; inside, the balconies were strung with chains of lights, now lit like constellations. The band was small and distant. She saw Dean – tall, handsome, and kind of jerky when he danced, but in a good way.

Bernadette was rotund, but elastic. She had a serious shimmy in her shoulders, loose knees, rocking hips. She was sugarfooting one minute, buck-and-winging the next. A restrained, ladylike cha-cha. It was too bad Dean was out there with her. He was obviously holding her back.

Sylvia locked the car in the parking garage and waited with Allegra for the elevator to the street. She was relaxed, relieved. Jocelyn had phoned to tell her that Daniel hadn't shown. Sylvia had forgiven Allegra for almost backing out on the evening (and now felt guilty for making her come). She'd even forgiven Allegra the serious crime of making Allegra unhappy.

Somewhere around the second floor she said, 'You know, I don't think there's anything truly unforgivable. Not where there's love,' but Allegra was reading an ad for Depo-Provera on the elevator wall, and she didn't answer.

Jocelyn spoke to Prudie, but pitched her voice so that Grigg and Mo would also hear. 'Don't you find that people who dance well don't usually go around telling people they dance well?'

'Any savage can dance,' Grigg said. He got up, walked over, held out his hand. Jocelyn's feet hurt all the way up to her knees, but she wouldn't give Grigg the satisfaction of saying so. If he wasn't too tired to dance, then neither was she. She would dance until it killed her.

She ignored the hand, rose without his help.

She didn't look at him. He didn't look at her. Prudie looked at them both, walking off together, angry backs, angry arms, perfectly synchronized angry steps.

Prudie's mood had been volatile since her mother's death. She'd had a pretty nice evening here, listening to Bernadette's stories, making a mockery of Mo. Now suddenly she felt abandoned by Dean and by Bernadette, Jocelyn, and Grigg. It was silly, they were only dancing, but there it was; they'd left her all alone. She was always being left behind.

'I feel untethered,' she told Mo. 'As if the rope tying me to this earth had snapped.' This wasn't something she could say to Dean. He'd be so hurt to think he wasn't her tether. She could say it to Mo only because she had had too much to drink and would never see him again. Or read his stupid books.

'Then it's time to soar,' Mo said. He leaned across the table to say it, so the zinnia centerpiece brushed the bottom of his chin. He came close enough to see that she was crying, then straightened up in a helpless, startled way. 'Don't do that!' he told her. 'Come dance instead. If you think Dean won't mind.' The band was playing the Beatles' 'Come Together,' which, out of all the hundreds of Beatles songs, was her mother's absolute favorite.

'Let's not and say we did,' Prudie almost answered, because that's what her mother would have done.

But it was such a nice thing for Mo to have said. It seemed, in its small way, like sound advice. A plan, even. *Dance instead.* She could stay here, alone if you didn't count Mo, who didn't count, or she could make herself join the party. She wiped her eyes with her napkin, folded it, and set it on the table. 'Okay,' Prudie said.

So what if she'd refused an earlier offer from the man she loved? He would ask again. In the meantime there were lights and flowers, glass rings and bronze fox faces. Rich men and nice men and absent men and men who just liked a good plot. If the music was good, why not dance with them all?

Bernadette told us:

By the end of *Pride and Prejudice*, Jane, Elizabeth, and Lydia Bennet are all married. This still leaves two Bennet girls, Mary and Kitty, unattached.

According to Austen's nephew, she married them off later. She told her family that Kitty Bennet eventually wed a clergyman who lived near the Darcy estate. Mary Bennet wed a clerk from her uncle Philips's office, which kept her close to her parents' home and part of the only sort of society in which she could distinguish herself. Both marriages, according to Austen, were good ones.

'I always like to know how a story ends,' says Bernadette.

PROMOTIONAL MATERIALS
for a new
TERRENCE HOPKINS MYSTERY
by Mo Bellington

MORE MO!

In his debut novel, THE DEAD FILES, a case gone horribly wrong sent urban cop, Terrence Hopkins, to the country to devote himself to THINGS THAT GROW.

In Bellington's much-loved LAST HARVEST, Terrence Hopkins hoped he'd seen his last dead body. But take one small-town politician with big-league ambitions, add one mysterious reclusive cult, and it's that season again.

A MURDER OF CROWS
by Mo Bellington

'May be Bellington's best ever.'
— STANDARD BEARER WEEKLY

Author available for interviews, readings, and book clubs.

AUGUST

AUGUST

SUBJECT: **Re: Mom**
DATE: 8/5/02 8:09:45 am PDT
FROM: Airheart@well.com
TO: biancasillman@earthlink.net; Catwoman53@aol.com

Hey, team Harris—

Mrs Grossman called this morning. She thought we ought to know that our seventy-eight-year-old mother with the new hip was on the second-story roof cleaning the gutters. I told her we'd hired Tony for the daredevil housework, but Mrs Grossman says Tony has already left for college, because he has soccer camp. So one of us should probably go down and find someone else.

(And what's up with little Grigg? He called me last night with that scraped-paint voice he gets, so obvious he wants me to know something's wrong, but then he won't say what.)

Amelia

SUBJECT: **Re: re: Mom**
DATE: 8/5/02 11:15:52 am PDT
FROM: Catwoman53@aol.com
TO: Airheart@well.com; biancasillman@earthlink.net

I just want us all to be clear that this is exactly what Mom wants. She knows Mrs Grossman will call and then we'll all look like shocking, neglectful daughters and someone will be dispatched posthaste. I mean, of course someone has to go, but she's a cunning old woman, and why can't she just ask us? I say she should be locked up in a nursing home until she promises to stay off the roof.

As to Grigg, am I the only one who thinks he's in love again? And about time? How long ago was Sandra?
ove all, Cat

SUBJECT: **Re: re: re: Mom**
DATE: 8/5/02 12:27:59 pm PDT
FROM: Airheart@well.com
TO: Catwoman53@aol.com; biancasillman@earthlink.net

I blame us for Grigg's love life. We set a standard no woman can possibly live up to.
    A

SUBJECT: Mom and Grigg
DATE: 8/5/02 1:02:07 pm PDT
FROM: biancasillman@earthlink.net
TO: Airheart@well.com; Catwoman53@aol.com

Things are slow here so I don't mind going and dealing with Mom. (We *are* shocking, neglectful daughters.)
    I'm pretty sure Grigg likes some woman in his book club. I'm not so sure she likes him back. He called me, too, last night, so very late, so very down. I worry that Sandra left him even more fragile than before. (What's that girl scout motto – Leave the campsite better than you found it? Sandra was no girl scout.) I always thought she was just using him for his computer skills.
    Love to the husbands and kiddies, Bianca

SUBJECT: **Re: Mom and Grigg**
DATE: 8/5/02 1:27:22 pm PDT
FROM: Catwoman53@aol.com
TO: Airheart@well.com; biancasillman@earthlink.net

Sandra was a piece of work. You remember your Christmas party, Amelia? Just step away from the mistletoe, lady. Keep your hands where we can see them. We did try to warn him. One pretty face and he just doesn't listen to his sisters anymore.
    XXXXXX, Cat

SUBJECT: **Re: re: Mom and Grigg**
DATE: 8/5/02 5:30:22 pm PDT
FROM: Airheart@well.com
TO: Catwoman53@aol.com;biancasillman@earthlink.net

If Grigg's in love again, one of us better go take care of that, too.
    A

CHAPTER SIX

in which we read
Persuasion
and find ourselves
back at Sylvia's house

At any given time, most of the people in the California History Room were looking up their own families. Sylvia had worked in the state library since 1989; she'd helped hundreds and hundreds of people load rolls of microfiche into the feeder, adjust the image, master the fast-forward. She'd opened the bride, groom, and death indexes and gone spelunking for great-great-great grandparents. Today had started with a failure – a common name (Tom Burke), a big city (San Francisco), a certain vagueness as to dates, all resulting in a pissed-off descendant who felt Sylvia simply wasn't trying hard enough. Her resources, her sheer will to succeed, were compared unfavorably with those of the Mormons.

It made Sylvia reflective. Had there always been this level of interest in genealogy, she wondered, even in the sixties, when everything was to be made from scratch? What did it mean, all this personal looking backward? What were people hoping to find? What bearing, really, did their ancestry have on who they were now?

She supposed she was no better than the rest. She felt a particular pleasure whenever anyone asked for Box 310, a collection of archived Spanish and Mexican documents. She herself had recently translated the 'Solemn Espousal of Manuel Rodríguez from Guadalajara, parents deceased, to María Valvanora E La Luz, daughter of a soldier and a resident of Cynaloa.' The date on the document was October 20, 1781. The information, dry. Did they love each other desperately? Were they friends, or did they eat each night in icy silence, have resentful sex? Did they, in fact, go on to marry? Were there children? Did one of the two then leave with little warning, and if so, who left and who was left behind?

Other items in the box included an invitation to a grand ball at the governor's house in honor of Antonio López de Santa Anna; a photocopy of Andrés Pico's Articles of Capitulation to John C. Frémont at Cahuenga; a letter to Fra José María de Zalvidea discussing marriage laws among the Indians. This last was tentatively dated 1811. A world away, Jane Austen was finally publishing *Sense and Sensibility*, on a similar subject.

We were here first, Sylvia's father used to say to her, although her mother was only second-generation, and even so, of course, they weren't even close to first, just earlier than some.

> *For California is a Poem!*
> *The land of romance, of mystery,*
> *of worship, of beauty and of song.*

Ina Coolbrith had written it, and the words were now chiseled into the wall near the staircase to the second floor. But the sign Sylvia preferred was upstairs and done in Magic Marker. *Quiet*, it read. *Research in progress.*

Sylvia had never come to this library as a child, but she'd grown up not far away, in a gray wood house on Q Street. They'd had a large yard with lemon trees in the front, tomatoes and chili peppers in the back. Her mother was always in the garden; she had the touch. Her mother's favorite saint was Thérèse, who had promised, after her death, to shower the world with roses.

Sylvia's mother was doing her bit. She had rosebushes and rose trees and roses that climbed on trellises. She washed them for aphids and fed them with compost and wrapped them in the winter. 'How do you know what to do?' Sylvia asked her once, and her mother said that if you only paid attention, the roses told you what they needed.

Sylvia's father wrote for the Spanish language paper *La Raza*. At night men would come and sit on the porch, play guitars, talk politics, farming, and immigration. It was Sylvia's job the next morning to clean up the bottles, the cigarette butts, the dirty dishes.

Her second job was to hurry straight to her grandmother's house after school and provide a running translation of the daytime soap *Young Dr Malone*. Such goings-on in the small town of Denison! Murder, incarceration, drink, and despair. Adultery and hysterical blindness. Thrombosis. Throat cancer. Crippling accidents. Forged wills. And then came episode two.

Afterward Sylvia's grandmother would analyze the show for character shadings, themes and symbols, useful moral lessons. The analysis took most of the rest of the afternoon. Women had affairs and went blind. Nurses loved doctors with quiet and unrequited devotion, opened pediatric clinics, did good works. Life was made up of medical emergencies, court cases, painful love affairs, and backstabbing relatives.

Sometimes Sylvia's father read her European fairy tales at bed-time, changing the heroines' hair from blond to black (as if Sylvia could be fooled by this, as if Diego Sanchez's daughter would identify with a brunette named Snow White anyway), pointing out class issues whenever they arose. Woodsmen grew up to marry princesses. Queens danced themselves to death in bloody shoes.

Sundays her mother read to her from *The Lives of the Saints*, about Saint Dorcas, and all the others who'd given away their fortunes, devoted themselves to charity. Her mother flipped hurriedly past the martyrs — Saint Agatha (her breasts were cut from her body), Saint Lucy (her eyes were put out), Saint Perpetua (she guided her executioner's blade to her throat with her own hand). For years Sylvia didn't even know those other stories were there. She merely suspected them.

But neither the fairy tales nor the saints had the lasting impact of *Young Dr Malone*. Sylvia dated her grandmother's decline from the day the show was cancelled.

Most of what we knew about Sylvia came from Jocelyn. They'd met at Girl Scout camp when they were eleven years old. Little Jocelyn Morgan and little Sylvia Sanchez. 'We were both in the Chippewa cabin,' Jocelyn said. 'Sylvia seemed very grown up compared with me. She knew stuff you would never have imagined a little girl would know. History and medicine. She could tell you more things about comas.

'But she always thought the counselors were scheming behind our backs. She was always seeing the most elaborate plots in everything they did. One day four of us Chippewas were taken on a hike away from camp and left to find our own way home. It was part of some merit badge we were getting, or so the counselors said. Sylvia was suspicious of the whole thing. "Is there any reason anyone would want you out of the way?" Sylvia asked each of us. What little girl thinks like that?'

No one in Sylvia's family knew that her father had stopped drawing a paycheck and started putting their money into the paper until the money was gone. They moved then to the Bay Area, where Sylvia's uncle gave her father a job working at his restaurant. Sylvia and her brothers traded their two-story Victorian for a small apartment, private school for the large public ones. Her older sister was already married and stayed behind in Sacramento to have babies her parents complained they now never saw.

Sometimes they drove all the way to Sacramento for Sunday with Sylvia's grandparents. More often Sylvia's father had to work, and they didn't. Her father wasn't used to waiting on people and struck the customers as unfriendly. He had to be reminded not to participate in their conversations, not to talk about unions with the busboys and cooks.

The whole tipping process is designed to humiliate. On her mother's birthday when he serenaded her at five-thirty in the morning just as the sun came up, as he'd done every year since their wedding, Sylvia had seen curious, irritated Anglo lights coming on in the house behind theirs.

One of the cooks at the restaurant had a daughter at the public high school. Sylvia's father arranged for them to meet so Sylvia would already have a friend when classes started. The daughter was named Constance; she was a year younger than Sylvia. She wore white lipstick and ratted her hair so it cushioned her head like packing material. She'd sewn the name of her boyfriend in the palm of her left hand. Sylvia could hardly look at this, though Constance said it hadn't hurt; the secret was in shallow stitches. It fell to Sylvia to explain the dangers of infection, the risk of amputation. Plus, it was really gross. Obviously they were not going to be the best of friends.

But there was Jocelyn. And then there was Daniel.

'Is he Catholic?' her mother asked the first time Daniel drove her home from school.

'I'm not going to marry him!' Sylvia had snapped back, because he wasn't and she didn't wish to say so.

After their wedding, on the night when Sylvia and Daniel had had their first big fight and she'd driven to her parents' house and stood on the doorstep with tears on her face and an overnight bag in her hand, her father wouldn't even let her in. 'You go home to your husband,' he said. 'You live there now. Work things out.'

Non-Catholics, on the other hand, *they* believed in divorce. They would become miserable for one reason or another, and then they would leave, and their parents wouldn't even try to stop them, which was why you didn't marry non-Catholics in the first place.

And sure enough, thirty-plus years later, wasn't that exactly what Daniel had done? It was a shame Sylvia's mother hadn't lived to see it. She so enjoyed being right.

In all fairness, probably no more than anyone else did.

A stout woman emerged from the Microforms Room and came to the desk. She was dressed in jeans and a green Squaw Valley sweatshirt. She had a pencil balanced between her ear and her head. Since she also wore glasses, the space behind that ear was crowded. 'There's a date missing from the 1890 *San Francisco Chronicle*,' she told Sylvia. 'It skips from May ninth to May eleventh. I looked at the *Alta*, too. And the *Wasp*. They just don't seem to have had a May tenth in 1890.'

Sylvia agreed that this was strange. Since the microfiche came from a central service, she guessed that nothing would be solved by going to another library. Sylvia sent Maggie to the basement to see if she could find the missing date among any of the actual papers.

In general, librarians enjoyed special requests. A reference librarian is someone who likes the chase. When librarians read for pleasure, they often pick a good mystery. They tend to be cat people as well, for reasons more obscure.

A black man in a gray turtleneck requested an oral-history interview regarding public policy in the Lieutenant Governor's Office from 1969 to 1972.

An elderly man in a velvet beret called Sylvia over to his table to show her his work. He was lettering his family tree in meticulous and beautiful calligraphy.

Maggie returned, having failed to find the missing date. She offered to put in a call to the Bancroft Library in Berkeley, but the woman who had asked for the *Chronicle* said she had to go; there was no more time on her parking meter. Maybe next week when she'd be back.

A man with bad skin asked for help printing a copy from the microfiche reader. It was Sylvia's turn to do this.

The main room was a lovely space, with curving walls, large windows, and red-tile-rooftop views. If you sat at one of the tables you could see the top of the Capitol dome.

The Rare Materials Reading Room was lined with glass book-cases filled with rare books and was, in its way, equally pleasant. You worked there with the door locked and outside noises hushed. Only the librarians could key you in and out.

But the Microforms Room was windowless, lit by overheads and by the screens of the readers. There was a constant hum, with images inevitably warped on one side or the other, no way to bring the whole into focus at once. All very headache-inducing. You had to love research to love the Microforms Room. Sylvia was threading the feeder when Maggie came to get her. 'You have a phone call from your husband,' Maggie said. 'He says it's urgent.'

Allegra had been having an excellent day. She'd spent the morning working and put several orders in the mail. She'd thought of a birthday present for Sylvia and was figuring out how to make it. To aid in this she went to the Rocknasium, a local climbing gym. You couldn't really think about anything but climbing when you climbed, but Allegra always found it a fruitful not-thinking.

She strapped herself into a harness. She was supposed to be meeting her friend Paul; they'd been belaying each other for the last couple of months. Allegra's level was somewhere in the 5.6 to 5.7 range, Paul's a bit better. The regulars were almost all men, but the few women who came were Allegra's sort of women – strong and athletic. The place smelled of chalk and sweat, and those were Allegra's sort of smells.

The Rocknasium had only nine full-sized walls. These were knobbed and creviced in many places, the holds marked with bright-colored drips like a Jackson Pollock painting. Each wall contained a variety of routes – a red route, a yellow, a blue. You were always passing up a closer hold to find the correct color for the course you were on. The correct hold was inevitably small and far away. Paul had called Allegra the night before to say the routes had just been changed. And about time.

When Allegra first started climbing, she would hang in one spot for too long, contemplating the best way to make her next grab. Her arms and fingers would begin to burn with exhaustion. She noticed that the experienced climbers moved very, very quickly. Staying still was more work than moving; thinking too much was fatal. Allegra supposed there was a lesson there. She learned things quickly, but she didn't much like lessons.

She'd never been to the Rocknasium during the day. Gone was the intimidating soberness of the regular climbers, the focused quiet. Instead someone was screaming. Someone was singing. Someone was throwing chalk. There was laughing, shouting, all the chaos of a ten-year-old's birthday party echoing off the fake paint-splotched rocks. Children, sugar coursing through their tiny veins, were everywhere, fastened to the walls on their ropes like spiders. There was so much chalk in the air it made Allegra sneeze. This was intimidation of a different sort.

Allegra liked being an aunt. Her brother Diego had two girls; that was all the kid time Allegra needed. Probably. All she wanted. Mostly. There would certainly be something challenging in a genetic code that made you gay but left your reproductive urge fully functional. Some days Allegra hardly noticed how the years were floating by. 'Come on,' some kid shouted impatiently to someone who wasn't coming on.

Allegra went to warm up on the solo wall while she waited for Paul. This wall was low enough to climb without ropes, no more than seven feet. At the bottom was a very thick mat. Allegra put her foot on a blue hold. She reached for a blue hold above her head. She pulled herself up. Blue hold to blue hold to blue hold. Toward the top she saw some enticing orange paint, farther than the next blue – she'd have to leap – but glittering at the edge of what might be possible. Things worked best if you didn't think about them. Just jump.

To her right the birthday girl came rappelling down at top speed, her belayer playing the rope out to give her a ride. 'Wire work,' someone called. 'Hello, Jet Li.'

An adult at another wall was giving instructions. 'Look up,' he said. 'The purple's just on your left there. You can reach it. Don't worry. I'll catch you.'

I'll catch you.

Nobody was catching Allegra, but Allegra had never needed catching. She reached back with one hand into the pouch on her harness for chalk. Kicked off and grabbed.

Sylvia called Jocelyn from the car. 'Allegra fell at the climbing gym,' she said. She was trying not to picture all the things that might happen to someone who fell. Wheelchairs. Comas. 'They've taken her to Sutter. I'm on my way, but I don't know anything. I don't know how far it was. I don't know if she's awake. I don't know if she's broken a nail or broken her neck.' She could hardly get the last part out, she was crying so hard.

'I'll call you as soon as I get there,' Jocelyn said. 'I'm sure it's fine. They don't let you climb in those gyms without a harness. I don't think it's possible to really hurt yourself.'

Jocelyn always thought things were fine. If they weren't fine when she got there, she made damn sure they were fine before she left. Jocelyn didn't think about those things she couldn't make fine until she was forced to. There were days when Sylvia thought about nothing else. Jocelyn had no children; Sylvia had three, plus two grandchildren; that was the difference. Why would Allegra be at the hospital if things were fine?

Bad things did happen, after all. You could be lucky only so long. Sylvia and Daniel had been parked in his car just a couple of blocks from his house on the day his brother died. It was their senior year of high school. They were kissing some and they were talking some. Both the kissing and the talking were fraught. They'd begun to have the same conversation over and over. Would they go to the same college? Should they go to the same college just to be together? If they both wanted to be at the same college, should one of them go elsewhere just to avoid being together? Could their relationship pass the test of a separation? Should it be made to? Who loved whom most? They heard sirens. They kissed.

Daniel's brother had been hit by a car driven by a sixteen-year-old. Andy was killed instantly, which was the only small mercy, so Daniel didn't have to spend the rest of his life thinking that if he'd gone home the minute he heard the fire trucks he could have said good-bye.

Sylvia had thought Daniel's mother a peculiarly affectless woman, polite but distant. This became even more obvious after Sylvia and Daniel were married and had children. Where were the constant complaints about never seeing the grandkids? And where was all the sobbing and hand-wringing when Allegra – such a beautiful girl! – turned out to be gay and would likely have no children of her own?

Sylvia was somewhat affectless herself, but in the general noise of her own dramatic family, no one, including Sylvia, had noticed this yet. She liked Daniel's mother okay – the woman hardly cast a shadow, what was not to like? – but she would have been insulted to be told they were similar. On the day Andy died she watched Daniel's mother crumple like paper. Something moved into her face that never moved out.

In *Persuasion*, Jane Austen mentions the death of a child. She is brief and dismissive. The Musgroves, she says, 'had had the ill fortune of a very troublesome, hopeless son; and the good fortune to lose him before he reached his twentieth year.' Dick Musgrove was not loved. When he went to sea, he was not missed. Assigned to a boat under Captain Wentworth's command, he died in a way never specified, and only death made him valuable to his family.

These are the parents Austen's heroine, Anne Elliot, describes later in the book as excellent. 'What a blessing,' Anne says, 'to young people to be in such hands!'

There was traffic on the causeway; the lanes were glutted. Sylvia inched along. Bad things did happen. Now there was glass, now a fractured car on the shoulder of the road, the back door on the driver's side folded nearly in two. The people had been removed, no way to guess what shape they were in. As soon as she passed this, Sylvia was able to resume a proper freeway speed.

It took Jocelyn fifteen minutes to get to the hospital, another five to find the nurse in the emergency room who'd admitted Allegra. 'Are you a relative?' the nurse asked, and then explained very politely that the hospital couldn't release information on Allegra's condition to anyone who wasn't.

Jocelyn believed in rules. She believed in exceptions to rules. Not only for herself, but for anyone just like her. She described with equal courtesy the scene she was capable of making. 'I don't get embarrassed,' she said. 'And I'm not tired. Her mother is waiting for me to call.'

The nurse noted that Allegra was also the name of an allergy medication. This was spitefully done and inappropriate, too. When Jocelyn looked back on it later, remembering everything but with the anxiety over Allegra removed, she was quite angry about this part. What a flippant thing to say under the circumstances. And it was a beautiful name. It was from Longfellow.

But then the nurse conceded that X rays had been taken. Allegra was in a brace. There was concern about a head injury, but she was conscious. Dr Yep was in charge of the case. And no, Jocelyn couldn't see Allegra. Only her relatives could see her.

Jocelyn was in the midst of explaining why the nurse was mistaken about this as well, when Daniel arrived. He walked in as if it hadn't been months since they'd spoken, and put his arms around Jocelyn. He smelled just exactly like Daniel.

Times came when you needed someone's arms around you. Mostly Jocelyn liked being single, but sometimes she thought about that. 'She's been X-rayed. Possible head injury. They won't tell me anything,' she said into his shoulder. 'I have to call Sylvia right away.'

By the time Sylvia saw her, Allegra had been immobile for almost two hours and was furious about it. Sylvia, Daniel, and Jocelyn circled her with white faces, forced smiles. They agreed that it always was Allegra getting hurt, never the boys. Remember how she'd broken her foot falling off the monkey bars? Remember how she'd dislocated her collarbone, tumbling from the elm tree? Remember how she'd crushed her elbow in that bike incident? Accident-prone, they agreed, which made Allegra madder and madder. 'I'm not hurt at all,' she said. 'I fell maybe four feet and I landed on a mat. I can't believe they brought me here. I didn't even black out.'

In fact she had lost consciousness, and she suspected as much. She'd no memory of the fall, nothing until the ambulance came. And certainly she must have dropped more than four feet. She knew about the mat only because she'd seen it. But since she couldn't remember the details, she felt free to adjust them. How was that lying?

And right then, in the hospital with everyone standing around her bed as though it were the last scene of *The Wizard of Oz* movie, it seemed that they were all colluding to make a big deal out of nothing. In the context of the white-water rafting, the snowboarding, the surfing, for God's sake the parachuting, Allegra had done, she felt her record was pretty clean. It looked bad to her parents only because they didn't know about the white-water rafting, the snowboarding, the surfing, the parachuting.

Finally Dr Yep entered with the X rays. Allegra couldn't move an inch to see, but she could never see anything on X rays anyway. She could never see the colors of stars through a telescope, never find birds through binoculars, paramecia through microscopes. This was irritating, but not on a daily basis.

Dr Yep was talking with her parents, showing them this and that on Allegra's ribs, her skull. The doctor had a very pleasant voice, which was nice because she talked for a long time. After cataloguing the many things that might have been on Allegra's X rays, but happily were not, Dr Yep came to the point. Just as Allegra had said, there was absolutely nothing wrong with her. Still, they wanted to keep her overnight for observation and maximum annoyance. Dr Yep claimed Allegra had given some bizarre answers to questions in the ambulance – what day of the week it was, what was the month. Allegra denied this.

'They just took me so literally,' she said. She didn't remember her answers, only that the emergency techs, buzzing about like gnats, had provoked her. Perhaps she'd quoted a little Dickinson. In what universe was that a crime? At least she could finally be unstrapped, move from side to side again. It was embarrassing, when she did this, to learn that she had a bandage on her temple, blood on her cheek. Apparently she'd gashed her head.

It took another forty minutes to finish the paperwork and get her checked in upstairs. She was in quite a bit of pain by then, bruised, stiff, with a dreadful headache beginning to stir. Nothing the couple of Tylenol she'd been offered were going to manage. She needed real drugs; she hoped she wasn't going to be the only one to think so just because no bones were broken.

The nurse on duty turned out to be Callie Abramson. Allegra had gone to high school with Callie, though they hadn't been in the same year or run in the same circles. Callie'd been yearbook and student government. Allegra, field hockey and art. Still it was nice to see a familiar face in a strange place. Sylvia, at least, was delighted.

While helping Allegra into bed, Callie told her that Travis Browne had become a Muslim. Hard-core, Callie said, whatever that meant. Allegra didn't suppose she'd ever exchanged two words with Travis. Brittany Auslander had been arrested for stealing computers from the language lab at the university. Everybody but Callie had always thought she was such a good girl. Callie herself was married – no one you'd know, she said – and had two boys. And Melinda Pande turned out gay.

'Hard-core?' Allegra asked. She remembered how Callie had gotten so thin everyone suspected she was anorexic. How she tried out for cheerleading anyway, like a stick figure in a short skirt, her sharp little face shouting to give her an F, give her an I. How she'd freaked out one spring during finals and been taken to the counselor's office in hysterics, and they'd found pills in her locker, either to help her diet or to kill herself; no one seemed to know, but it didn't stop them from saying.

Now here she was, thin but not too thin, working, smiling like someone's mom, and telling Allegra how nice it was to see her again. Allegra was very happy for her. She looked at Callie's photos of her boys and she got a whole vibe off them of a tolerant, loving, noisy home. She thought Callie was probably a very good mother.

Callie didn't seem to remember much about Allegra at all, but wasn't that really what you wanted from the kids at your high school?

Sylvia and Daniel drove back to the house together to collect some things for Allegra – her toothbrush, her slippers. She'd asked for a milk shake, so they'd pick that up, too. 'She was very emotional,' Dr Yep had told Sylvia privately. Clearly she thought it a matter of some concern.

Sylvia heard it as a reassurance. Relief turned to happiness. There was her Allegra, then, undamaged, unchanged. She would rather have taken Allegra home, yet there was nothing, absolutely nothing, to complain about. A narrow escape. Another lucky, lucky day in Sylvia's lucky, lucky life.

'How's Pam?' she asked Daniel charitably. Sylvia still hadn't met Pam. Allegra said she was every bit as tough and opinionated as a family-practice lawyer would have to be.

'Pam's good. Did Jocelyn seem a bit subdued to you? Of course, she was worried. We were all worried.'

'Jocelyn's fine. Busy running the world.'

'Thank God,' Daniel said. 'I wouldn't want to live in any world Jocelyn wasn't running.' As if that weren't exactly what he'd done, left the world Jocelyn ran, for one she didn't. Sylvia thought this, but was too relieved, too grateful (though not to Daniel) to say it.

Seeing him in the house again gave Sylvia a peculiar feeling, as though she were dreaming or waking up and couldn't tell which. Who was she, really – the Sylvia without Daniel or the Sylvia with? In some ways she felt that she'd aged years in the months he'd been gone.

In other ways she'd become her parents' daughter again. After Daniel had left, she'd found herself remembering things from her childhood, things she hadn't thought of in forever. As though Daniel had been an interruption that went on most of her life. Suddenly she was dreaming in Spanish again. She found herself thinking more and more about her mother's roses, her father's politics, her grandmother's soaps.

Divorce itself was an inevitable soap opera, of course. The roles were prewritten, no way to do them differently, no way to make them your own. She could see how it was killing Daniel not to be the hero in his own divorce.

'You have to remind yourself that it isn't just the good Daniel who left,' Jocelyn had told her. 'The bad Daniel is gone, too. Wasn't he insufferable sometimes? Make a list of everything you didn't like.'

But when Sylvia tried, the things she didn't like often turned out also to be the things she did like. She would focus on some unpleasant memory – how she'd set out a punishment for one of the children, only to have him grant a parole. How he would ask her what she wanted for Christmas and then shake his head and tell her she didn't want that, after all. 'You'll put it in the cupboard and never use it,' when she wanted a bread machine. 'It looks just like the coat you already have,' when she'd shown him a winter jacket she liked. It was so smug. She really couldn't stand it.

Then the memory would turn on her. The children had grown up fine; she was proud of them all. The present Daniel would get her would be something she would never have thought of. Usually it would be wonderful.

One night several weeks before Daniel had taken her out to dinner and asked for a divorce, she'd woken up and seen that he wasn't in bed. She found him in the living room, in the armchair, looking out at the rain. The wind was shrill against the windows, rocking the trees. Sylvia loved a storm at night. It made everything simple. It made you content just to be dry.

Obviously it was having a different effect on Daniel. 'Are you happy?' he had asked.

This sounded like the start of a long conversation. Sylvia didn't have on her robe or her slippers. She was cold. She was tired. 'Yes,' she said, not because she was, but because she wanted to keep things short. And she might be happy. She couldn't think of anything making her unhappy. She hadn't asked herself that question for a very long time.

'I can't always tell,' Daniel said.

Sylvia heard this as a criticism. It was a complaint he'd made before – she was too subdued, too reticent. When would she learn to let go? Water poured from the gutters onto the deck. Sylvia could hear a car pass on Fifth Street, the *shhh* of its tires. 'I'm going back to bed,' she said.

'You go on,' Daniel told her. 'I'll be along in a minute.'

But he wasn't, and she fell asleep. She had a familiar dream. She was in a foreign city and no one spoke the languages she spoke. She tried to call home, but her cell phone was dead. She put the wrong money in the pay phone, and when she finally got it right, a strange man answered. 'Daniel's not here,' he told her. 'No, I don't know where he went. No, I don't know when he'll be back.'

In the morning she tried to speak to Daniel, but he was no longer willing. 'It was nothing,' he said. 'I don't know what that was about. Forget it.'

Now Daniel was down the hallway in Allegra's room, packing her things. 'Should we take her a book?' he called. 'Do you know what she's reading?'

Sylvia didn't answer immediately. She'd gone into the bedroom to phone the boys and noticed she had five messages. Four were hang-ups, telemarketers presumably, and one was from Grigg. 'I was wondering if we could talk,' he said. 'Would you have lunch with me this week? Give me a call.'

Daniel entered just in time to hear the end. She could tell he was surprised. Sylvia, less so. She saw Jocelyn's fingers all over this. Sylvia had always suspected Grigg was intended for her. Of course, she didn't want him, but when had that ever stopped Jocelyn? He was far too young.

She could see Daniel not asking her who that was. 'Grigg Harris,' she told him. 'He's in my Jane Austen book club.' Let Daniel think another man was interested in her. A suitable man. A man who read Jane Austen.

A man with whom she now had to have an awkward lunch. Damn Jocelyn.

'Should we take Allegra a book?' Daniel asked again.

'She's rereading *Persuasion*,' Sylvia said. 'We both are.'

Daniel phoned Diego, who was their oldest, an immigration lawyer in L. A. Diego had been named for Sylvia's father and was the one with his grandfather's political passions. In other ways, Diego was the child most like Daniel, an early adult, dependable, responsible. The way Daniel used to be.

Sylvia phoned Andy, named for Daniel's brother. Andy was their easygoing child. He worked for a landscaping firm in Marin and called on his cell whenever he was eating a really great meal or looking at something beautiful. In Andy's life these things happened frequently. 'The most amazing sunset!' he would say. 'The most amazing tapas!'

Diego offered to come home and had to be convinced it wasn't neccessary. Andy, who could have made the trip in little more than an hour, didn't think to make the offer.

Daniel and Sylvia went back to the hospital and sat with Allegra. They stayed all night, dozing in their chairs, because mistakes could happen in hospitals – doctors got distracted by their personal lives, there were romances and jiltings, people went in with fevers and came out with amputations. That was Sylvia's motivation, anyway. Daniel stayed because he wanted to be there. It was the first night he and Sylvia had spent together since he'd moved out.

'Daniel,' Sylvia said. It was two in the morning, or else it was three. Allegra was sleeping, her face turned toward Sylvia on her pillow. She was dreaming. Sylvia could see her eyes move under her lids. Allegra's breath was quick and audible. 'Daniel?' Sylvia said. 'I'm happy.'

Daniel didn't answer. He, too, might have been asleep.

The next Saturday, Sylvia organized a trip to the beach. She proposed sushi at Osaka in Bodega Bay, because Allegra would never say no to sushi and Osaka was the best they'd ever had. She proposed a run on the sand for Sahara and Thembe, because Jocelyn would never say no to that. There were so few places a Ridgeback could safely run off-leash. They weren't the kind of dogs who came when they were called. Unless they belonged to Jocelyn.

A trip to the beach would get everyone out of the Valley heat for a day. 'And I think I'll invite Grigg,' Sylvia told Jocelyn, 'instead of having lunch with him.' Group activities, your key to avoiding unwanted intimacy.

This was a conversation on the phone, and there'd been a noticeable pause on Jocelyn's end. Sylvia hadn't told Jocelyn about the lunch, so perhaps she was just surprised. 'All right,' she said finally. 'I guess we can fit another person into the car.' Which made no sense. If they took Jocelyn's van, as they surely would with the dogs, they could fit a couple more people in.

And a good thing, too, because first Grigg said he couldn't. His sister Cat was visiting. And then he called back and said Cat really wanted to go to the beach, was in fact insistent on it, and could they both come? Cat turned out to look a lot like Grigg, only fatter and without the eyelashes.

The tide had left the graceful curves of its going etched into the sand. The wind came in off the water and the surf was wild. Instead of tidy sets, the waves were broken to bits, white water and green and brown and blue, all battered together. A few shells were washed over at the water's edge, small and perfect, but everyone was too ecologically well behaved to pick these up.

Allegra was looking out to the ocean, her hair blowing into her eyes, a delicate tattoo of butterfly stitches on her temple. 'Austen is so in love with sailors in *Persuasion*,' she said to Sylvia. 'What profession would she admire today?'

'Firemen?' Sylvia guessed. 'Just like everyone else?' And then they stopped talking because Jocelyn was approaching, and discussing the book in advance of the meeting, though tolerated, was not encouraged.

The dogs were ecstatic. Sahara raced along the sand with a rope of seaweed in her mouth, dropping it to bark at some sea lions sunning on a rock in the surf. The sea lions barked back; it was all very friendly.

Thembe found a dead gull and rolled over it, so that Jocelyn had to drag him into the icy water and scrub him down with wet sand. Her feet turned white as a fish belly; her teeth chattered – a rare achievement in August. She was looking very nice, her hair tied back with a scarf, her skin polished by the wind. At least Sylvia thought so.

Sylvia was managing never to be alone with Grigg. Jocelyn, she noticed, almost seemed to be doing the same thing. They sat together on the sand while Jocelyn toweled off with her sweat-shirt. 'When I was driving to the hospital,' Sylvia said, 'I thought if Allegra was all right I would be the happiest woman in the world. And she was, and I was. But today the sink is backed up and there are roaches in the garage and I don't have the time to deal with any of it. The newspaper is filled with misery and war. Already I have to remind myself to be happy. And you know, if it were the other way, if something had happened to Allegra, I wouldn't have to remind myself to be unhappy. I'd be unhappy the rest of my life. Why should unhappiness be so much more powerful than happiness?'

'One difficult member spoils a whole group,' Jocelyn agreed. 'One disappointment ruins a whole day.'

'One infidelity wipes out years of faithfulness.'

'It takes ten weeks to get into shape and ten days to get out of it.'

'That's my point,' said Sylvia. 'We don't stand a chance.' Jocelyn was closer and more dear to Sylvia than her own sister ever had been. They had quarreled over Sylvia's tardiness and Jocelyn's bossiness and Sylvia's malleability and Jocelyn's righteousness, but they had never had a serious fight. All those years before, Sylvia had taken Daniel from Jocelyn, and Jocelyn had simply gone on loving them both.

Cat came and sat down beside them. Sylvia had liked Cat instantly. She had a loud laugh, like a duck quacking, and she laughed a lot. 'Grigg just loves dogs,' she said. 'We were never allowed to have one, so when he was three he decided to be one. We had to pat him on the head and tell him what a good dog he was. Give him little treats.

'And there was this book he absolutely loved. *The Green Poodles*. Kind of a mystery, took place in Texas, a long-lost cousin from England, a missing painting. And lots and lots of dogs. Our sister Amelia used to read it to us at bedtime. Books and dogs, that's our Grigg.'

Allegra had discovered tide pools in the hollows of rocks and shouted for the others to come see. Each pool was a world, tiny but complete. The pools had the charm of dollhouses without inspiring the urge toward rearrangement. They were lined with anemones, so thick they were squeezed together, there were limpets and an occasional urchin, abalone the size of fingernails, and a minnow or two. It was a preview of lunch.

On the way home Jocelyn made a wrong turn. They were lost in the wilds of Glen Ellen for half an hour, which was so unlike Jocelyn. Sylvia was in the front with the MapQuest map, which, now that it was needed, appeared to bear no relationship to the realities of roads and distances. In the back, Cat suddenly turned to Grigg. 'Oh my God,' she said. 'Did you see that sign? To Los Guilicos? You remember the Los Guilicos School for wayward girls? I wonder if it's still there.'

'My folks were always threatening my sisters with the Los Guilicos School,' Grigg told the rest of the car. 'It was a family joke. They'd read about it in the paper. It was supposed to be a pretty tough place.'

'There was a riot there,' Cat said. 'I don't think I was even born yet. It was started by some girls from L.A., so I guess it got a lot of play in the L.A. papers. It lasted four whole days. The police kept arresting girls and taking them away and saying now it was all under control, and the next night the girls who were left would start in again. They broke windows and got drunk, fought with knives from the kitchen and bits of broken glass. They tore up the toilets and threw them out the windows with the rest of the furniture. Went into town and broke the windows there, too. Eventually the National Guard was called in, and even they couldn't control things. Four days! Gangs of rampaging teenage girls. I always thought it would make a great movie.'

'I never heard of that,' Sylvia said. 'What started it?'

'I don't know,' Cat said. 'It was blamed on violent lesbians.'

'Ah,' Allegra said, 'of course,' when Sylvia could see no *of course* about it. How many riots blamed on violent lesbians had Allegra heard about?

Or maybe that had been an impressed 'of course.' Maybe Allegra felt a sneaking admiration for toilet-hurling lesbians.

'I used to have nightmares,' Grigg said, 'where I was being chased by wayward girls with knives.'

'Of course,' Cat said. 'You would. Doesn't it make you wonder where all those girls are now? What they went on to be?'

'Turn here,' Sylvia told Jocelyn, just because they'd come to a yard filled with roses.

Jocelyn turned. Let Saint Thérèse guide them home.

Or let them all end up at the Los Guilicos School for wayward girls. Sylvia was fine with it either way.

Jocelyn was being very quiet. This was partly because she couldn't hear the conversation in the backseat. But it was mostly because while they were on the beach, while Allegra and Sylvia were still poking about the tide pools and Grigg was throwing bits of driftwood for the dogs, learning that Ridgebacks weren't fetchers like that, Cat had abruptly, without warning, had a word with her. 'My brother likes you,' she'd said. 'He'd kill me if he knew I told you so, but I figure this is for the best. This way it's up to you. God knows it can't be left up to him. He'll never make a move.'

'Did he tell you he liked me?' Jocelyn immediately regretted having asked. How high school had that sounded?

'Please. I know my brother,' which Jocelyn supposed meant he hadn't. She turned away, looked down the beach toward Grigg and her dogs. They were headed to her, coming at a gallop. She saw that Thembe, at least, was smitten, couldn't take his eyes off Grigg.

Ridgebacks are hounds, which means friendly, but independent. Jocelyn liked them for the challenge; there's no glory in a well-behaved shepherd. She liked independent men as well. Before the library fundraiser Grigg had always seemed so eager to please.

And then he joined them and nothing more could be said. He was obviously fond of his sister; that was attractive. The two of them stood together, his arm around her shoulder. Cat had an open, outdoorish face. She looked her age and then some. But the sun was full on her, which hardly one woman in a thousand could stand the test of. It was obviously a good bloodline. Both brother and sister had good teeth, neat little ears, deep chests, long limbs.

When she dropped Sylvia off, Jocelyn told her what Cat had said. Grigg and Cat had already been taken home. Allegra had gone straight inside to make a phone call. 'I'm not at all convinced Cat knew what she was talking about,' Jocelyn said. 'Grigg and I had a big fight the other night. Apologies all around, but still . . . Anyway, I kind of had Grigg in mind for you. You're the one he asked to lunch.'

'Well, I don't want him,' Sylvia answered. 'I took your boyfriend away from you back in high school and it all came to nothing. I'm not doing it again. Do you like him?'

'I'm too old for him.'

'And yet I'm not.'

'He was to be a fling.'

'You fling him.'

'I think I'll read those books he gave me,' Jocelyn said. 'If they turn out to be good books, well then, maybe. Maybe I'll give it a try.' At least she'd never been, thank God, the kind of woman who stopped liking a guy just because he maybe liked her back.

There was a letter pushed under Sylvia's door, picked up by Allegra and left on the dining room table. 'I want to come home,' the letter said. 'I made the most terrible mistake and you should never forgive me, but you should also know that I want to come home.

'I've always felt that making everyone happy was my job, and then like a failure if you or the kids couldn't produce that happiness for me. I didn't figure this out for myself. I'm seeing a counselor.

'So I was stupid enough to blame you for not being happier. Now I think, if I could come home again, I'd let you have your own moods, your lovely, loving alarms.

'Last week I knew I never wanted to be with a woman I couldn't bring to my child's hospital room. I had this dream while we were in those awful chairs. In my dream there was a forest. (Remember how we took the kids to the Snoqualmie National Park and Diego said, 'You said we were going to a forest. There's nothing here but trees'?) I couldn't find you. I got more and more panicked, and then I woke up and you were right across the room from me. It was such a relief I can't even say. You asked me how Pam was. I haven't seen Pam for two months. She wasn't the woman for me after all.

'I've been unjust, weak, resentful, and inconstant. But in my heart it's always been you.'

Sylvia sat folding and unfolding the letter, trying to see how she felt about it. It made her happy. It made her angry. It made her think that Daniel was no prize. He was coming home, because no one else turned out to want him.

She didn't show the letter to Allegra. She didn't even tell Jocelyn. Jocelyn would respond however Sylvia wished, but Sylvia didn't know yet what response that would be. It was too important a moment to ask Jocelyn to go through it unguided. Sylvia wanted things simple, but they refused to simplify. She carried the letter about, rereading and rereading, watching her feelings rearrange about it, sentence by sentence, like a kaleidoscope.

*

The last official meeting of the Jane Austen book club took place at Sylvia's again. It had been in the low nineties all day, which is not so bad for August in the Valley. The sun sank and a Delta breeze came up. We sat on Sylvia's deck, underneath the big walnut tree. She made peach margaritas and served homemade strawberry sherbet with homemade sugar cookies. Really, no one could have asked for a prettier evening.

The meeting began with an unveiling. Sylvia had a birthday coming. It was still a few weeks off, but Allegra had made something she wanted us all to see, so she gave it to Sylvia early, wrapped in last week's funny papers. It was about the size and shape of a holiday cheese-ball. We would have guessed Sylvia was the sort to unknot the ribbon, carefully remove and fold the paper. Instead she tore it apart. Sahara and Thembe couldn't have opened it faster, even working together.

Allegra had bought one of those black Magic 8-Balls, reamed it open, replaced the answers, and sealed it. She'd painted it a dark green, and over the old 8, she'd transferred a reproduction of Cassandra Austen's sketch of her sister, set in a framed oval like a cameo. It wasn't a very attractive portrait; we were certain she had been prettier than this, but when you need a picture of Jane Austen you don't have a lot of choices.

A ribbon wound about the ball. *Ask Austen* was painted in red on the ribbon. Allegra had matched Austen's writing from a facsimile in the university library.

'Go ahead,' Allegra said. 'Ask a question.'

Sylvia got up to give Allegra a kiss. It was the most fantastic present! Allegra was so very clever. But Sylvia couldn't think of a question benign enough for its maiden forecast. Later, when she was alone, she thought she had some things to ask.

'I'll go,' Bernadette offered. Bernadette was nicely dressed tonight, not a hair out of place. Her socks didn't match, but why should they? Her shoes did. It was rakish.

'Should I take a trip?' Bernadette asked Austen. She'd been contemplating a birding expedition to Costa Rica. Pricey, but not if you calculated it bird by bird. She shook the ball, upended it, and waited. *It is not everyone who has your passion for dead leaves*, she read.

'Go in autumn,' Jocelyn translated.

Prudie took the ball next. Something about Prudie just looked right with an object of divination. Her snow-white skin, sharp features, dark, bottomless eyes. We thought how she should always be holding one, like a fashion accessory. 'Should I buy a new computer?' Prudie asked.

Austen answered, *My good opinion once lost is lost for ever.*

'I guess that's no,' Allegra said. 'You have to squint a bit. It's sort of a Zen experience.'

Next was Grigg. All summer, his hair and lashes had been bleaching at the ends. He obviously tanned easily; even that short trip to the beach made him browner. He looked five years younger, which was unfortunate if you were an older woman and contemplating dating him. 'Should I write my book?' Grigg asked. 'My *roman à clef* ?'

Austen ignored this, answered a different question, but Grigg was the only one of us who knew it. *He advances inch by inch, and will hazard nothing till he believes himself secure.*

'I bet you could sell a bunch of these,' Grigg said. 'You could put out a whole line, different writers. The Dickens ball. Mark Twain. Mickey Spillane. I'd pay a lot for access to daily advice from Mickey Spillane.'

There was a time when we might have bristled at the devolution from Austen to Spillane. But we were very fond of Grigg now. Probably he was making a joke.

He passed to Jocelyn. Jocelyn was also looking exceptionally good. She was wearing a blouse even Sylvia had never seen, so it must have been brand-new. A long, light khaki skirt. Makeup. 'Should I take a chance?' Jocelyn asked.

It is not everyone who has your passion for dead leaves, Austen told her.

'Well, that answer works equally well for any question,' Allegra noted. 'Anyway, you should always take a chance. Ask Allegra.'

Jocelyn turned directly to Grigg. 'I read those two Le Guins you gave me. In fact, I bought a third. I'm halfway through *Searoad*. She's just amazing. It's been forever since I found a new writer I love like that.'

Grigg blinked several times. 'Le Guin's in a league of her own, of course,' he said cautiously. He gained enthusiasm. 'But she's written a bunch. And there are other writers you might like, too. There's Joanna Russ and Carol Emshwiller.'

Their voices dropped; the conversation became intimate, but the bits we could hear were still about books. So Jocelyn was a science fiction reader now. We had no objection. We could see how it might be unsafe for people prone to dystopian fantasies, but as long as science fiction wasn't all you read, as long as there was a large allowance of realism, what was the harm? It was nice to see Grigg looking so happy. Perhaps we would all start reading Le Guin.

The globe came back to Sylvia. 'Should we talk about *Persuasion* now?' she asked it. Her answer: *It is not everyone who has your passion for dead leaves.*

'You didn't shake it,' Allegra complained. The phone rang and she got up, went inside. 'Go ahead and start,' she said as she left. 'I'll be right back.'

Sylvia put down the ball, picked up her book, paged through for the passage she wanted. 'I was troubled,' she began, 'by the difference in the way Austen talks about the death of Dick Musgrove and the way she talks about the death of Fanny Harville. It's very convenient to the plot that Fanny's fiancé falls in love with Louisa, since this leaves Captain Wentworth free to marry Anne. Still, you can see Austen doesn't entirely approve.' Sylvia read aloud. ' "Poor Fanny!" her brother says. "She would not have forgotten him so soon!" '

'But there are no tears at all for Dick Musgrove. The loss of a son is less important than the loss of a fiancée. Austen was never a mother.'

'Austen was never a fiancée,' said Bernadette. 'Or just overnight. Not long enough to count. So it's not son versus fiancée.'

There was a fly on the porch, humming about Bernadette's head. It was large and loud and slow and distracting. Distracting to us, anyway. It didn't seem to be bothering Bernadette. 'What matters is the worthiness of the person deceased,' she said. 'Dick was a useless, incorrigible boy. Fanny was an exceptional woman. People earn the way they're missed. *Persuasion* is all about earning your place. The self-made men of the navy are so much more admirable than the high-born Elliots. Anne is so much more valuable than either of her sisters.'

'But Anne earned more than she got,' Grigg said. 'Up until the very end. As does poor dead Fanny.'

'I guess I think we all deserve more than we earn,' said Sylvia, 'if that makes any sense. I'd like the world to be forgiving. I feel sorry for Dick Musgrove, because no one loved him more than he deserved.'

We were quiet for a minute, listening to the fly buzz, thinking our private thoughts. Who loved us? Who loved us more than we deserved? Prudie had an impulse to go right home to Dean. She didn't, but she would tell him she'd thought to.

'There aren't so many deaths in the other Austen novels,' Jocelyn said. She was already helping herself to a bite of Grigg's sugar cookie without even asking. That was fast! 'One wonders how much her own death was on her mind.'

'Did she think she was dying?' Prudie asked, but no one knew the answer.

This is too grim a beginning,' Bernadette said. 'I want to talk about Mary. I absolutely love Mary. Except for Collins in *Pride and Prejudice*, and Lady Catherine de Bourgh, too, and Mr Palmer in *Sense and Sensibility*, and I love Mr Woodhouse, of course, in *Emma*, but except for those, she's my favorite of all the comic Austen characters. Her constant complaints. Her insistence on being neglected and put-upon.'

Bernadette supported her case with quotes. '"You, who have not a mother's feelings." "Everybody is always supposing that I am not a good walker!"' and so on and so on. She read several paragraphs aloud. No one was arguing; we were in complete agreement, listening drowsily in the sweet, cool evening. Allegra might have said something sour – she so often did – but she hadn't come back from her phone call, so not a person there did not love Mary. Mary was an exceptional creation. Mary deserved a toast. Sylvia and Jocelyn were sent to the kitchen for a second round of margaritas.

They passed Allegra, who was gesturing while she talked, as if she could be seen. '. . . tore out the toilets and threw them out the windows,' she was saying. What a waste of her pretty expressions, her silent-film-star gestures. She had a face made for the videophone. She covered the receiver. 'Dr Yep says hello,' she told Sylvia.

Dr Yep? Jocelyn waited until Sylvia had finished with the blender to lean in and whisper. 'So! What mother doesn't want her daughter dating a nice doctor?'

Such a thing to say! Obviously Jocelyn had never seen a single episode of *Young Dr Malone*. Sylvia knew how these things worked. Any minute now someone would fall into a coma. There'd be an accident in the kitchen with the blender. A suspicious death followed by a trial for murder. Hysterical pregnancies followed by unnecessary abortions. The many, many braided chains of disaster.

'I'm very happy for her,' Sylvia said. She poured the largest margarita for herself. She deserved it. 'Dr Yep seemed like a really lovely woman,' she added insincerely, although, in fact, Dr Yep had.

Bernadette was still talking when they returned. She'd shifted from Mary to the older sister, Elizabeth. Equally well drawn, but far less funny. Not intended to be, of course. And then the conniving Mrs Clay. But how was she worse than Charlotte in *Pride and Prejudice*, and hadn't they all agreed they loved Charlotte?

Sylvia started to argue on behalf of her adored Charlotte. She was interrupted by the doorbell. She went to answer it and there was Daniel. He had a gray, nervous look, which Sylvia liked better than the lobbyist's smile he tried immediately to paste over it. 'I can't talk to you now,' Sylvia said. 'I got your letter, but I can't talk. My book club is here.'

'I know. Allegra told me.' Daniel held out his hand, and in it was a book with a woman on the cover, standing in front of a leafy tree.

Allegra's copy of *Persuasion*. 'I looked it over in the hospital. Anyway, I read the afterword. Apparently it's all about second chances. That's the book for me, I thought.'

He stopped smiling and the nervous look came back. The book in his hand was shaking. It softened Sylvia. 'Allegra thought you were feeling forgiving,' Daniel said. 'I took a chance she was right.'

Sylvia had no recollection of having said anything that would give Allegra this impression. She couldn't remember talking about Daniel much at all. But she stood aside and let him in, let him follow her back to the deck. 'Daniel wants to join us,' Sylvia said.

'He's not in the club.' Jocelyn's voice was stern. Rules were rules, and no exceptions were made for philanderers and abandoners.

'*Persuasion*'s my favorite Austen,' Daniel told her.

'Have you read it? Have you read any of them?'

'I'm fully prepared to,' said Daniel. 'Every single one. Whatever it takes.'

He had a rosebud, short-stemmed, in the top pocket of his jeans. He pulled it out. 'I know you won't believe this, but I found it lying on the sidewalk in front. Honest to God. I hoped you'd think it was a message.' He gave it to Sylvia, along with a couple of petals that had come loose. '*Te echo de menos,*' he said. '*Chula.*'

' "*Les fleurs sont si contradictoires,*" ' Prudie answered coldly, to remind him we didn't all speak Spanish. Grigg had wanted only a single margarita, so she had taken his second and made it her third. You could hear this on the '*sont si.*' She gave Daniel the courtesy of a translation, which was more than he had done for her. 'From *Le Petit Prince*. "You should never listen to flowers." '

No one was more of a romantic than Prudie, you could ask anyone that! But the rose was a cheap move, and Prudie thought less of Daniel for making it. Added to this was the guilt of knowing the rose was hers. Dean had picked it for her, and the last time she'd looked it had been pinned to her blouse.

She wasn't sure that *Persuasion* wasn't a cheap move, too, but who would put Jane to an evil purpose?

'Ask Austen,' Bernadette suggested.

'Shake it up,' Grigg said. 'Shake hard.' Clearly he was rooting for Daniel. So predictable. So tediously Y to Y.

Sylvia set the rose down. It was already limp on its stem; the heavy head rolled from side to side. If it was an omen, it was an unclear one. She cupped the globe and shook. The answer began to settle: *My good opinion once lost is lost for ever*; but Sylvia didn't want that. She tipped secretly past it and got: *When I am in the country, I never wish to leave it; and when I am in town it is pretty much the same.*

'So what does that mean?' Jocelyn asked Sylvia. 'Your call.'

'It means he can stay,' Sylvia said, and saw, on Jocelyn's face, for just one moment, a flash of relief.

Allegra came back outside. *'Hola, papá,'* she said. 'You've got my book. You've got my margarita. You're in my chair.' Her voice was suspiciously light. She had the face of an angel, the eyes of a collaborator. Daniel moved to make room for her.

Sylvia watched them settle together, Allegra leaning against her father, her cheek on his shoulder. Sylvia found herself suddenly, desperately missing the boys. Not the grown-up boys who had jobs and wives and children or, at least, girlfriends and cell phones, but the little boys who'd played soccer and sat on her lap while she read *The Hobbit* to them. She remembered how Diego had decided over dinner that he could ride a two-wheeler, and made them take the training wheels off his bike that very night, how he sailed off without a single wobble. She remembered how Andy used to wake up from dreams laughing, and could never tell them why.

She remembered a ski trip they'd all taken the year of the big floods. 'Eighty-six? They'd rented a cabin in Yosemite and barely gotten home after. Interstate 5 had closed while they were on it, but they'd been able to shift to 99. Highway 99 flooded an hour after they'd driven over it.

While they were in the mountains, it snowed and snowed. This would have been lovely if they'd been sitting in some expensive ski lodge with their feet propped next to a fire. Instead they were standing in the Badger Pass parking lot with hundreds of other families, waiting for the bus to take them down.

It was a long, cold wait, and everyone was unhappy to be doing it. An announcement told them one of the buses had stalled and wouldn't arrive at all. This worsened the collective mood. The boys were hungry. Allegra was starving. The boys were cold. Allegra was freezing. They hated skiing, they all said, and why had they been made to come?

When a bus did arrive, almost thirty minutes later, a man and a woman pushed their way into line in front of Sylvia. There was little point to this. None of them was close enough to the front to have a shot at this first bus. But Sylvia had been shoved aside and, in her efforts not to step on Diego, had fallen onto the icy pavement. 'Hey,' Daniel had said. 'That's my wife you just pushed over.'

'Fuck you,' the man answered.

'What did you say?'

'Fuck your wife,' the woman added.

The kids had scarves wound around their necks, covering their mouths. Over these, their eyes were shiny with excitement. There was going to be a fight! Their father was going to start it! The people nearest gave way so that there was empty space around Daniel and the other man.

'Daniel, don't,' said Sylvia. One thing she'd always loved about Daniel was his lack of machismo. The boys she'd grown up with were such *caballeros*. Such cowboys. She'd never found it attractive. Daniel was like her father, self-confident enough to take an insult if one was offered. (On the other hand, she had been pushed and cursed, entirely without provocation. That wasn't right.)

'I'll deal with this,' Daniel told her. He was wearing ski pants, soft après-ski boots, and an enormous parka. That was the top layer, but there were many strata beneath. He looked as if he were about to be shot from a cannon. The other man was equally padded, the Michelin man in Patagonia blue. They squared off. Daniel was as angry as Sylvia had ever seen him.

He took a swing, but the ice was so bad he almost went down from his own momentum. He missed the other man's chest by many inches. The other man rushed him and Daniel side-stepped, so the man slid past and crashed into a pile of skis and poles.

Both regained their balance, turned around. 'You'll be sorry for that,' the man said. He walked toward Daniel, setting each foot onto the ice with care. Daniel took another swing and a miss. His boots slid out from under him; he went down hard. The other man stepped in to hold him there, pin him with a knee, but in his haste slid past again. His wife caught him and propped him upright. Daniel got to his feet, lumbered forward. He took a third swing; it spun him halfway around to face Sylvia.

He was smiling. Fat as a Santa in his big dark parka, there he was, fighting for her honor, but never managing to land a single punch. Windmilling, slipping, falling. Laughing.

Is Anne Elliot really the best heroine Austen ever created?' Daniel asked. 'That's what it says here in the afterword.'

'She's a little too innately good for my taste,' said Allegra. 'I prefer Elizabeth Bennet.'

'I love them all,' Bernadette answered.

'Bernadette,' Prudie said. She'd reached that pensive, sentimental state of drunkenness that everyone watching so enjoys. 'You've done so many things and read so many books. Do you still believe in happy endings?'

'Oh my Lord, yes.' Bernadette's hands were pressed against each other like a book, like a prayer. 'I guess I would. I've had about a hundred of them.'

On the deck behind her was a glass door, and behind the door a dark room. Sylvia was not a happy-ending sort of person herself. In books, yes, they were lovely. But in life everyone has the same ending, and the only question is who will get to it first. She took a drink of peach margarita and looked at Daniel, who was looking back, and didn't look away.

What if you had a happy ending and didn't notice? Sylvia made a mental note. Don't miss the happy ending.

Above Daniel's head, one leaf, and only one leaf, ticked about on the walnut tree. How exacting, how precise the breeze! It smelled of the river, a green smell in a brown month. She took a deep breath.

'Sometimes a white cat is just a white cat,' Bernadette said.

NOVEMBER

EPILOGUE

The Jane Austen book club did meet one more time. In November we gathered at the Crêpe Bistro to have lunch and take turns looking at the pictures from Bernadette's Costa Rican trip on her laptop. It was too bad she'd done no editing. Every time she saw something breathtaking, she took two or three identical shots. There were also two photos of headless people, and one in which you saw nothing but two red spots, which Bernadette said were jaguar eyes, and we couldn't prove they weren't. They were very far apart, though.

She told us how one day the tour bus had broken down in front of a plantation named The Scarlet Macaw. The owner of the plantation, the courtly Señor Obando, had insisted the group all stay there until a new bus could arrive. In the fourteen hours that took, they hiked around the plantation. Bernadette saw a bare-necked umbrella bird, a torrent tyrannulet, a rufous mot-mot, a harpy eagle (a cause for considerable celebration), a stripe-breasted this, and a red-footed that.

Señor Obando was a great enthusiast, had enormous energy for a man his age. He was determined to get his plantation on the ecotour circuit, and not for himself, but for the birders. It was his dream, he said. Surely there was no plantation anywhere with better birds or better trails. They could see for themselves how good the accommodations were, how varied the feathered denizens.

He and Bernadette sat on the veranda, drank something minty, and talked about everything under the sun. His relatives in San José – sadly infirm. They wrote often, but he rarely saw them. Books – 'I'm afraid we don't have the same taste in novels,' Bernadette said – and music. The relative merits of Lerner and Loewe versus Rodgers and Hammerstein. Señor Obando knew the songs from a dozen Broadway musicals. They sang 'How Are Things in Gloccamora?' and 'I Loved You Once in Silence,' and 'A Cockeyed Optimist.' He encouraged Bernadette to talk more; he said listening to her would improve his English. A week later Bernadette had added Señor Obando to her Life List.

She was married again. She showed us a ring set with a large aquamarine. 'I really think this is the one,' she said. 'I love a man with a vision.'

She'd come back to see the kids, the grandkids, the great-grandkids, and to pack up her apartment. She was grabbing her coat and getting her hat. Just forward her mail to The Scarlet Macaw.

We were happy for her, of course, and lucky Señor Obando, but we were a little sad, too. Costa Rica is far away.

Grigg said that he, in particular, missed our meetings. Grigg and Jocelyn were just back from the World Fantasy Convention in Minneapolis. It was a serious convention, Jocelyn said. For serious readers. She'd liked everyone she'd met, and seen nothing of which to disapprove. Grigg said that she hadn't been looking too closely.

In fact, he'd thought her awkward and uncomfortable, surrounded by so many people she didn't know. It didn't worry us. Give her time to relax, give her time to see what was needed, and Jocelyn would have the whole community in order. The match-making alone could occupy her for years.

'We could read someone else,' Grigg suggested. 'Patrick O'Brian? Some of his books are very Austenish. More than you'd expect.'

'I'm a big fan of boats,' Prudie told Grigg. 'Ask anyone.' Her tone was polite, at best.

Grigg never had quite gotten it. If we'd started with Patrick O'Brian, we could have then gone on to Austen. We couldn't possibly go the other direction.

We'd let Austen into our lives, and now we were all either married or dating. Could O'Brian have done this? How? When we needed to cook aboard ship, play a musical instrument, travel to Spain dressed like a bear, Patrick O'Brain would be our man. Till then, we'd just wait. In three or four years it would be time to read Austen again.

Sylvia and Daniel had stayed at Jocelyn's to watch the kennel while Jocelyn was at World Fantasy. Afterward, Daniel moved back home. Sylvia told us she picked up some useful marital tips from Sahara and the matriarchal Ridgebacks. She says that she's happy, but she's still Sylvia. Who can really tell?

We see a lot less of Allegra these days. She moved back to San Francisco and back with Corinne. None of us expects this to last. Daniel told Sylvia the things Corinne had done, and Sylvia told Jocelyn, and now we all sort of know. It's hard to like Corinne much now; it's hard to have a good feeling about the relationship. You have to believe in fundamental reform. You have to trust Allegra. You remind yourself that no one can push Allegra around.

There's a whole story involving Samantha Yep, but Allegra says she's never telling it, not to us, not to Corinne. It's a good story, that's why. She has no intention of finding it in *The New Yorker* some day.

We all ordered a glass of Crêpe Bistro's excellent hard cider and toasted Bernadette's marriage. Sylvia brought out the Ask Austen, not to ask a question, just to give the last word to the right person.

South or north, I know a black cloud when I see it.
Except that Austen wouldn't want us to end things that way.

A single woman, of good fortune, is always respectable.
Better. A good sentiment. Not so true, though, as other things she said. We're sure you can think of exceptions.

The mere habit of learning to love is the thing.
There.

In honor of Bernadette, with best wishes for her future health and happiness, Austen repeats herself:

The mere habit of learning to love is the thing.
                                        — JANE AUSTEN, 1775–1817

READER'S GUIDE

Jane Austen is weirdly capable of keeping everybody busy. The moralists, the Eros-and-Agape people, the Marxists, the Freudians, the Jungians, the semioticians, the deconstructors – all find an adventure playground in six samey novels about middle-class provincials. And for every generation of critics, and readers, her fiction effortlessly renews itself.

— MARTIN AMIS, 'JANE'S WORLD,' *The New Yorker*

THE NOVELS

Emma was written between January 1814 and March 1815, published in 1815. The title character, Emma Woodhouse, is queen of her little community. She is lovely and wealthy. She has no mother; her fussy, fragile father imposes no curbs on either her behavior or her self-satisfaction. Everyone else in the village is deferentially lower in social standing. Only Mr Knightley, an old family friend, ever suggests she needs improvement.

Emma has a taste for matchmaking. When she meets pretty Harriet Smith, 'the natural daughter of somebody,' Emma takes her up as both a friend and a cause. Under Emma's direction, Harriet refuses a proposal from a local farmer, Robert Martin, so that Emma can engineer one from Mr Elton, the vicar. Unluckily, Mr Elton misunderstands the intrigues and believes Emma is interested in him for herself. He cannot be lowered to consider Harriet Smith.

Things are further shaken by the return to the village by Jane Fairfax, niece to the garrulous Miss Bates; and by a visit from Frank Churchill, stepson of Emma's ex-governess. He and Jane are secretly engaged, but as no one knows this, it has no impact on the matchmaking frenzy.

The couples are eventually sorted out, if not according to Emma's plan, at least to her satisfaction. Uninterested in marriage at the book's beginning, she happily engages herself to Mr Knightley before its end.

Sense and Sensibility was written in the late 1790s, but much revised before publication in 1811. It is primarily the story of two sisters, Elinor and Marianne Dashwood. The death of their father has left them, with their mother and younger sister, financially pressed. Both women fall in love, each in her own characteristic way – Marianne is extravagant and public with her emotions, Elinor restrained and decorous.

The object of Elinor's interest is Edward Ferrars, brother to Fanny Dashwood, her odious, stingy sister-in-law. Elinor learns that Edward has been for some time secretly, unhappily, and inextricably engaged to a young woman named Lucy Steele. She learns this from Lucy, who, aware of Elinor's interest though pretending not to be, chooses Elinor as her special confidante.

Marianne hopes to marry John Willoughby, the book's only sexy man. He deserts her for a financially advantageous match. The surprise and disappointment of this sends Marianne into a dangerous decline.

When Lucy Steele jilts Edward for his brother Robert, Edward is finally free to marry Elinor. Edward seems quite dull, but is at least her own choice. Marianne marries Colonel Brandon, the dull man Elinor and her mother have picked out for her.

Mansfield Park was written between 1811 and 1813, and published in 1814. It marks Austen's return to novel writing after an interruption of more than a decade.

Ten-year-old Fanny Price is taken from her impoverished home to the estate of her wealthy aunt and uncle Bertram. There she is tormented by her aunt Norris, disliked by her cousins Tom, Maria, and Julia, and befriended only by her cousin Edmund. Her position is less than a daughter, more like a servant. Years pass. Fanny grows up shrinking and sickly (though very pretty).

While Uncle Bertram is away on business, Henry and Mary Crawford come to stay at the nearby parsonage. The Crawfords, brother and sister, are lively and charming. Both Maria and Julia are taken with Henry. Edmund is equally smitten with Mary.

Amateur theatricals are planned, then canceled by Uncle Bertram's return. But the rehearsals have already encouraged several damaging flirtations. Maria, humiliated by Henry's lack of real interest, marries Mr Rushworth, a wealthy buffoon.

Henry then falls in love with shy Fanny. She refuses the advantageous match and, as punishment, is sent back to her parents. Henry pursues her for a time, then has an affair with Maria that results in her disgrace. Edmund's eyes are opened by Mary's casual response to this.

Tom, the eldest Bertram cousin, nearly dies of vice and dissipation; Fanny is fetched back to Mansfield Park to help nurse him. At the end of the book Edmund and Fanny marry. They seem well suited to each other, though not, as Kingsley Amis has pointed out, the sort of people you would like to have over for dinner.

Northanger Abbey was written in the late 1790s, but published only post-humously. It is the story of a deliberately ordinary heroine named Cath-erine Morland. The book is divided into two parts. In the first, Catherine travels with family friends, the Allens, to Bath. There she meets two brother-sister pairs – John and Isabella Thorpe, and Henry and Eleanor Tilney. Her own brother, James, joins them and becomes engaged to Isabella. Catherine is attracted to Henry, a clergyman with witty and unorthodox manners.

General Tilney, father to Henry and Eleanor, invites Catherine to visit them at home; this visit makes up the second half of the book. The General is at once solicitous and overbearing. Under the spell of the gothic novel she has been reading, Catherine imagines he has murdered his wife. Henry discovers this and sets her humiliatingly straight.

Catherine receives a letter from James telling her that Isabella has ended their engagement. General Tilney, upon returning from London, has Catherine thrown out, to make her own way home. It is eventually understood that Catherine and James had been mistaken for people of great wealth, but the situation has been clarified.

Henry is so outraged by his father's behavior that he follows immediately after Catherine and proposes marriage. They cannot proceed without his father's permission, but this is finally given in the happy madness of Eleanor's marriage to a viscount.

Pride and Prejudice was originally entitled *First Impressions*. It was written between 1796 and 1797, and heavily revised before its publication in 1813. It is the most famous of the novels. Austen herself characterized it as 'rather too light and bright, and sparkling,' suggesting it needed some 'solemn specious nonsense' for contrast. In an inversion of the classic Cinderella fairy tale, when the hero, Fitzwilliam Darcy, first sees the heroine, Elizabeth Bennet, at a ball, he refuses to dance with her.

Elizabeth is one of five Bennet daughters, second in age only to the beautiful Jane. The Bennet estate is entailed on a male cousin, and although the girls are comfortable enough as long as their father lives, their long-term financial survival depends on their marrying.

The story revolves around Elizabeth's continued dislike of Darcy and Darcy's growing attraction to Elizabeth. When she meets the rake Wickham, she dislikes Darcy intensely; she is quickly won over by their shared distaste.

A subplot involves her father's heir, the Reverend Collins, who attempts to amend his financial impact on the family by asking Elizabeth to marry him. Elizabeth rejects him – he is pompous and stupid – so he proposes to Charlotte Lucas, Elizabeth's best friend, who accepts.

Darcy proposes to Elizabeth, but rudely. Elizabeth rudely rejects him. Wickham elopes with Lydia, the youngest Bennet sister, and Darcy is instrumental in finding the couple and buying Lydia a marriage. This, along with his steadfast love and improved manners, convinces Elizabeth that he is the man for her after all. Jane marries Darcy's friend Mr Bingley on the same day Elizabeth and Darcy are married. Both sisters end up very rich.

Persuasion was, like *Northanger Abbey*, published posthumously. It begins in the summer of 1814; peace has broken out; the navy is home. A vain and profligate widower, Sir Walter Elliot, is forced as an economy to let the family estate to an Admiral Croft, and move with his eldest daughter, Elizabeth, to Bath. A younger daughter, Anne Elliot, visits her delightfully whiny married sister, Mary, before joining them.

Many years before, Anne was engaged to Admiral Croft's brother-in-law, now Captain Frederick Wentworth. Her family's disapproval and the advice of an old friend, Lady Russell, caused her to cancel the match, but she is still in love with him.

Wentworth comes to call on his sister and begins a series of visits to see the Musgroves, the family into which Mary Elliot has married. This keeps him often in Anne's path. She must watch as Wentworth appears to wife-hunt among the Musgrove daughters, favoring Louisa. On a trip to Lyme, Louisa suffers a bad fall, from which she is slow to recover.

Anne joins her family in Bath, though they seem neither to miss her nor to want her. A cousin, the heir to her father's title, has been attentive to her oldest sister. When Anne arrives, he turns his attentions to her.

He is revealed by Anne's old school chum Mrs Smith to be a villain. Louisa's engagement is announced, not to Wentworth, but rather to Benwick, a bereaved navyman who saw her often in Lyme. Wentworth follows Anne to Bath, and after several more misunderstandings, they marry at last.

THE RESPONSE

IN WHICH JANE AUSTEN'S FAMILY AND FRIENDS COMMENT
ON *Mansfield Park*, OPINIONS COLLECTED AND RECORDED
BY AUSTEN HERSELF [1]

My Mother – not liked it so well as P. & P. – Thought Fanny insipid. –
Enjoyed Mrs Norris. –

Cassandra [sister] – thought it quite as clever, tho' not so brilliant as P.& P.
– Fond of Fanny. – Delighted much in Mr Rushworth's stupidity. –

My Eldest Brother [James] – a warm admirer of it in general. – Delighted
with the Portsmouth Scene.

M^r & Mrs Cooke [godmother] – very much pleased with it – particularly
with the Manner in which the Clergy are treated, – Mr Cooke called it
'the most sensible Novel he had ever read.' – Mrs Cooke wished for a
good Matronly Character. –

Mrs Augusta Bramstone [elderly sister of Wither Bramstone] – owned
that she thought S & S. – and P. & P. downright nonsense, but expected
to like M P. better, & having finished the 1st vol. – flattered herself she
had got through the worst.

Mrs Bramstone [wife of Wither Bramstone] – much pleased with it;
particularly with the character of Fanny, as being so very natural. Thought
Lady Bertram like herself. – Preferred it to either of the others – but
imagined *that* might be her want of Taste – as she does not understand
Wit. –

IN WHICH JANE AUSTEN'S FAMILY
AND FRIENDS COMMENT ON *Emma*[2]

My Mother – thought it more entertaining than M. P. – but not
so interesting as P. & P. – No characters in it equal to Ly Catherine &
Mr Collins. –

Cassandra – better than P. & P. – but not so well as M. P. –

M^r & Mrs J. A. [James Austen] – did not like it so well as either of the
3 others. Language different from the others; not so easily read. –

Captn. Austen [Francis William] – liked it extremely, observing that
though there might be more Wit in P & P – & an higher Morality in M P
– yet altogether, on account of it's [*sic*] peculiar air of Nature throughout,
he preferred it to either.

Mr Sherer [vicar] – did not think it equal to either M P – (which he liked
the best of all) or P & P. – Displeased with my pictures of Clergymen. –

Miss Isabella Herries – did not like it – objected to my exposing the sex
in the character of the Heroine – convinced that I had meant M^{rs} & Miss
Bates for some acquaintance of theirs – People whom I never heard of
before. –

Mr Cockerelle – liked it so little, that Fanny w^d not send me his opinion. –

Mr Fowle [friend since childhood] – read only the first & last Chapters,
because he had heard it was not interesting. –

Mr Jeffery [editor of the *Edinburgh Review*] was kept up by it three nights.

IN WHICH CRITICS, WRITERS, AND LITERARY FIGURES COMMENT
ON AUSTEN, HER NOVELS, HER ADMIRERS, AND HER DETRACTORS
THROUGH TWO CENTURIES

1812 – Unsigned review of *Sense and Sensibility*[3]

We will, however, detain our female friends no longer than to assure
them, that they may peruse these volumes not only with satisfaction
but with real benefits, for they may learn from them, if they please,
many sober and salutary maxims for the conduct of life, exemplified
in a very pleasing and entertaining narrative.

1814 – Mary Russell Mitford, review of *Pride and Prejudice*[4]

It is impossible not to feel in every line of *Pride and Prejudice*, in every
word of 'Elizabeth,' the entire want to taste which could produce so
pert, so worldly a heroine as the beloved of such a man as Darcy.
Wickham is equally bad. Oh! they were just fit for each other, and I
cannot forgive that delightful Darcy for parting them. Darcy should
have married Jane.

1815 – Sir Walter Scott, review of *Emma*[5]

Upon the whole, the turn of this author's novels bears the same
relation to that sentimental and romantic cast, that cornfields and
cottages and meadows bear to the highly adorned grounds of a show
mansion, or the rugged sublimities of a mountain landscape. It is
neither so captivating as the one, nor so grand as the other, but it
affords to those who frequent it a pleasure nearly allied with the
experience of their own social habits; and what is of some importance,
the youthful wanderer may return from his promenade to the ordinary
business of life, without any chance of having his head turned by the
recollection of the scene through which he has been wandering.

1826 – Sir Walter Scott eleven years later, after Austen's death, his
enthusiasm having grown[6]

Also read again and for the third time at least Miss Austen's very
finely written novel of *Pride and Prejudice*. That young lady had a talent
for describing the involvement and feelings and characters of ordinary
life which is to me the most wonderful I ever met with. The Big Bow
Bow-wow strain I can do myself like any now going, but the exquisite
touch which renders ordinary commonplace things and characters

interesting from the truth of the description and the sentiment is
denied to me. What a pity such a gifted creature died so early!

1826 – Chief Justice John Marshall, letter to Joseph Story[7]

I was a little mortified to find you had not admitted the name of Miss
Austen into your list of favorites ... Her flights are not lofty, she
does not soar on an eagle's wings, but she is pleasing, interesting,
equable, yet amusing. I count on your making some apology for this
omission.

1830 – Thomas Henry Lister[8]

Miss Austen has never been so popular as she deserved to be. Intent
on fidelity of delineation, and averse to the commonplace tricks of
her art, she has not, in this age of literary quackery, received her
reward. Ordinary readers have been apt to judge of her as Partridge,
in Fielding's novel, judged of Garrick's acting. He could not see the
merit of a man who merely behaved on the stage as any body might
be expected to behave under similar circumstances in real life. He
infinitely preferred the 'robustious periwig-pated fellow,' who
flourished his arms like a wind-mill, and ranted with the voice of
three. It was even so with many of the readers of Miss Austen. She
was too natural for them.

1848 – Charlotte Brontë, letter to G. H. Lewes[9]

What a strange lecture comes next in your letter! You say I must
familiarise my mind with the fact that 'Miss Austen is not a poetess,
has no "sentiment"' (you scornfully enclose the word in inverted
commas), 'no eloquence, none of the ravishing enthusiasm of poetry';
and then you add, I *must* 'learn to acknowledge her as *one of the greatest
artists, one of the greatest painters of human character*, and one of the writers
with the nicest sense of means to an end that ever lived.'

   The last point only will I ever acknowledge.

   Can there be a great artist without poetry?

1870 – Unsigned review of James Edward Austen-Leigh's *A Memoir of
Jane Austen*[10]

Miss Austen has always been *par excellence* the favourite author of
literary men. The peculiar merits of her style are recognised by all,
but, with the general mass of readers, they have never secured what
can fairly be called popularity ... It has always been known that Miss
Austen's private life was unruffled by any of the incidents or passions

which favour trade of the biographer ... It fits in with our idea of
the authoress, to find that she was a proficient in the microscopic
needle-work of sixty years since, that she was never in love, that she
'took to the garb of middle age earlier than her years or her looks
required.' ...

The critics of the day were ... in the dark ... She was not conscious
herself of founding a new school of fiction, which would inspire new
canons of criticism.

1870 – Margaret Oliphant [11]

Miss Austen's books did not secure her any sudden fame. They stole
into notice so gradually and slowly, that even at her death they had
not reached any great height of success ... We are told that at her
death all they had produced of money was but seven hundred pounds,
and but a moderate modicum of praise. We cannot say we are in the
least surprised by this fact; it is, we think, much more surprising that
they should at length have climbed into the high place they now hold.
To the general public, which loves to sympathise with the people it
meets in fiction, to cry with them, and rejoice with them, and take a
real interest in all their concerns, it is scarcely to be expected that
books so calm and cold and keen, and making so little claim upon
their sympathy, would ever be popular ... They are rather of the
class which attracts the connoisseur, which charms the critical and
literary mind.

1870 – Anthony Trollope [12]

Emma, the heroine, is treated almost mercilessly. In every passage of
the book she is in fault for some folly, some vanity, some ignorance,
– or indeed for some meanness ... Nowadays we dare not make our
heroines so little.

1894 – Alice Meynell [13]

She is a mistress of derision rather than of wit or humour ... Her
irony is now and then exquisitely bitter ... The lack of tenderness
and of spirit is manifest in Miss Austen's indifference to children.
They hardly appear in her stories except to illustrate the folly of their
mothers. They are not her subjects as children; they are her subjects
as spoilt children, and as children through whom a mother may
receive flattery from her designing acquaintance, and may inflict
annoyance on her sensible friends ... In this coldness or dislike Miss
Austen resembles Charlotte Brontë.

1895 – Willa Cather[14]

I have not much faith in women in fiction. They have a sort of sex consciousness that is abominable. They are so limited to one string and they lie so about that. They are so few, the ones who really did anything worth while; there were the great Georges, George Eliot and George Sand, and they were anything but women, and there was Miss Brontë who kept her sentimentality under control and there was Jane Austen who certainly had more common sense than any of them and was in some respects the greatest of them all ... When a woman writes a story of adventure, a stout sea tale, a manly battle yarn, anything without wine, women and love, then I will begin to hope for something great from them, not before.

1898 – Unsigned article in *The Academy*[15]

It is sometimes my fortune at a week-end to ... have discovered a cosy old inn on the Norfolk coast where there are no golf-links, some flight shooting, an abundance of rabbits to pop at, a plain, good dinner to be had, and a comfortable oak room in which to spend the evening. For the sake of convenience I will call my friends ... Brown and Robinson ...

Brown is a flourishing journalist, and therefore, entirely destitute alike of definite opinion and principle ... It is his business to keep a finger on the public pulse and allot space accordingly.

Robinson is an ardent young student, busily employed in devouring literature wholesale ... It was he that started the talk about Jane Austen ...

'I like Di [Vernon],' said the student, 'but [Sir Walter] Scott did not take her through her paces as well as Lizzie [Elizabeth Bennet] is taken. She is not shown in as many different moods and tempers. She is too perfect. It was the way of Scott. All his heroines ... are spotless. Elizabeth has a thousand faults ... is often blind, pert, audacious, imprudent; and yet how splendidly she comes out of it all! Alive to the very tips of her fingers ...'

'It does my heart good to see that youth is still capable of enthusiasm,' said the journalist, 'but my dear chap, after another twenty years, when I hope to see you a portly husband and father who has ceased to think much of heroines either in fact or fiction, your ideals will be completely changed. You will like much better to read about Mrs Norris saving three-quarters of a yard of baize out of the stage-curtain, and Fanny Price will be more interesting to you than Elizabeth.'

'Not a bit of it,' stoutly rejoined the student. 'Mrs Norris is quite interesting to me now . . .'

1898 – Mark Twain [16]
Every time I read 'Pride and Prejudice' I want to dig her up and hit her over the skull with her own shin-bone.

1901 – Joseph Conrad to H. G. Wells [17]
What is all this about Jane Austen? What is there *in* her? What is it all about?

1905 – Henry James [18]
Practically overlooked for thirty or forty years after her death, she perhaps really stands there for us as the prettiest possible example of that rectification of estimate, brought about by some slow clearance of stupidity . . . This tide has risen high on the opposite shore – risen rather higher, I think, than . . . her intrinsic merit and interest . . . Responsible . . . is the body of publishers, editors, illustrators, producers of the pleasant twaddle of magazines; who have found their 'dear,' our dear, everybody's dear Jane so infinitely to their material purpose . . .

The key to Jane Austen's fortune with posterity has been in part the extraordinary grace of her facility, in fact of her unconsciousness: as if, at the most, for difficulty, for embarrassment, she sometimes over her work basket . . . fell . . . into woolgathering, and her dropped stitches . . . were afterwards picked up as . . . little master-strokes of imagination.

1905 – Unsigned review of *Jane Austen and Her Times*, by G. E. Mitton [19]
Miss Mitton . . . reveals many virtues which we salute. She is a lover of books. She is hard-working . . . Her expressions of opinion are naive and abundant and likely to give much pleasure to those who contradict her: for example, in her mention of 'Sense and Sensibility,' she says very little and that of a disparaging kind about Mrs Jennings; we, on the other hand, bow down to Mrs Jennings as one of the few persons in fiction whom it is equally delightful to have met on paper and not to have met in the flesh.

1908 – Unsigned review in *The Academy*[20]

Northanger Abbey is not the best example of Jane Austen's work, but the fact that the scene is mostly laid in Bath, one of the few towns in England which retain their proper character, makes it particularly attractive to foreigners. It has also a stronger romantic element than is usual with Jane Austen, which adds interest for young people.

1913 – Virginia Woolf[21]

Here was a woman about the year 1800 writing without hate, without bitterness, without fear, without protest, without preaching. That was how Shakespeare wrote, I thought … and when people compare Shakespeare and Jane Austen, they may mean that the minds of both had consumed all impediments; and for that reason we do not know Jane Austen and we do not know Shakespeare, and for that reason Jane Austen pervades every word that she wrote, and so does Shakespeare.

1913 – G. K. Chesterton[22]

Jane Austen was born before those bonds which (we are told) protected women from truth, were burst by the Brontës or elaborately untied by George Eliot. Yet the fact remains that Jane Austen knew more about men than either of them. Jane Austen may have been protected from truth: but it was precious little of truth that was protected from her.

1917 – Frederic Harrison, letter to Thomas Hardy[23]

[Austen was] a rather heartless little cynic … penning satires about her neighbours whilst the Dynasts were tearing the world to pieces and consigning millions to their graves … Not a breath from the whirlwind around her ever touched her Chippendale chiffonier or escritoire.

1924 – Rudyard Kipling, epigraph to 'The Janeites'[24]

Jane lies in Winchester – blessed be her shade!
Praise the Lord for making her, and her for all she made!
And while the stones of Winchester, or Milsom Street, remain,
    Glory, love, and honour unto England's Jane.

1924 – E. M. Forster [25]

I am a Jane Austenite, and therefore slightly imbecile about Jane Austen. My fatuous expression, and airs of personal immunity – how ill they sit on the face, say, of a Stevensonian! But Jane Austen is so different. She is my favourite author! I read and re-read, the mouth open and the mind closed ... The Jane Austenite possesses little of the brightness he ascribes so freely to his idol. Like all regular churchgoers, he scarcely notices what is being said.

1925 – Edith Wharton [26]

Jane Austen, of course, wise in her neatness, trim in her sedateness; she never fails, but there are few or none like her.

1927 – Arnold Bennett [27]

Jane Austen? I feel that I am approaching dangerous ground. The reputation of Jane Austen is surrounded by cohorts of defenders who are ready to do murder for their sacred cause. They are nearly all fanatics. They will not listen. If anybody 'went for Jane,' anything might happen to him. He would assuredly be called on to resign from his clubs. I do not want to resign from my clubs ...

   She is marvellous, intoxicating ... [but] she did not know enough of the world to be a great novelist. She had not the ambition to be a great novelist. She knew her place; her present 'fans' do not know her place, and their antics would without doubt have excited Jane's lethal irony.

1928 – Rebecca West [28]

Really, it is time this comic patronage of Jane Austen ceased. To believe her limited in range because she was harmonious in method is as sensible as to imagine that when the Atlantic Ocean is as smooth as a mill-pond it shrinks to the size of a mill-pond. There are those who are deluded by the decorousness of her manner, by the fact that her virgins are so virginal that they are unaware of their virginity, into thinking that she is ignorant of passion. But look through the lattice-work of her neat sentences, joined together with the bright nails of craftsmanship, painted with the gay varnish of wit, and you will see women haggard with desire or triumphant with love, whose delicate reactions to men make the heroines of all our later novelists seem merely to turn signs, 'Stop' or 'Go' toward the advancing male.

1931 – D. H. Lawrence [29]

This, again, is the tragedy of social life today. In the old England, the curious blood-connection held the classes together. The squires might be arrogant, violent, bullying and unjust, yet in some ways they were *at one* with the people, part of the same blood-stream. We feel it in Defoe or Fielding. And then, in the mean Jane Austen, it is gone. Already this old maid typifies 'personality' instead of character, the sharp knowing in apartness instead of knowing in togetherness, and she is, to my feeling, thoroughly unpleasant, English in the bad, mean, snobbish sense of the word, just as Fielding is English in the good generous sense.

1937 – W. H. Auden [30]

You could not shock her more than she shocks me;
   Beside her Joyce seems innocent as grass.
It makes me most uncomfortable to see
   An English spinster of the middle class
   Describe the amorous effects of 'brass,'
Reveal so frankly and with such sobriety
The economic basis of society.

1938 – Ezra Pound, letter to Laurence Binyon [31]

I am inclined to say in desperation, read it yourself and kick out every sentence that isn't as Jane Austen would have written it in prose. Which is, I admit, impossible. But when you *do* get a limpid line in perfectly straight normal order, isn't it worth any other ten?

1938 – Thornton Wilder [32]

[Jane Austen's novels] appear to be compact of abject truth. Their events are excruciatingly unimportant; and yet, with *Robinson Crusoe*, they will probably outlast all Fielding, Scott, George Eliot, Thackeray, and Dickens. The art is so consummate that the secret is hidden; peer at them as hard as one may; shake them; take them apart; one cannot see how it is done.

1938 – H. G. Wells, dialogue from a character in a novel, perhaps expressing Wells's own opinion, perhaps not [33]

'The English Jane Austen is quite typical. Quintessential I should call her. A certain ineluctable faded charm. Like some of the loveliest butterflies – with no guts at all.'

1940 – D. W. Harding[34]

I gathered, she was a delicate satirist revealing with inimitable lightness of touch the comic foibles and amiable weaknesses of the people whom she lived amongst and liked . . . This was enough to make me quite certain I didn't want to read her. And it is, I believe, a seriously misleading impression . . .

In order to enjoy her books without disturbance, those who retain the conventional notion of her work must always have had slightly to misread what she wrote.

1940 – MGM plug for the movie *Pride and Prejudice*[35]

Five charming sisters on the gayest, merriest manhunt that ever snared a bewildered bachelor! Girls! Take a lesson from these husband hunters!

1944 – Edmund Wilson[36]

There have been several revolutions of taste during the last century and a quarter of English literature, and through them all perhaps only two reputations have never been affected by the shifts of fashion: Shakespeare's and Jane Austen's . . . She has compelled the amazed admiration of writers of the most diverse kinds, and I should say that Jane Austen and Dickens rather queerly present themselves today as the only two English novelists . . . who belong in the very top rank with the great fiction-writers of Russia and France . . . That this spirit should have embodied itself . . . in the mind of a well-bred spinster, the daughter of a country clergyman, who never saw more of the world than was made possible by short visits to London and a residence of a few years in Bath and who found her subjects mainly in the problems of young provincial girls looking for husbands, seems one of the most freakish of the many anomalies of English literary history.

1954 – C. S. Lewis[37]

She is described by someone in Kipling's worst story as the mother of Henry James. I feel much more sure that she is the daughter of Dr Johnson: she inherits his commonsense, his morality, even much of his style. I am not a good enough Jamesian to decide the other claim. But if she bequeathed anything to him it must be wholly on the structural side. Her style, her system of values, her temper, seem to me the very opposite of his. I feel sure that Isabel Archer, if she had met Elizabeth Bennet, would have pronounced her 'not very cultivated,' and Elizabeth, I fear, would have found Isabel deficient in both 'seriousness' and in mirth.

1955 – Lionel Trilling [38]

The *animality* of Mark Twain's repugnance is probably to be taken as the male's revulsion from a society in which women seem to be at the center of interest and power, as a man's panic fear at a fictional world in which the masculine principle, although represented as admirable and necessary, is prescribed and controlled by a female mind. Professor Garrod, whose essay 'Jane Austen, A Depreciation,' is a *summa* of all the reasons for disliking Jane Austen, expresses a repugnance which is very nearly as feral as Mark Twain's; he implies that a direct sexual insult is being offered to men by a woman author.

1957 – Kingsley Amis [39]

Edmund and Fanny are both morally detestable and the endorsement of their feelings and behaviour by the author . . . makes *Mansfield Park* an immoral book.

1968 – Angus Wilson [40]

As to the trickle of critics hostile to Jane Austen, from Victorian times onwards, they have been either temperamentally off key like Charlotte Brontë, Mark Twain, or [D. H.] Lawrence, or insufficiently informed like Professor Garrod, or critical only partially, like Mr Amis in his unwillingness lightly to undertake inviting Mr and Mrs Edmund Bertram to dine; her less intelligent, more fulsome admirers have been more an embarrassment to her high reputation than her hostile critics.

1974 – Margaret Drabble [41]

There are some writers who wrote too much. There are others who wrote enough. There are yet others who wrote nothing like enough to satisfy their admirers, and Jane Austen is certainly one of these. There would be more genuine rejoicing at the discovery of a complete new novel by Jane Austen than any other literary discovery, short of a new major play by Shakespeare, that one can imagine.

1979 – Sandra M. Gilbert and Susan Gubar [42]

Austen's story is especially flattering to male readers because it describes the taming not just of any woman but specifically of a rebellious, imaginative girl who is amorously mastered by a sensible

man. No less than the blotter literally held over the manuscript on
her writing desk, Austen's cover story of the necessity for silence and
submission reinforces women's subordinate position in patriarchal
culture ... At the same time, however ... under this cover story,
Austen always stimulates her readers 'to supply what is not there.'
[This last quotation is from Virginia Woolf.]

1980 – Vladimir Nabokov [43]

Miss Austen's is not a violently vivid masterpiece ... *Mansfield Park*
... is the work of a lady and the game of a child. But from that
workbasket comes exquisite needlework art, and there is a streak of
marvelous genius in that child.

1984 – Fay Weldon [44]

I also think ... that the reason no one married her was the same
reason Crosby didn't publish *Northanger Abbey*. It was just all too
much. Something truly frightening rumbled there beneath the bub-
bling mirth: something capable of taking the world by its heels, and
shaking it.

1989 – Katha Pollitt, from her poem 'Rereading Jane Austen's Novels' [45]
This time round, they didn't seem so comic.
Mama is foolish, dim or dead. Papa's
a sort of genial, pampered lunatic.
No one thinks of anything but class.

1989 – Christopher Kent [46]

An Oxford tutor, H. F. Brett-Smith, served during World War I as
an advisor to hospitals on reading matter for wounded soldiers. 'For
the severely shell-shocked,' a former student recalled, 'he selected
Jane Austen.' ...

   While the French Revolution raged, Jane Austen barely looked up
from her literary petit point. Who better to soothe minds unhinged
at Passchendaele or the Somme? In the therapeutic calm of her pages
history's victims could escape from their nemesis.

1993 – Gish Jen [47]

I think the next writer to have a really big influence on me was Jane
Austen. *Pride and Prejudice* was one of the books that I read backwards
and forwards. I really wanted to be Elizabeth Bennet. Of course
today, there are people who would say, 'Oh, that's so Anglo'; they

think I should have been more influenced by Chinese opera or something.

1993 – Edward W. Said [48]

Where *Mansfield Park* is concerned, however, a good deal more needs to be said . . . Perhaps then Austen, and indeed, pre-imperialist novels generally, will appear to be more implicated in the rationale for imperialist expansion than at first sight they have been.

1995 – Article about an essay by Terry Castle [49]

Was Jane Austen gay? This question, posed by the normally staid *London Review of Books*, was the headline for an essay by Stanford professor Terry Castle that subtly explored the 'unconscious homoerotic dimension' of Austen's letters to her sister Cassandra. The implication has caused quite a kerfuffle among Austenites.

1996 – Carol Shields [50]

Austen's heroines are compelling because in a social and economic system that conspires to place them at a disadvantage, they exercise real power . . . We look at Jane Austen's novels . . . and see that her women not only know what they want, they have evolved a pointed strategy for how to go about getting it.

1996 – Martin Amis [51]

Jane Austen is weirdly capable of keeping *everybody* busy. The moralists, the Eros-and-Agape people, the Marxists, the Freudians, the Jungians, the semioticians, the deconstructors – all find an adventure playground in six samey novels about middle-class provincials. And for every generation of critics, and readers, her fiction effortlessly renews itself.

Each age will bring its peculiar emphasis, and in the current Austen festival our own anxieties stand fully revealed. We like to wallow in the accents and accoutrements of Jane's world, but our response is predominantly sombre. We notice, above all, the constriction of female opportunity: how brief was their nubility, and yet how slowly and deadeningly time passed within it. We notice how plentiful were the occasions for inflicting social pain, and how interested the powerful were in this infliction. We see how little the powerless had to use against those who might hate them. We wonder who on earth will marry the poor girls. Poor men can't. And rich men can't. So who can?

1996 – Anthony Lane [52]

No burden weighs more heavily on a writer's shoulders than that of being much loved, but something unreachable in Austen shrugs off the weight.

1997 – Editorial in *Forbes* [53]

'Drucker's not a management theorist in the narrow, academic sense,' says Lenzner . . . 'He compares the strategic corporate alliances with the matrimonial alliances in Jane Austen novels.'

1997 – Susan M. Korba [54]

For years, critics of *Emma* have been circling around the apparently disconcerting issue of the protagonist's sexuality . . . Claudia Johnson finds that . . . 'transparently misogynist, sometimes even homophobic, subtexts often bob to the surface of the criticism about her.' Johnson cites Edmund Wilson's ominous allusions and Marvin Mudrick's dark hints about Emma's infatuations with and preference for other women as examples of the unease aroused by this particular Austen heroine.

1999 – David Andrew Graves [55]

For the last two years I have been using software as a tool for analyzing texts for patterns in word sequence and word frequency . . . From the viewpoint of word frequency by semantic category, *Emma* stands as Jane Austen's lightest and brightest novel, strongly positive, and with the lowest incidence of negative feeling, just as she promised us from the very first sentence.

1999 – Andy Rooney, correspondence with Emily Auerbach, quoted in Natalie Tyler [56]

I have never read anything Austen wrote. I just never got at reading *Pride and Prejudice* or *Sense and Sensibility*. They seemed to be the Bobbsey Twins for grown-ups.

1999 – Anthony Lane [57]

Nudity, sexual abuse, lesbianism, a dash of incest – will we never tire of Jane Austen?

2000 – Nalini Natarajan [58]

A 'commonsense' perception on the popularity of Austen in India would point to the translatability of Austenian situations into the context of the emergent Indian middle class . . . The issues raised by my metacritique, or reading of recent criticism of the Austenian daughter, while quite removed from the specificities of women's reform and its narrativization in colonial Bengal, suggest a paradigm within which to discuss the interlocking of two cultures.

2002 – Shannon R. Wooden, on the Austen movies [59]

Food control, a culturally pervasive defining feature of 'femininity,' also pervades Ang Lee's *Sense and Sensibility*, Roger Michell's *Persuasion*, Douglas McGrath's *Emma*, and Amy Heckerling's *Clueless* . . . Without exception the heroine does not eat . . . Conspicuous food consumption invariably signals the 'bad' or ridiculous woman.

2002 – Elsa Solender, past president of the Jane Austen Society of North America [60]

Having reviewed all the available films and critical reactions to them in the specialized libraries of London, Los Angeles, and New York, and having begged, bought, or borrowed a library of books and articles on adaptation from literature to film, I have reached one definitive conclusion about trying to re-create 'Jane Austen's World' faithfully and authentically on film in a way to satisfy Janeites. In a single word: Don't!

2003 – J. K. Rowling [61]

I never wanted to be famous, and I never dreamt I would be famous . . . There's a slight disconnect with reality which happens a lot with me. I imagined being a famous writer would be like being like Jane Austen. Being able to sit at home in the parsonage and your books would be very famous and occasionally you would correspond with the Prince of Wales's secretary.

NOTES

1. Jane Austen, *The Works of Jane Austen*, vol. 6: *Minor Works*, ed. R. W. Chapman (Oxford, London, and New York: Oxford University Press, 1969), pp. 431–435.

2. Ibid., pp. 436–439.

3. B. C. Southam, ed., *Jane Austen and the Critical Heritage* (London and New York: Routledge & Kegan Paul, 1968), vol. 1, p. 40.

4. Mary Russell Mitford, *Life of Mary Russell Mitford*, ed. A. G. L'Estrange (New York: Harper & Brothers, 1870), vol. 1, p. 300.

5. David Lodge, ed., *Jane Austen's Emma: A Casebook* (Houndsmill, Basingstoke, Hampshire, and London: Macmillan Education, 1991), p. 42.

6. Southam, *Jane Austen and the Critical Heritage*, vol. 1, p. 106.

7. A. J. Beveridge, *Life of John Marshall* (Boston: Houghton Mifflin, 1916–1919), vol. 4, pp. 79–80.

8. [Thomas Henry Lister], unsigned review of Catherine Gore, *Women As They Are*, in *Edinburgh Review*, July 1830, p. 448.

9. T. J. Wise and J. A. Symington, eds., *The Brontës: Their Friendships, Lives and Correspondence* (Philadelphia: Porcupine, 1980), vol. 2, p. 180.

10. *The Academy*, 1 (February 12, 1870), pp. 118–119.

11. Southam, *Jane Austen and the Critical Heritage*, vol. 1, pp. 224–225.

12. Anthony Trollope, 'Miss Austen's Timidity,' in Lodge, *Jane Austen's Emma: A Casebook*, p. 51.

13. Alice Christiana Thompson Meynell, *The Second Person Singular and Other Essays* (London and New York: H. Milford, Oxford University Press, 1921), p. 66.

14. Willa Cather, 'The Demands of Art,' in Bernice Slote, ed., *The Kingdom of Art* (Lincoln: University of Nebraska Press, 1966), p. 409.

15. *The Academy*, 53 (January/June 1898), pp. 262–263.

16. Mark Twain, *Mark My Words: Mark Twain on Writing*, ed. Mark Dawidziak (New York: St. Martin's, 1996), p. 128.

17. John Wiltshire, quoted in B. C. Southam, ed., *Critical Essays on Jane Austen* (London: Routledge & Kegan Paul, 1968), p. xiii.

18. Henry James, 'The Lesson of Balzac,' in Leon Edel, ed., *The House of Fiction* (London: Rupert Hart-Davis, 1957), pp. 62–63.

19. *The Academy*, 69 (November 11, 1905), p. 1171.

20. *The Academy*, 74 (January/June 1908), p. 622.

21. Virginia Woolf, *A Room of One's Own* (New York: Harcourt, Brace, Jovanovich, 1957), pp. 50–51.

22. Gilbert Keith Chesterton, *The Victorian Age in Literature* (New York: Henry Holt, 1913), p. 109.

23. Quoted in Christopher Kent, 'Learning History with, and from, Jane Austen,' in J. David Grey, ed., *Jane Austen's Beginnings: The Juvenilia and Lady Susan* (Ann Arbor, MI, and London: UMI Research Press, 1989), p. 59.

24. Rudyard Kipling, 'The Janeites,' in Craig Raine, ed., *A Choice of Kipling's Prose* (London: Faber and Faber, 1987), p. 334.

25. E. M. Forster, 'Jane Austen,' in *Abinger Harvest* (New York: Harcourt, Brace, 1936), p. 148.

26. Penelope Vita-Finzi, *Edith Wharton and the Art of Fiction* (New York: St Martin's, 1990), p. 21.

27. Arnold Bennett, *The Author's Craft and Other Critical Writings of Arnold Bennett*, ed. Samuel Hynes (Lincoln: University of Nebraska Press, 1968), pp. 256–257.

28. Rebecca West, *The Strange Necessity* (London: Jonathan Cape, 1928), pp. 263–264.

29. D. H. Lawrence, *Apropos of Lady Chatterley's Lover* (London: Martin Secker, 1931), pp. 92–93.

30. W. H. Auden and Louis MacNeice, *Letters from Iceland* (New York: Random House, 1937), p. 21.

31. Ezra Pound, *Letters from Ezra Pound*, ed. D. D. Paige (New York: Harcourt, Brace, and World, 1950), p. 308.

32. Thornton Wilder, 'A Preface for *Our Town*' (1938), in *American Characteristics and Other Essays* (New York: Harper & Row, 1979), p. 101.

33. H. G. Wells, *The Brothers: A Story* (New York: The Viking Press, 1938), pp. 26–27.

34. D. W. Harding, 'Regulated Hatred: An Aspect of the Work of Jane Austen,' *Scrutiny*, 8 (March 1940), pp. 346–347.

35. Quoted by Anthony Lane, 'Jane's World,' *The New Yorker*, September 25, 1995, p. 107.

36. Edmund Wilson, 'A Long Talk About Jane Austen,' *The New Yorker*, June 24, 1944, p. 69.

37. C. S. Lewis, 'A Note on Jane Austen,' in *Essays in Criticism: A Quarterly Journal of Literary Criticism*, 4, no. 4 (Oxford: Basil Black-well, 1954), p. 371.

38. Lionel Trilling, '*Mansfield Park*,' in Ian Watt, ed., *Jane Austen: A Collection of Critical Essays* (Englewood Cliffs, NJ: Prentice-Hall, 1963), p. 126.

39. Kingsley Amis, 'What Became of Jane Austen?' in Watt, *Jane Austen: A Collection of Critical Essays*, p. 142.

40. Angus Wilson, 'The Neighbourhood of Tombuctoo: Conflicts in Jane Austen's Novels,' in Southern, *Critical Essays on Jane Austen*, p. 186.

41. Margaret Drabble, 'Introduction,' *Lady Susan; The Watsons; Sanditon* (Great Britain: Penguin, 1974), p. 7.

42. Sandra M. Gilbert and Susan Gubar (1979), *The Madwoman in the Attic: The Woman Writer and the Nineteenth-Century Literary Imagination* (New Haven, CT, and London: Yale University Press, 1984), pp. 154–155.

43. Vladimir Nabokov, *Lectures on Literature*, ed. Fred Bowers (New York: Harcourt, Brace, Jovanovich, 1980), p. 10.

44. Fay Weldon (1984), *Letters to Alice on First Reading Jane Austen* (New York: Taplinger, 1985), p. 97.

45. Katha Pollitt, 'Rereading Jane Austen's Novels,' *The New Republic*, August 7 and 14, 1989, p. 35.

46. Kent, 'Learning History with, and from, Jane Austen,' p. 59.

47. Y. Matsukawa, 'Melus Interview: Gish Jen,' *Melus*, 18, no. 4 (Winter 1993), p. 111.

48. Edward W. Said, *Culture and Imperialism* (New York: Alfred A. Knopf, 1993), p. 84.

49. Belinda Luscombe, 'Which Persuasion?' *Time*, August 14, 1995, p. 73.

50. Carol Shields and Anne Giardini, 'Martians in Jane Austen?' *Persuasions*, 18 (December 16, 1996), pp. 196, 199.

51. Martin Amis, 'Jane's World,' *The New Yorker*, January 8, 1996, p. 34.

52. Anthony Lane, 'The Dumbing of Emma,' *The New Yorker*, August 5, 1996, p. 76.

53. James W. Michaels, 'Jane Austen Novels as Management Manuals,' *Forbes*, 159, no. 5 (March 10, 1997), p. 14.

54. Susan M. Korba, ' "Improper and Dangerous Distinctions": Female Relationships and Erotic Domination in *Emma*,' *University of North Texas Studies in the Novel*, 29, no. 2 (Summer 1997), p. 139.

55. David Andrew Graves, 'Computer Analysis of Word Usage in *Emma*,' *Persuasions*, 21 (1999), pp. 203, 211.

56. Quoted in Natalie Tyler, ed., *The Friendly Jane Austen* (New York: Penguin, 1999), p. 231.

57. Anthony Lane, 'All over the Map' (review of the film *Mansfield Park*), *The New Yorker*, November 29, 1999, p. 140.

58. Nalini Natarajan, 'Reluctant Janeites: Daughterly Value in Jane Austen and Sarat Chandra Chatterjee's *Swami*,' in You-me Park and Rajeswari Sunder Rajan, eds., *The Postcolonial Jane Austen* (London and New York: Routledge, 2000), p. 141.

59. Shannon R. Wooden, ' "You Even Forget Yourself": The Cinematic

Construction of Anorexic. Women in the 1990's Austen Films,' *Journal of Popular Culture*, Fall 2002, p. 221.

60. Elsa Solender, 'Recreating Jane Austen's World on Film.' *Persuasions*, 24 (2002), pp. 103–104.

61. Quoted at www.bloomsburymagazine.com.

QUESTIONS FOR DISCUSSION

Jocelyn's Questions

1. Austen's books often leave you wondering whether all of her matches are good ideas. Troubling couples may include: Marianne Dashwood and Colonel Brandon, Lydia Bennet and Wickham, Emma and Mr Knightley, Louisa Musgrove and Captain Benwick. Do any of the matches in *The Jane Austen Book Club* create disquiet?

2. Do you like any of the movies based on Austen's books? Do you ever like movies based on books? Have you seen any of the adaptations of Austen's novels that star a Jack Russell terrier named Wishbone? Do you want to?

3. Is it rude to give a person a book as a gift and then ask later if the person liked it? Would you ever do that?

Allegra's Questions

1. We seldom go to elegant balls anymore, but high school proms still play a prominent – too prominent – role in our personal histories. Especially if we didn't attend them. Why does every teen romance movie end up at the prom?

2. Does any part of your answer have to do with dancing?

3. In *The Jane Austen Book Club*, I take two falls and visit two hospitals. Did you stop to wonder how a woman who supports herself making jewelry affords health insurance? Do you think we will ever have universal coverage in this country?

Prudie's Questions

1. What I meant in that section about irony is that just because everyone finds their social level at the end of *Emma* doesn't mean Austen approves of it. Like with Shakespeare, it's hard to read Austen and know what her opinions really were about much of anything. Can the same be said of Karen Joy Fowler?
2. *Il est plus honteux de se défier de ses amis, que d'en être trompé.* Agree or disagree?
3. Which of the women in *Sex in the City* is Dean *really* most like?

Grigg's Questions

1. Jane Austen's books were initially published without the author's name and tagged 'An Interesting Book,' which alerted the reader that romance was involved. If Austen were publishing today, would she be considered a romance writer?
2. Austen lovers and science fiction readers feel a similar intense connection to books. Are there more book communities you know of that engage with a like passion? Why these and not others?
3. Many science fiction readers also love Austen. Why do you suppose this is true? Do you think many Austen readers love science fiction?

Bernadette's Questions

1. One of the reasons we don't know more about Austen is that her sister, Cassandra, destroyed many of her letters, finding them too personal, or feeling they reflected badly on her. How does this make you feel about Cassandra?
2. Do you think it adds to a book to know about the author? Do you care if no author photo is included? Do you assume the author looks nothing like her photo anyway?
3. Do you believe in happy endings? Are they harder to believe in than sad ones? When do you generally read the ending of a book? After the beginning and middle, or before? Defend your choice.

Sylvia's Questions

1. How many generations back can you go in your own family tree? Are you interested in genealogy? Why or why not?
2. Is love better the second time around? Is a good book better the second time around? Is the book you love the most also the one you reread the most? Is the person you love most the person you want to spend the most time with?
3. Do you ever wish your partner had been written by some other writer, had better dialogue and a more charming way of suffering? What writer would you choose?

ACKNOWLEDGMENTS

I owe many people more than I can say.

Thanks to my daughter, Shannon, who not only read and advised, but also did all my skydiving for me.

Thanks to Kelly Link and Gavin Grant, who each looked over the emerging manuscript more often than any friend should have to, always with encouragement, and always with smart, smart advice.

Thanks to Sean Stewart and Joy Johannessen for their enormous help on the home stretch.

Thanks to Susie Dyer and Catherine Hanson-Tracy, each so generous with her time and expertise.

Thanks to Christopher Rowe for the book's invisible vampires.

Thanks to Christien Gholson for a stolen image, to Dean Karnhopp for a stolen anecdote.

Thanks to the MacDowell Colony and also the Davis Crêpe Bistro for time, space, and really good food.

Thanks as always to Marian Wood and Wendy Weil for so many things over so many years.

And special thanks to the incomparable Anna Jardine.

Everyone has a private Austen. Mine is the Austen who showed her work to her friends and family and took such obvious pleasure in their responses. Thanks most of all to her, then, for those renewable, rereadable, endlessly fascinating books and everything that's been written about them.

THE SWEETHEART SEASON

THE SWEETHEART SEASON
KAREN JOY FOWLER

It is 1947 and America has once again made the world safe for democracy. A can-do optimism governs the land – nowhere more so than in America's heartland, the picture-perfect town of Magrit, Minnesota, headquarters to one of the nation's largest manufacturers of breakfast cereal.

But the boys who marched off to war have not returned and without young men to marry, the future of the young women of Magrit is uncertain. Until the company founder decides to form them into a baseball team. What could be better for business than a group of lovely young women playing the great American game? And if, while on the road, the players should happen to meet up with eligible young men, so much the better. And so the Sweetwheat Sweethearts were born. But as the young women tour the land, it becomes clear that all is not quite as it seems …

'A remarkable treasure – hilarious. Smart, wry, and just this side of insane'
Washington Post

'Full of sparkling wit. In territory long ago staked out by Garrison Keillor, *The Sweetheart Season* reads like the best of *Lake Wobegon* and then some'
Philadelphia Inquirer

Don't miss out on the delicious new novel from bestselling author

Karen Joy Fowler

By the author of
THE JANE AUSTEN BOOK CLUB

Karen Joy Fowler

The
**Sweetheart
Season**

'Fowler's light touch and sly wit are a delight'
Sunday Times

'A joy to read' *USA Today*

'A remarkable treasure — often wistful and
hilarious at once ... Smart, wry, and just this
side of insane' *Washington Post Book World*

OUT IN PENGUIN PAPERBACK JULY 2006

'EXQUISITE. IT'S THAT RARE BOOK
THAT REMINDS US WHAT READING IS ALL ABOUT'
The New York Times Book Review

'I WAS ENCHANTED. A CHARMING AND
INTELLIGENT READ, WITH THE BEST APPENDIX I'VE
COME ACROSS SINCE MARK HADDON'S *THE CURIOUS
INCIDENT OF THE DOG IN THE NIGHT-TIME*'
Kate Long, author of *The Bad Mother's Handbook*

'SO WINNING, SO TOUCHING, SO DELICATELY,
SLYLY WITTY ... JUST WONDERFUL'
Washington Post

'MISS AUSTEN WOULD BE PROUD'
Scotland on Sunday

'THIS WONDERFUL NOVEL SHOWS HOW
SOME BOOKS ENTER OUR BLOODSTREAM'
Independent

'PLAYFUL AND GRIPPING'
Eve